HIT FOR HIRE

ISBN-13: 978-1-63696-093-7
ISBN-10: 1-63696-093-6

Cover design by: Damonza
Printed in the United States of America

DAVID ARCHER

HIT FOR HIRE

A
NOAH WOLF
THRILLER

R

RIGHT HOUSE

NOAH WOLF THRILLERS

"There are nights when the wolves are silent and only the moon howls."

- George Carlin

PROLOGUE

The red-haired man sat at the bar, seeming completely oblivious to everything that was going on around him, but Sam Little knew better. He'd been watching this fellow for weeks, and there was no possibility, in his mind, that he had not been made. The knowledge ran cold through Sam's veins, because it was likely going to lead to his death.

The only thing Sam couldn't figure out was why he hadn't met with some kind of tragic accident already. He knew good and well that bastard was aware he was following him around; why hadn't he done something about it?

Of course, thinking like that was based at least partly on the public perception of what a spy did. If Sam were the kind of spy Ian Fleming wrote about, then he probably would have had to survive a dozen assassination attempts already, but those spies were not in his department. Men and women like those were in the more clandestine departments of MI6, CIA and Mossad, and didn't associate with the likes of Mrs. Little's little boy.

All that told him that his prey was doing everything possible to avoid looking like what he was. Red hair and all, he was trying to look like the same kind of average bloke who always frequented pubs like this one, and it was working as far as everyone else was concerned. Half the other patrons had exchanged some sort of pleasantry with him, and a couple had even bought him drinks.

Sam wasn't fooled, though. The red-haired chap was the one he'd been sent out to find, no doubt about it, and it was finally time to take him. If everything went according to plan, the bloke'd shortly be trussed up like a Christmas goose. The little earpiece shoved into Sam's right auditory canal was chirping incessantly as the rest of the team moved into place, ready for the biggest arrest of their careers. All of them were scared but they were ready to do whatever it took to finish this job, because this chap was far too important to let slip away.

"This is three, I'm in position near the loo."

"Two is ready, end of the bar."

"This is four, I've got sights on the target."

"Affirmative, four, do not fire unless ordered," Sam whispered.

"This is six, I'm in position at the rear door."

"Five, I'm entering the pub now. Target is still in place at the bar. Taking a seat at his seven o'clock."

"This is seven. I'm on the window, ready to move on command."

He turned his head and looked at the red-haired man then, and for the first time the fellow looked him in the eye. There was a slight nod, and then the barest hint of a smile, and Sam sighed and whispered, "One here. Target is hot, I say again, target is hot." The man sitting just behind the red-haired man rose and stepped up to stand just on his right.

"Sir," agent five said softly, "we have you completely surrounded and snipers are prepared to fire if you resist. Please come with me quietly."

The man turned his eyes to five, looking surprised. "Me," he said. "What for?"

"Let's not play games, shall we? There are a lot of innocent people in here..."

The red-haired man moved suddenly, thrusting his right elbow back into five's solar plexus. It wasn't a hard impact, but five's face suddenly looked startled as he stumbled backward. He looked down at his chest at the spreading red stain on his pale yellow shirt, placed a hand over it and then collapsed to the floor. His eyes stared at the short blade that was protruding from the elbow of the red-haired man's sleeve as he realized he'd been killed by one of the oldest tricks in the assassin's book.

"Take him, take him," Sam shouted as he leapt to his own feet. He lunged toward the red-haired man just as the latter spun on his stool, a pistol appearing in his hand. Sam dived for the floor as three shots rang out, and suddenly all hell broke loose in the pub. People were screaming and trying to run in every direction, and the ear bud was going crazy.

"This is four, I have no shot, I repeat, I have no shot!"

"This is three, two and five are down, I say again, two and five are down!"

Sam was scrambling across the floor, keeping his eyes on the red-haired man's feet even as he waited for death. Another shot came from the far right and the red-haired man spun and snapped off a shot in response. Sam risked a glance in that direction and saw number three fall to the floor.

This was it, he knew; he had come to the moment of his own death. He wrenched his eyes back toward the man with the gun even as he finally got his own revolver out of its holster on his back, then pointed it and fired twice in rapid succession.

Me guardian angel be doin' his job, Sam thought just then, as the red-haired man fell back against the bar. That's what Sam's old Nana used to say when something that seemed miraculous happened just as it was needed. The automatic in the red-haired man's hand had been pointing at Sam, but Sam's own bullets had taken him in the chest just before he could squeeze his trigger.

"Target is hit!" Sam didn't know who shouted it, he was too busy keeping his gun aimed as he rose onto his knees, but then the red-haired man stumbled forward off the edge of the bar and aimed at Sam once again. Everything seemed to go into slow motion, and Sam suddenly noticed that the man was not bleeding. He instinctively squeezed off another shot, stunning the target again, even as he realized the gunman must be wearing body armor.

Number six had come running from the back of the pub, and threw himself at the red-haired man even as Sam tried to aim for a headshot. The target saw him at the last possible second and snapped a shot that took six between the eyes. Sam fired, but the bullet was low and struck the red-haired man in the flesh of his right shoulder. The automatic fell from his hand, and Sam lunged from the floor.

They collided and crashed against the bar, then both of them were on the floor, tangled in the legs of the bar stools. Sam got the barrel of his short-nosed revolver against the man's head and screamed, "Go on, give me a reason! Those were my mates, you sorry bastard, give me a reason to blow your bloody brains out!"

Then number four landed on top of them, and a moment later the last man, seven, joined them, as well. Between the three of them, they got their captive onto his belly and Sam put him into cuffs. Four searched him thoroughly, removing a second pistol and a pair of throwing knives, as well as the knife that was strapped onto the back of his forearm and hidden in the now-torn sleeve of his jacket. That was the knife that had pierced the heart of number five. Sam and the others dragged their prisoner to his feet just as policemen rushed into the pub.

Sam flashed his ID. "MI6," he said. "This is our prisoner. Do what you can for the wounded." The police sergeant snapped a brisk salute and began barking orders at his own men.

The red-haired man had been wearing body armor, right enough, but it didn't protect his shoulder. Sam's bullet had only torn through the flesh, but the shock and pain had been enough to make him drop his pistol. They dragged him out of the pub to one of the ambulances that had responded, and rode with him to the hospital.

There, doctors decided the wound was not as serious as it looked, so they cleaned and stitched it and released him back to Sam. An SIS car had arrived, and the prisoner was taken away. Sam and his remaining agents were picked up moments later and dragged back to Vauxhall for debriefing.

Three hours later, in a sub-basement at Vauxhall Cross, the MI6 headquarters building, Sam was finally allowed into the interview room with the red-haired man. The fellow was seated on a metal stool with both hands clamped into restraints that were chained to the top of the table between them. The short chains allowed only enough movement to let the man sign his name if needed.

The red-haired man looked up at Sam as he entered. "Well," he said, "at last we meet face-to-face. I kept expecting you to make your move long before this, but you never did."

"Sorry to keep you in suspense, old boy," Sam said as he took the chair at the opposite side of the table. "I was having too much fun following you about to let it all end too quickly, y'see?"

The red-haired man chuckled. "Ah, yes, the thrill of the chase, the hunt, yes? Well, then, shall we proceed?"

"Yes, let's," Sam said. "Shall we dispense with introductions? I know basically who you are, insofar as you're the assassin known as Adrian."

Adrian smiled and tilted his head in acquiescence. "Ah, but I don't know your name. That is not equitable, is it?"

Sam allowed himself a cold smile. "I'm Samson Little, case officer on the operation to identify and capture you. I've been working on this for two solid years, and it's sort of nice to think I can now move on to other things."

"I'm sure it seems that way, right now," Adrian said, "but what about next week? Will you ever have an assignment of such importance again? Will you ever again feel such fear, such excitement? I could have killed you any number of times, you know. Do you not wonder why I left you alive, knowing how this must end?"

Sam swallowed to thrust back the nervousness he

felt. "I've wondered," he admitted. "Would you care to tell me?"

Adrian leaned forward, a smile on his face. "I'd be delighted to," he said. "You see, Samson Little, I am dedicated to my work. I have been making preparations for what might have been my greatest assassination ever. Since you seemed content to merely follow me, and I was certain that you were unaware of what I was actually doing, I did not want to create any distractions or difficulties until all of my preparations were ready. Had you waited only one more day to try to take me into custody, the outcome would have been very different. My final preparations would have gone into effect by morning, and within hours after that, you would have been dead."

A chill went down Sam's spine, but he kept any expression from reaching his face. "Good for me we decided not to wait another day, then, right? Would you mind telling me who it was you were planning to assassinate?"

Adrian laughed, throwing his head back. "Oh, I cannot do that. I'm sure that someone else will take my place when the news of my arrest is made public. In my profession, one never interferes with the work of his successor."

Sam laughed as well, but his own laugh was sarcastic. "Ha, ha, well, then I've got one on you. If the coppers had got you, they'd already be holding press conferences, showing your bloody face to the press and bragging about how they took you down. Not your luck, though, you got nicked by the Foreign Espionage Group of SIS. We've enough evidence of who you are to keep you on ice as long as we want, under the Terrorism Act of 2000.

We are going to wring you bloody dry, we're going to do whatever it takes to learn every sodding thing you know, and when we finally get to the point we can't get any more, then we'll put a bullet through your brain and shove you into the furnace. No press, no funeral, nothing. As far as the world is concerned, Adrian is dead as of now."

Adrian shrugged. "Ah, now do you see what you've done? You have eliminated any possibility of my cooperation. You have opted for the stick, rather than the carrot. In this world, you can only accomplish so much by trying to use fear, and I do not fear death. It is a natural consequence of the life I have lived, and while I do not wish to die so soon, I am not going to give you anything you want as long as there is nothing in it for me." He smiled and leaned back, making himself a little more comfortable. "Now, there are certain things I could give you, details about some of my past work, information regarding future threats to your national security and such, but only if there is some reward I can hope to gain. If I'm going to die anyway, I have no motive to offer you any kind of cooperation. If, on the other hand, that cooperation might gain me a stay of execution, then we may find a common ground."

Sam looked him in the eye for a long moment. "So you'd trade information for the chance to stay alive somewhat longer, even though you'll never leave a cell again?"

Adrian smiled broadly. "Tell me, Samson Little, did you ever read Burroughs?"

Sam nodded. "Doesn't every lad?"

"Then you'll remember the motto of John Carter of Mars: 'I still live.' Those three simple words express the essence of man, don't you think? With those three words, Burroughs expressed the human condition, because as long as life exists—there is hope."

Sam exploded onto his feet and slammed both fists onto the table. "Well, let me tell you something, you arrogant son-of-a-bitch," he said loudly. "I don't care if you live bloody forever, I can personally guarantee that hope is the last thing you will ever know. I know you've killed dozens of important figures, but those deaths are nothing to me but statistics. Earlier tonight, though, you killed three of my very good friends, men I've worked with and fought with for years. Two of those men had wives and children, and now they are widows and orphans because of you. I don't give a flying fig how many political figures you killed, but when you kill my friends, that means I'm going to dedicate my life to making you as miserable as I fucking can! Now, my superiors might agree to keeping you alive in order to get the information you might be willing to give up, but I'll tell you something right now. You'll be kept in a basement cell, with no windows, no telly, the same boring food every sodding day and not a single thing in the world to break up the monotony. You think you're willing to give up information to stay alive? Trust me when I tell you it won't be long before you'll be willing to give us everything you know, but only if we promise to kill you."

Adrian chuckled at him. "You may be correct," he said. "But remember this: even if I do reach the point where I am begging for death, the fact remains that I still live."

ONE

Noah's phone rang, snapping him instantly out of sleep. He grabbed it up quickly, before its ringing could waken Sarah.

"Hello?"

"Camelot," came a voice he knew well. "It's Allison. We've got a situation and I'm afraid your team is up. Briefing at oh nine thirty."

The line went dead without waiting for him to respond, so he turned and looked at Sarah. She had been snuggled up against him as he slept and felt him move. One eye was open and peering at him through a tuft of her own hair.

"Mission," Noah said. "We got briefing in two hours." He glanced at his phone. "Let's get a shower and go have some breakfast on the way."

"Mmm, can't I just stay in bed? You go to the briefing and come back and tell me what it's all about."

"I have my doubts whether Allison would approve of that. Come on, it's shower time."

Sarah grumbled again but rolled over and managed to get her feet onto the floor. "Fine," she said, "but just for that, you can wait till I get done and shower by yourself." She stumbled into the bathroom and shut the door behind herself. A moment later, Noah heard the shower begin to run.

He rose from the bed and began laying out clothes for himself and Sarah. He knew that she liked it when he chose her clothing and so he tried to do it every day when they were not on mission. This would be the last chance for a while, he was sure, so he decided to make it count. When she came out a few moments later and found the low-cut blouse and short skirt he had selected, she stared at him as he walked past her into the bathroom, but then put them on.

Fifteen minutes later, Noah came out of the bathroom with a towel around his waist to find Sarah blow-drying her hair. He slid quickly into his own clothes and then went to the kitchen to make coffee. He had just poured two cups when she came into the kitchen and sat down at the table across from him.

"Allison's gonna raise her eyebrows at me, you know," she said.

"So will the guys," Noah replied, "but no one will say anything. Allison will just figure you're trying to flirt with me and the guys in the room will just enjoy the view."

The grin she had been trying to hold back suddenly escaped onto her face. "I think you like it when they look at me," she said. "I know you don't really get jealous, but somehow I think there's something about it that tickles your fancy in some way."

Noah picked up his coffee and took a sip. "Well, I have noticed that they all seem to be in better moods when you're looking sexy."

She chuckled. "Noah, you're terrible."

They drank their coffee and headed out to Noah's car.

Noah held Sarah's door as she slid into the passenger seat of the Corvette, then went around and got behind the wheel. A moment later they were on the road and headed toward the office of the Dragon Lady.

Allison Peterson was the absolute head of the US agency that was known simply as Elimination and Eradication. Her job required her to decide whether or not to send an assassin to terminate the life of a particular individual or group of individuals. Other agencies submitted requests for assassination to her, with a complete and detailed dossier on why they believed that assassination was necessary. If she approved the request, she personally assigned the mission to an operative who worked directly for her. Noah Wolf was one of those operatives.

Each assassin had a three-person support team that consisted of a transportation specialist, an intelligence specialist and a weapons and combat specialist. All of them were under the command of their team leader, and it was their job to make sure that their team leader was able to carry out his or her mission.

Sarah was Noah's transportation officer, and one of the best drivers he had ever seen. The girl could handle absolutely anything on wheels, and better than anyone else. When she had been assigned to him almost a year earlier, she had been aloof and resistant to even the slightest possibility of friendship, but as she got to know him that reluctance turned into attraction. They had begun a relationship not long afterward, and after a particularly rough mission a couple of months earlier, Sarah had given up her own apartment and moved in permanently with Noah.

Noah was, in Allison's words, the superstar of the organization. Because of something tragic that happened in his childhood, Noah Wolf had no normal, detectable emotions. This meant that he could not be baited into an emotional response, such as with anger or jealousy, but could always make his decisions based entirely on a clear and logical understanding of the situation. Of course, it also meant that he had no conscience, and was capable of doing whatever had to be done without any feelings of guilt or recriminations. He was extremely intelligent and could often take a mission that seemed impossible and turn it into success.

It was his lack of emotion that had originally caused Sarah to want little to do with him, but it was that same lack of emotion that finally drew her closer. Noah wondered occasionally if she considered him a challenge, if she was trying to get through to him in a way that no other woman ever had. Considering that she was the only woman he had ever truly wanted to be with for more than a very short time, he had to believe that she was accomplishing at least some part of that goal. He still didn't feel anything that might be construed as a romantic attachment to her, but he had conceded that he preferred living in a world that had her in it. That had twice caused him to walk into deadly traps in order to recover her from an enemy who had taken her hostage.

They got to the office in plenty of time and parked in the underground garage, then rode the elevator up to Allison's offices. Katie Gamble, Allison's secretary, smiled at them as they walked past her toward the conference room where briefings always took place.

The door was open, so Noah and Sarah walked in to find Neil Blessing and Moose Conway already there and snacking on the doughnuts that were always present in the room. Allison was sitting at the head of the table, and Donald Jefferson, her second-in-command, was beside her. Neil, Moose and Don all smiled when they got a look at Sarah, then nodded to Noah.

"Mr. Jefferson," Noah said, "it's good to have you back. How are you doing, Sir?"

"I'm still a little sore in spots," Jefferson said, "but I'm getting around okay. Lost some feeling in my chest and lower legs, and the doctors swear they took out part of one of my lungs, but I can't tell it. Thanks for asking."

"We're all pleased that you're back, Sir. I don't think this place would run right without you." He turned to Allison. "What have we got?"

Allison smiled as Sarah handed Noah a paper plate with two doughnuts and a cup of coffee. "The situation we're going to tell you about is one that has been developing over the last few months, but is suddenly taking center stage. There's plenty in the news about terrorist groups and the threats they are presenting to so many Western nations, but there is one particular group that has been in the shadows for some time. This group has been responsible for inciting many of the attacks attributed to the better-known organizations, sometimes just by manipulating their leaderships, but often by providing direct funding, personnel and equipment. The group is known as IAR, which stands for Independent Armies of Revolution, and their goal is to cripple several European nations by fostering terrorist activities. IAR and their puppets have been behind literally hundreds of terrorist actions, from suicide bombers to blowing airliners out of the sky. Most of their activities have been particularly evil because they tend to target civilians, especially children. In the last six months alone, groups that answer to them have bombed at least a dozen schools in different countries. CIA and NSA have both been working with British and European agencies, monitoring their activities for quite some time, but it's been almost impossible to find out who was truly behind them, who was pulling the strings. Now we've come across some intelligence that seems to indicate one individual, Pierre Broussard, as the mastermind running the group."

Donald Jefferson leaned forward as a black-haired and bearded face appeared on the screen mounted on the wall behind him. "Broussard was born in Marseille, France, forty-six years ago, but his family moved to England and settled in Wilshire when he was very young. He was raised there, then attended Cambridge before joining the Royal Navy. He served one tour of duty aboard a ship, and then was transferred to the SAS, where he received extensive antiterrorism training. He served with honor and distinction for eight years with SAS, then left the military to take a post as an assistant to the British ambassador to Libya. It was while he was in Libya that he seems to have begun some of his earlier activities, mostly just arranging the sale of weapons to various revolutionary groups. That led to some even bigger deals, negotiating weapons sales between various countries, and in 2002 he decided to leave diplomatic service and become an independent. He calls London home, but he's only there two or three days a week. The rest of the time, he's flying around the world in one of several private jets as he conducts his business."

The picture on the screen changed to another man, this one with blonde hair and whiskers. "This is Walter Wyndham. As far as we know, Wyndham is nothing more than a messenger, maybe a bag-man, for Broussard and IAR. He was recently identified in some spy photos taken at a training camp for Islamic militants, and it's been determined that he arrived there with several large suitcases filled with French and Italian currency. An MI6 operative was able to mark some of that money with an invisible, slightly radioactive chemical, and a significant amount of it has been turning up in Germany and Switzerland in the hands of known terror suspects that have been rounded up. From interrogation, we learned that Wyndham has been delivering money and explosives to a number of such groups, so when he turned up in London two weeks ago he was put under surveillance. Care to guess who he met with?"

"Broussard, obviously," Noah said.

"Exactly. And when he left, on one of Broussard's private jets, he had three more suitcases than when he arrived. Those captured terrorists have confirmed that they were receiving money from IAR, and since we know the money is actually coming from Broussard, it looks like he's the elusive mastermind we've been trying to track down."

Noah nodded his head. "So, you want him taken out."

"Not necessarily," Allison said. "The question of whether Broussard is the true head of the organization is a matter of debate among the relevant intelligence circles, so this could possibly be a bit more complicated. Donald and I have come up with a mission plan that is designed to find out for sure and then eliminate him if he is. If not, then the plan will need to be modified on the fly. Donald?"

Jefferson cleared his throat as he tore his eyes away from Sarah. "There is a known assassin who goes by the name Adrian, but no one seems to know who he is or, other than generally, what he looks like. What we do know is that IAR has been trying to recruit him, sending out cryptic messages that are obviously aimed at him. What nobody is aware of is that Adrian was recently captured by MI6, and is being quietly interrogated, after which he will be equally quietly executed. Since he's out of the picture, what we're going to propose is that you assume his identity and make contact with IAR. Whatever they want Adrian to do, it's likely to be big enough to get you into contact with their highest levels, so you'll be able to confirm whether Broussard is in fact running the show. If that's the case, then yes, we want you to take him out. If not, then we need you to stay in deep cover until you can determine who gives him his orders."

Noah's eyebrows went up slightly. "I'm going out alone, then?"

"Not a bit," Allison said emphatically. "One of the interesting things about Adrian is that he always seemed capable of being in more than one place at a time. During his interrogation, it came out that he always had a few accomplices, essentially people he could use like the same kind of support team that you work with. They've been identified and eliminated, so there's no one out there who can prove you aren't him. You are built enough like him that it shouldn't be hard for Wally to help you pass for him. It'll take some hair color and contacts, and Wally can make your nose seem a little bigger. Again, no one before now has ever gotten a photo of him and lived to tell about it, so it's highly unlikely anyone will be able to spot you as a doppelgänger."

"What about us?" Moose asked. "You said he had a

team. Did anyone know them? Will anybody be able to say whether we're it?"

"That's doubtful," Jefferson said. "We can't say for sure that nobody knew who they were, but it's kind of a moot point. There were actually four of them, and they're all dead. You will each be given a backstory that indicates Adrian recruited you only recently. In other words, if it should become necessary for anyone to have to know about you, then you were simply their replacements."

"And were they like us? Driver, computer nerd and overgrown leg breaker?" Neil asked.

"Nobody knows for sure precisely what they did for Adrian," Allison said, "but there were definitely some intel and combat skills among them. Each of them, just as when you were recruited for E & E, would have been recruited by Adrian for particular skills and abilities. As far as we know, his accomplices were never in contact with any of his clients, so it's highly unlikely anyone could identify them. All that being true, it shouldn't be hard for you to pull off the same kind of roles you already live, now should it?"

"What about those messages that were sent to Adrian?" Noah asked. "I'm assuming there was some kind of code word or phrase, something Adrian was supposed to use in order to identify himself?"

"Yes," Jefferson replied, "and there are copies of each of them in the file we're going to give you. You'll be able to study them for yourself, so that you can refer to them easily when you need to."

Noah nodded once again. "So when do we leave?"

Allison smiled. "We've obtained some video of Adrian's interrogation from the Brits, and you'll need to study it, practice imitating his voice and speech peculiarities, just in case someone you meet has spoken to him on the phone before. There's very little chance you'll run into anyone who actually met him face-to-face. Adrian had a habit of not leaving people alive once they actually saw his face when he was on a mission. He was also pretty adept at staying out of the line of sight of any cameras, including security cameras and traffic cameras and all that sort of thing. If he had to meet someone, it was always in the dark, and he always wore a disguise or something that could hide his face. As we said, nobody really knows exactly what he looks like, other than being a tall, red-haired man with a large nose. The tapes are out at Mission ID Development, and there's an acting coach who will work with you there starting tomorrow morning. I'd say you'll need a couple of days to work on the voice, and Wally can get you set up with hair color, contacts and such during that time. Today is Monday, so I'd like to see you head out by Thursday."

"We're going to give you," Jefferson said, "the usual identity kits, but of course they're for use only in an emergency. Anyone who believes you to be Adrian won't expect you to be using a real name on identification, anyway, so you should only need them for hotels or if you happen to be pulled over by local police. You'll be going to Spain first, to Madrid. That's where you will make your initial contact with IAR. One of those messages suggested that Adrian post an ad in the newspaper in one of seven different cities. Madrid is one of them. You'll place an ad and wait for one of their people to respond to it."

"Okay, no problem. And if it turns out Broussard is

not the head guy? How long do you want me to pretend I'm going to take whatever contract they offer?"

Allison made a grimace and cocked her head slightly to the left. "Probably as long as you can. Depending on the contract, you may have to actually carry it out to maintain your cover. This is the first chance any of us have had to get somebody inside that organization, and we can't afford to let the opportunity slip away. If we can cut off the head, it's possible this is a snake that will actually wither and die."

"Then that's what I'll try to do," Noah said.

"One other thing," Allison said. "You're going to be mostly on your own with this one. We're providing you with ample financing through the credit cards we're giving you, but we won't be able to use many of our assets to help you out, once you leave. Adrian worked independent of any government or organization, always arranging anything he needed on his own. We'll give you contact information for a few of our people who aren't directly affiliated with any embassy or agency, of course, and you can use them to get weapons, equipment and such. Other than that, you have to stay away from any American agents. Can't risk anyone spotting you talking to them, it's always possible they've been identified." She smiled sadly. "If stopping IAR wasn't so important, we probably would have refused this mission. As it is, you're the only team that has a chance of actually pulling it off, or I wouldn't have given it to you. I can't afford to lose you, Noah, so whatever you do, you make sure you come back. We're down to only three teams, and I don't know how long it will be before we can resurrect any of the others. Don't let this become a suicide mission."

"Understood. I guarantee I'll do my best."

Jefferson passed out the wallets and files, while Allison handed a large purse to Sarah. The two of them whispered over the contents for a few minutes, and Noah couldn't help noticing that Sarah's eyes widened at one point, and then narrowed suspiciously. On their last assignment, Sarah had been given an engagement ring to wear, posing as Noah's fiancé. He found himself wondering what surprise Allison had given the girl this time.

TWO

T he team left the briefing room and headed back to Noah's place. When they arrived, they gathered in his dining room to talk the situation over.

"I'm scheduled to spend the next two days with Mission ID and Wally," Noah said, "learning how to talk like Adrian and getting a makeover. I'm assuming we're going to fly out sometime early Thursday, so I want you guys to study the files on IAR and Broussard while I'm tied up. Moose, we won't be taking weapons or equipment. I'm going to ask Wally to send a message to our contacts to get us what we need. Glocks for you and me, we'll get Sarah a Beretta like the one she normally uses and let's get Neil another MP 9. That worked well for him on the last mission, so go by the armory and get him one today to practice with." He turned to Neil. "Neil, I want you to spend some time on the range with it today and tomorrow. Try to get comfortable with it. I know you have a little problem with typical handguns, but I think the three-round burst from the MP 9 might help you overcome it."

"Hey, I put all three rounds into Andropov's chest," replied the tall, skinny young man. "Wasn't my fault the son-of-a-bitch was already dead."

"Nope," Sarah said, "it was mine." She shuddered and looked at Noah. "I still have trouble believing I did that, but I just couldn't bear the thought of spending the rest of my life waking up and knowing he was still alive. I think it would have ruined me, I would've been constantly looking over my shoulder."

"I understand," Noah said. "I think we all sleep better knowing he's dead. I'm just glad you were able to cope with it."

"I have nightmares sometimes," she admitted, "dreams where I see myself doing it all over again, but I think it would've been worse if he were still alive. I'd be dreaming of him coming after me again, over and over and over. I just couldn't handle that thought."

Moose knuckled her shoulder gently. "Hey, look at it this way. You'll probably never have to do anything like that again, but at least you know you could if you had to."

Sarah rolled her eyes and grinned at him. "Oh, trust me, there's no doubt in my mind now that I can pull the trigger if I have to. I used to wonder if I really could if it came down to it, but not anymore."

"That's what's important, then," Noah said. "You got through it and came out stronger."

"I got something more important," Neil said. "Hasn't anybody but me noticed that it's getting close to lunchtime?"

Sarah glanced at the clock on the wall and smiled. "Neil, it's just barely eleven o'clock. Didn't you eat enough doughnuts this morning?"

"Not really," he said. "I like those cream-filled long johns, and there were only three of them. I can't help it if I'm still hungry."

Moose grinned and ruffled the boy's hair. "You're always hungry," he said. "Truth be told, I could stand an early lunch, myself. What do you say we all head out to the Sagebrush and put down a steak?"

Sarah looked at Noah, who nodded. "Sounds good," he said. "Might be the last chance we get for a while."

Neil got to his feet quickly. "Lacey's over at the trailer, she's off today. Let me get her and we can all ride out in the Hummer."

"Uh-uh, no way," Sarah said. "I've seen how you drive. We'll just meet you out there."

Moose chuckled and announced that he would take his own car, so Noah and Sarah went out to get into the Corvette. Noah and Moose started their cars up and pulled over by the trailer to wait for Neil and Lacey. They came out a moment later and got into Lacey's vintage Mustang, and then all three vehicles headed for the Sagebrush Saloon.

The Sagebrush was their favorite restaurant, just a few miles away from Noah's place, and sort of in the middle of nowhere. It was part restaurant and part tavern, the sort of roadhouse that has been made famous in novels and movies over the years. They had started frequenting it not long after their team was formed a year earlier, and Moose's girlfriend Elaine worked there. She was on duty when they walked in and the hostess smiled as she led them to one of Elaine's tables.

"Hey, gang," Elaine said as she put glasses of water in front of each of them. "Glad you came by. Dad tells me you're getting ready to go out on a business trip, that right?" Elaine was the daughter of Donald Jefferson and actually worked part-time for E & E, herself, so she was cleared for general information about the organization and its missions.

"Yep," Moose said. "Might be a long one, so I suggested we come out for lunch."

"We don't leave 'til Thursday," Sarah said. "Just seemed like a good time to come grab a bite to eat."

Since they all were there fairly often, it didn't take long for them to decide on what to order. Their mealtime chatter was casual and friendly, with Lacey and Neil spending a lot of the time talking between themselves. Lacey was barely an inch shorter than Neil's six-foot-five, and the two of them had hit it off the first time they met. Noah and the others had gotten accustomed to the way they mooned over each other, and had learned to ignore them.

When they had finished eating, they headed back to Noah's house and then started working on their individual agendas. Neil dropped Lacey off at the trailer, then he and Moose headed for the armory. Noah and Sarah sat down in their living room and began going over the files on IAR and Pierre Broussard.

IAR had only come on the scene a few years previously, and while the name wasn't well known publicly, most government agencies were fully aware of it. In the past five years, just about every major terrorist action, even those without Islamic influences, had some kind of tie back to IAR. In many cases it was only money, but there was mounting evidence that weapons, explosives and even chemical weapons were being provided. That seemed to explain the fact that many of the smaller terror cells, who simply didn't have the people or assets necessary to make some of the explosive or chemical devices they had been using, were getting their hands on them.

The file on Broussard was actually pretty small. Until this latest intelligence had come to light, he had been considered a fairly reputable arms dealer and negotiator. Despite the fact that he had made more than a billion dollars trading in weapons, there had been no evidence anywhere that he was dealing illegally, or working with any known terrorist groups.

Now, it appeared that he had been funneling many such transactions through IAR, keeping them completely off of most government radars. By running them through intermediaries like Wyndham, he avoided having any contact with organizations that might have exposed him to risk.

The same was true of his financial dealings. It was apparent that there were many accounts scattered throughout several countries that could be tapped for resources as needed, including right near his home in England. There was little doubt that Wyndham had left his meeting with Broussard carrying a large amount of cash, and yet there were no financial records connected to Broussard showing any kind of transfers or withdrawals. Neither MI6 nor CIA had been able to determine how Broussard managed to have large amounts of currency in his possession, but it was clear that he had found a way.

"This guy's some kind of magician," Sarah said. "None of the agencies have any idea how he's getting his hands on so much hard currency."

"By wearing it," Noah said. "He's got an entourage of more than a dozen people that travels everywhere with him, and he's in a different country almost every day. All he's got to do is have his people gather up all the national currency they can in each location, and then they can just strap it to themselves when they get off the plane back in London. Slip on some big overcoats and climb into a car, then walk into his house. It's that simple. Nobody watching would see a thing."

Sarah looked hard at him for a moment, then suddenly burst out laughing. "Have you ever been to a magic show where you couldn't figure out how they did it?"

Noah's eyebrows scrunched downward. "No, I don't think so," he said. "Some things are just obvious to me."

The girl shook her head. "You're just amazing, do you know that?"

"Look at the list of people who have been seen going in and out of his house. We've got businesspeople from just about every industry, we've got lawyers and politicians from numerous countries, we've even got known intelligence agents from countries that are sympathetic to Islamic terrorism. How has this guy managed not to be outed long before this? According to this file, MI6 has been keeping tabs on him for the last three years. None of these visitors set off any alarm bells?"

"Page 17. One of their analysts said that even the most legitimate arms dealer would have contact with such people from time to time. He's even made reports to the government about being approached by intelligence agents, just the way he should. They didn't figure it was anything to worry about, I guess."

Noah cocked his head to the right. "Too bad our CIA didn't get to look those lists over. Those guys are so paranoid they would have automatically suspected him."

"Probably. The question is, is he actually the head of

IAR, or is he just a front man for somebody else?"

"That's what I've got to figure out. By going in as Adrian, I'm sure they're hoping I'll get some sort of feeling about it, something I can prove or act on."

Sarah put down the folder she was reading through and looked at him. "Noah, this mission worries me. If Broussard or his people suspect for a moment that you're not really Adrian, I doubt they're going to let you walk out of whatever meeting you have with them alive."

"Then I'd better get my act down pat," Noah said. "I don't have any intention of letting them bring an end to my short career."

Sarah stared at him for almost a full minute before speaking again. "You'd better not," she said softly.

THREE

Moose and Neil joined Sarah the next day as they continued studying the folders, while Noah went to Mission ID. A security guard in the building checked his ID and then directed him to an office where he met Gary Mitchell.

"Camelot, right?" Mitchell asked. "Come on in and have a seat, I'm getting everything set up for you. Take that chair, and put on those headphones."

Noah sat where he was told to and slipped the headphones over his ears. A microphone on a boom extended from one of them and he adjusted it so that it was just to the right of his mouth. "I take it you're the one who's supposed to help me learn to sound like this guy?" he asked.

Mitchell nodded. "Yep, I'm the acting coach for ID Development. Whenever you guys have to impersonate someone, they send you out to me to give you some pointers on how to accomplish it. You have an advantage with this character in that almost nobody knows what he looks like, other than general things like build and such, and you're a pretty close match in that regard. All we have to do is retrain your speaking and physical mannerisms so that you can impersonate him, in case you run into anyone who might've spoken with him in the past." He tapped on a keyboard in front of him while staring at a computer monitor, then turned to Noah again. "Watch that monitor in front of you. What you're going to be seeing and hearing is part of his interrogation. This guy was cocky and kept his cool, so there isn't a lot of stress in his voice. If you can mimic his voice and speaking manner at all, you should be able to pull this off with no trouble. Ready?"

Noah nodded, and a second later he heard the sounds through the headset as the video began to play.

Interrogator: Tell me about your most recent target.

Adrian: What do you want to know? I mean, the fellow is dead already, so it won't do you a lot of good.

Noah noticed instantly that Adrian spoke with a trace accent, something that sounded slightly Germanic, possibly Austrian. His *w's* were very clearly enunciated, while his *s's* seemed to have a slight *sh* sound to them.

In the video, he was unrestrained, sitting in a wingback chair. He had a habit of cocking his head slightly to one side when he spoke, and tended to use his hands quite a bit to emphasize points he was making.

Interrogator: Just humor me, please. What was his name?

Adrian: His name? His name was Alexander Lifshitz. He was the Israeli ambassador to Costa Rica, but he was creating problems for someone who wanted him eliminated.

Interrogator: And who hired you to eliminate him?

Adrian: Oh, now that would be the Brazilian government, in the person of their attaché for foreign affairs at their own embassy there. It seems he once knew another of my clients, who told him how to get word to me.

Interrogator: So you agreed to assassinate the Israeli Ambassador so easily?

Adrian: Of course. That's my work, is it not?

Interrogator: Yes, I suppose it was. Tell me, Adrian, did your conscience never bother you at all?

Adrian: Conscience? Oh, yes, I've heard of that. Frankly, I don't seem to have one. I am telling you things you want to know simply because I want something from you in return. Incidentally, would you like to know the name of the target I was going after when you interrupted me?

Interrogator: I actually would.

Adrian: (laughing) I was certain you might. Her name is Emily Carriker. And before you even ask, I was hired by the wife of her married lover. Some people, it seems, will pay anything to get what they want.

Interrogator: An assassin of your stature takes such simple assignments? I would have thought you would concentrate yourself on those in the political world.

Adrian: I usually do, I confess. However, I have never turned down anyone who was willing to meet my price.

The playback suddenly ended and Mitchell looked at Noah. "Can you repeat that last line, just the way he said it?"

Noah looked up at him. "I usually do, I confess. However, I have never turned down anyone who was willing to meet my price." He mimicked the facial expressions and hand gestures that Adrian had used.

Mitchell was watching his monitor and smiled, nodding his head. "That was actually incredibly close," he said. "Let's do some more."

The playback resumed and Noah studied Adrian's responses to his interrogator for another ten minutes, after which Mitchell had him repeat the last line once again. Again the acting coach was pleased, and they continued these exercises throughout the morning.

At shortly before noon, Mitchell called a break. "You're an incredibly fast study, Camelot," he said. "I think we need to move on to improvisation this afternoon. Come on, I'll buy you lunch in our cafeteria."

Noah took off the headset and laid it on the table beside the chair, then followed Mitchell out of the office and down a hallway. The cafeteria turned out to be rather large, and the food choices were as good as anything at the Sagebrush Saloon. Noah opted for a grilled chicken breast with a baked potato and salad, while Mitchell chose roast beef with mashed potatoes and gravy. The two of them carried their choices to a table and sat down together.

"You know, I've heard a lot about you," Mitchell said. "I've been told, for instance, that you have a mind like a computer. After your performance this morning, I think I tend to believe it. I've never seen anyone pick up the nuances of an individual's speech patterns so quickly."

Noah shrugged. "When I was a kid, I had a friend who figured out that my brain isn't wired like everybody else's. She used to give me these little exercises to do, basically pattern recognition tricks. I learned to watch for recognizable patterns in just about everything, it makes it easier to pick up accents, remember phone numbers, all sorts of things."

"Yeah, I can see where it would. That would explain today. What about languages? Do you speak other languages?"

"I'm fairly fluent in Spanish and French," Noah said.

"I studied both in high school and had the opportunity to work with Hispanic soldiers at times. While I was in the Army, there was a French girl who was attracted to me. She was a clerk on our base and we dated for a while. I got to practice my French a lot with her and she helped me perfect it to some degree. I picked up a little bit of several Arabic dialects while I was in the Middle East, but not enough to say that I actually speak the language."

Mitchell was nodding again. "Yeah, I suspected you might have. I don't think you'd have too much trouble learning a language if you wanted to."

"You're probably right," Noah said. "Again, it's really just a matter of finding the patterns. I think most languages have some words that are similar to those in other languages, and if I can spot an identifiable root, then I could probably pick up a lot of it pretty quickly. Maybe not fluency, but at least enough to get by."

Mitchell shook his head as if amazed. "Man, that's incredible," he said.

"I don't think so," Noah replied. "I think it just boils down to the fact I got the right kind of training for it. That friend of mine who came up with it is an incredible genius—she works for a big Washington think tank, now. I was pretty lucky to have her in my life at that time."

"Yeah, I'd say so. Okay, let's try something. We're in a social setting, no real stress on either of us at the moment, so I'd like you to try speaking as Adrian. Can you do that?"

Noah looked at him with one eyebrow raised slightly. "You want me to speak as he would? With his inflections, his mannerisms?"

Mitchell stared at him for a moment and then a big smile broke across his face. "Wow, that was about perfect. You slid into character like you'd been doing it all your life."

"Well," Noah said, still in character as Adrian, "you could say that I have been. I have always had to wear a mask, so to speak, in order to conceal the fact that I do not think as others do. To me, this is nothing but another mask that I must wear. As I come to understand it, it simply becomes another persona that I can turn on or off as needed."

Mitchell laughed. "You've got it, you've got it down pat. That slight accent of his, the slurring of the sibilants, it's perfect. Come on, let's finish eating and get back to the lab. I'm supposed to drill you through the rest of today and tomorrow, so we'll just use up the time in practice. I don't really think you need it, but orders are orders."

The two of them stopped talking and finished their meals, then headed back to Mitchell's office. They spent the afternoon with Noah listening to other recordings of Adrian and practicing his impersonation. By the time they broke at four o'clock, Mitchell was convinced that Noah had the characterization down perfectly.

"I think that's enough for today," he said. "Let's start again tomorrow around nine, that be okay?"

"I'll be here," Noah replied.

The two men shook hands and Noah made his way back to the hallway and out to his car. He fired it up and started toward home, then took out his phone to call Sarah.

"Hey, baby," she said as she answered. "How'd it go?"

"Pretty well, I think. My teacher says I'm the best

pupil he's ever had. What are you guys doing?"

"We just finished up the file on Broussard," she said. "If you're done, we'll stop and pick up again tomorrow with the IAR files."

"That sounds good," Noah said. "I was thinking we should pack up some sandwiches and stuff and go out on the boat for a while. This might be the last chance we get before the weather turns cold, especially when we don't know how long we'll be gone."

He heard Sarah asking the guys if they liked that idea, then she spoke to him again. "Elaine is off tonight," she said. "You don't mind if she and Lacey come along, do you?"

"Of course not. We'll be packing tomorrow night, so let's just have some fun this evening."

"Holy cow, did I just hear Noah Wolf say he wanted to have fun? Who are you and what have you done with my boyfriend?"

"Very funny. Call the girls and tell them to head that way, I should be there in twenty minutes."

"Okay, babe. See you then, love you."

"See you then." Noah ended the call and slipped the phone back into his pocket.

FOUR

L acey had recently moved into the trailer that Neil rented from Noah, so she was already there when he got home. Elaine was on the way, and arrived only a few minutes later.

Despite the fact that it was mid-fall, the sun was shining brightly and the air was warm. All of them were dressed in shorts and T-shirts as they carried the cooler full of sandwiches and soft drinks down to the boathouse. Noah started up the big Mercury engine and backed the boat carefully out of its slip, then gave it power as they moved out to open water.

"I'm going back for more voice practice in the morning," Noah said, "and then I'm going out to R&D for a makeover. Apparently, he had red hair and green eyes, so I get hair color and contacts. Something about a big nose, too."

Sarah grimaced. "I'm having a little trouble seeing you as a redhead," she said. "Make sure he gives you enough that you can touch it up as needed."

"I'm sure he will. Wally knows what he's doing, and if anyone could anticipate what we might need, I'd say it's him."

"Hey," Neil said suddenly, "maybe he's come up with

a shot that can turn your hair red and your eyes green. Then you wouldn't have to worry about keeping up with it."

Moose smacked him playfully on the back of his head. "You're reading too much science fiction," he said. "I don't think we're anywhere close to doing that kind of thing yet."

Neil stuck out his tongue at the bigger man. "Did you not see that bomb-making 3D printer he gave us last time? I'm not too sure there's anything Wally's gang can't do if they set their minds to it."

"Yeah," Lacey put in, "and stop hitting my boyfriend or I'll tell my dad to make you miserable on your next workout."

The banter continued throughout the evening, and all six of them seemed to enjoy the outing. Noah called it a night when the air began cooling enough that the girls were occasionally shivering and took them back to the boathouse. Thirty minutes later, he and Sarah were alone once again.

Morning came on schedule and Noah let Sarah sleep in. He showered quickly and slipped out, then drove back to Mission ID for another morning of practicing his impersonation of Adrian. Mitchell was waiting for him when he arrived.

"Ready to go at it again? I wrote up some particular phrases I want you to work on today, see if you can do them as Adrian well enough to fool my computer program."

Noah nodded as he took his seat and slipped on the headset. "Let's do it," he said.

"Okay, try this," Mitchell said. "Say, 'my name is Adrian and I've been told you want to talk to me.'"

"My name is Adrian and I've been told you want to talk to me."

"Geez, that was dead on." Mitchell shook his head. "Blows my mind how you picked this up so easily. Let's try another one."

For three hours, Mitchell fed lines to Noah, which he repeated back into the headset microphone. Over and over the computer registered a nearly perfect emulation of Adrian's voice and speech patterns, so that by the time they ended the exercises at noon he stated that Noah had it down pat.

"I don't think there's anything else I can do for you," he said at last. "You're so good at this it's incredible."

Noah took off the headset and shook the hand that Mitchell extended to him. "I really appreciate all of this," he said. "I understand it's essential to the mission and that you're just doing your job, but having you and your technology available is undoubtedly beneficial."

It was almost noon, so Noah said goodbye and drove back into Kirtland to find lunch. He decided to hit the McDonald's that was close to the main office and grab a burger and fries to eat on his way out to R&D. He finished his lunch as he pulled up to the guard shack outside the big building.

The guard checked his ID as thoroughly as always, then waved him on in. Noah parked the Corvette near the entrance and walked inside, where another guard checked his ID and then notified Wally that he was there.

"Camelot!" Wally called as he stepped into the lobby. "Man, it's great to see you again! I understand we got to pretty you up a bit, that right?"

Noah shrugged. "Well, you've got to make me look

different. I'll have to let Sarah decide if it improves my looks any."

Wally laughed, throwing his head back. "I think she's crazy about you the way you are," he said. "She probably won't like what we're about to do, but I got everything all set up so let's get to it."

He led Noah down the hallway and into what looked for all the world like a beauty salon. Two women looked up and smiled as they entered.

"Camelot, this is Carol and Lizzie," Wally said. "Girls, this is Camelot. You got everything ready?"

"Yes, Sir," Lizzie said. "Camelot, if you'll have a seat in the chair right here, we'll get started on turning you into a ginger."

Noah took the seat she indicated and a moment later he was leaning back into a sink as she washed his hair. She scrubbed hard enough to make it hurt, explaining that she had to get all of the natural oils out of his hair in order for the special dye she was going to use to work properly. When she was finished scrubbing his scalp raw, she used a blow dryer to get all of the moisture out.

Once his hair was dried, she turned the chair so that he was looking into a mirror. "This is a very special hair dye, something we developed that will completely cover your natural color without bleaching your hair. It's about as permanent as permanent can get, so once we get finished, the only way you get your natural color back is to either let it grow out and trim off the red or stop back in and let us repeat this procedure."

She picked up a tube and uncapped it, then attached what looked like a comb to the open end. Little by little, she combed through his hair, and Noah watched with curiosity in the mirror as his hair went from blonde to red.

"Okay," she said after about fifteen minutes, "that about does it. I'm going to give you a couple of tubes of this stuff to take with you, so you can touch up roots as they start to grow out. Be sure to check yourself carefully every morning for any sign of blonde growing in under the red. It wouldn't do for someone to figure out that you're coloring your hair."

Noah agreed, and then Carol moved in beside him. "Camelot, have you ever worn contacts before?"

"Nope," Noah said. "My eyes seem to work just fine the way they are."

Carol nodded. "These don't have any kind of correction to them, they'll just turn your naturally blue eyes to green. These are very specially made, designed to let plenty of oxygen get through them to your cornea so that your eyes don't dry out too badly, but you may need to moisten them occasionally. You can leave these in for up to two weeks at a time, but try not to go past that. What I'm going to do is show you how to put them in and take them out yourself, just in case you ever have to. Are you ready?"

Noah said he was, and the girl began explaining how to put a couple of drops of saline solution into his eyes and then use the tip of a finger to carefully place the lens against his eyeball. Noah got it on the first try with his right eye, then again with his left. Once he had them both in place, she talked him through removing them, then had him rinse them in saline and put them back in. He did it again with no problem, and she pronounced him ready to go.

At that point, another woman entered the room. This one was carrying a hypodermic needle, and Noah was reminded of Neil's comments about shots to change hair and eye color.

"Hi, there," the woman said. "I'm Jackie, and you're probably not going to like me too much. I understand we need to make your nose a little bigger for your next mission, and that's my job. I'm going to give you a series of small shots in the skin of your nose that will make it swell a bit. The effect will last about a month, so hopefully you'll be done with your mission by then."

"If I'm not," Noah said, "it probably won't matter."

Jackie gave him a wry grin and leaned close to swab his nose with alcohol pads, and then she began poking the needle into various parts of the skin. Noah made no sound and did not flinch, and she was finished after less than a minute.

"Now, that may feel strange for a couple hours, as the swelling takes effect and sort of locks itself in. Once you get used to it, though, I don't think it will even be noticeable." She turned around without even saying goodbye and left the room.

Wally had taken a seat in the room and waited while the transformation was made, and he jumped to his feet as Noah rose from the chair. "Wow, Camelot," he said with a grin, "you do look different. I don't know, that girl of yours might decide she likes this look. Let me know how that goes, will you?"

Noah looked at himself in the mirror one more time, then turned to Wally. "Just being honest, but I don't think I like this look very much, myself. It makes me look like a guy I knew in the Army, and he wasn't exactly a friend of mine. A real jerk, if you want to know the truth."

"Yeah, well, everybody looks like somebody," Wally

said. "Wait and see what your girlfriend thinks before you decide not to keep this look after the mission."

Noah shook his hand and then Wally escorted him out of the building. He looked just different enough that the guards might have had trouble accepting his ID, so Wally even called out to the gate to clear his departure.

Noah climbed into the Corvette and headed for home. Sarah, Moose and Neil were all at his place, going through the files once more and looking for ideas they might suggest to Noah on how to handle various aspects of the mission. The three of them were at the table when he walked through the front door, and all of them stared when he entered the kitchen.

"Who are you and where the hell is my boyfriend?" Sarah said after a long moment's pause.

"Holy crap," Neil said, staring at Noah's hair. "That's really red."

"Yeah, and check out that schnoz!" Moose added in.

"Supposedly this makes me look more like Adrian," Noah said. He looked at Sarah. "Wally actually thought you might like this look. Can I tell him he was full of shit?"

Sarah nodded slowly. "About three tons of it," she said. "I don't like that at all. Good Lord, Noah, you don't even look like you."

Moose chuckled. "Yeah, you look like an Irish mobster."

Noah walked over to the counter and poured himself a cup of coffee, then took a seat at the table with them. "I knew a guy who looked a lot like this in the Army," he said. "His name was Monahan, and he was about as Irish as you can get. A real asshole." He took a sip of coffee and set the cup down. "So, where are we?"

Moose picked up a sheet of paper from one of the files and slid it over to him. "We noticed something," he said. "MI6 has been monitoring all of Broussard's phone calls for more than a year, but they say they've never heard anything that could implicate him with IAR. We thought that seemed a little odd..."

"So I got my computer and started searching for any photos of Broussard using a phone," Neil broke in. "I found a lot of them in different databases, and it seems he has a phone they haven't discovered yet. Look at these pictures." He turned the computer around so that Noah could see the screen. There were two photos on it. "In the first picture, you see him using the phone he's known for. It's an expensive Vertu, one of the most expensive cell phones you can get. In the other picture, he's using a blocky old sat phone, though, you see that?"

"Yes," Noah said. "I take it there's no record of a sat phone?"

"None at all," Moose said. "That struck us as odd, since there are at least three photos taken by MI6 and NSA that show him using this one or one like it, but somehow their people never caught it."

Noah lowered his eyebrows. "So you're thinking that he's using a sat phone to communicate with his IAR associates?"

"That's possible," Neil said, "but he uses it so rarely that I can't help wondering if it's for a special purpose only. What if he's actually using it to talk to someone above him? I mean, the Dragon Lady said they aren't certain he's the top guy, right?"

Noah looked closely at the two photos for another moment. "You may have just stumbled onto something important," he said. "I don't suppose there's any way you can track down the number of that phone, maybe get a tap on it?"

Neil scowled and shook his head. "Unfortunately, no. There are so many variables to a sat phone that it would be impossible to find any record of it. And before you ask, I already tried. There are no records anywhere of him purchasing one, but it's not like he'd do it under his own name, anyway, right?"

"I'm sure he wouldn't. Still, it gives us something to work on when we get close to him. And speaking of that, we need to get packed. We're booked on a KLM flight that leaves Denver at eight in the morning. We need to pull out of here around two o'clock, that should give us plenty of time to get checked in and go through security."

"We're already packed," Neil said. "You're the only one who hasn't gotten there yet. Soon as you do, we can load your bags into Hummer-stein with all of ours."

Noah nodded his head. "Give me fifteen minutes," he said, "and I'll have them ready. We can kick back and watch some TV, maybe heat up some pizzas for dinner later."

FIVE

T heir flight took off a few minutes late the next morning and landed two hours later in Chicago. It was a short layover, and they were back in the air in only thirty minutes. In order to keep their place of origin a secret, they would land in Belgium and use their mission IDs to purchase tickets on a smaller European airline that would take them to Madrid. They had used temporary, throwaway IDs for the flight out of Denver, and ditched them as soon as they landed in Brussels.

Overall, the trip took twenty hours. A taxi took them from the Madrid airport to the Wellington Hotel. They checked into four separate rooms, but no one was surprised when Sarah followed Noah into his.

They slept in the next morning and then gathered around lunchtime in the hotel's restaurant. Neil had done some research and selected the newspaper that Noah should place his ad in, so he took out a phone and called their offices.

The ad was simple. *"Available to discuss business. AD229."* Noah added the number of a throwaway phone he had picked up in Brussels, and paid for the ad with one of several disposable Visa cards.

"That's done," he said as he ended the call. "The ad will appear in tomorrow morning's newspaper, so we've got the rest of the day to ourselves. Now let's get some equipment." He took a business card out of his wallet and dialed a number. The card was for a rare book dealer, but it was part of the camouflage they used on a mission. The dealer was actually an E & E station officer.

"Intrigue Books," a British voice said. "How may I help you?"

"I'm looking for a copy of one of Kurt Saxon's books," Noah said. "Would you have a copy of *Granddad's Wonderful Book of Chemistry*? It's for a friend."

"How interesting," the man said. "I believe I might have just exactly what you're looking for. Could you come by my shop?"

"Yes, I'd be glad to. Shall we say in about an hour?"

"Very good, Sir. I look forward to meeting you." The line went dead.

"We meet with supply in an hour," Noah said to the team. "After that, how about we act like tourists?"

"I'm for that," Sarah said. "Will you buy me souvenirs?"

"Of course he will," Neil said. "Otherwise you'll just pester him all day."

"I do not pester," Sarah said, glaring at him. "I don't pester you, do I, Noah?"

"Of course not, Babe," Noah said. "I don't know why anyone would ever think so."

Sarah stared at him for a moment. "Did you forget what we said about not trying to be funny?"

They finished up their late lunch and headed out of the hotel. Noah spotted a taxi van and ushered them all in.

"We need to visit the Intrigue Books shop on Calle de la Bola," he said, using Adrian's speech mannerisms, "and then we are interested in doing some sightseeing. Would you be able to show us around?"

"Oh, yes, Señor," the driver replied. "I am Ernesto, I am the best for sightseeing. Come, let me take you to the bookstore, and then I shall show you the Royal Palace of Madrid!"

It only took about fifteen minutes to get to the bookstore, and they left Ernesto waiting with the taxi while they went inside. The proprietor looked up and smiled as they entered.

"Greetings, gentlemen, and lovely lady," he said. "How might I help you today?"

"I called a little while ago about a Kurt Saxon book," Noah said. "Do you have one in stock?"

"I do," the proprietor said. "I take it you're looking for the first edition?"

"Actually, the one my friend wanted me to look for was the revised edition from the 1980s," Noah said. "I guess it has more of Tesla's projects in it."

At the mention of Tesla, the proprietor smiled again, then motioned for them to follow him into a back room. Once the door was closed behind them, he picked up a box and set it on a table.

"My name is Henry. I was told you would be looking for these particular items," the Englishman said. He opened the box to reveal two Glock forty-caliber pistols, a 9-mm Beretta and a single MP9 machine pistol. Each of them came with three extra magazines, and the Glocks had concealable holsters. The MP9 had a lanyard attached that was designed to let it hang from the shoulder.

"These will be ideal," Noah said. He and Moose slid the special holsters down inside their slacks, while Neil shrugged into the shoulder harness. His light jacket would keep the gun concealed, since it hung slightly behind him. Sarah picked up the Beretta and looked it over, then slid it into her purse with the extra magazines. The men stuffed their spare magazines into their jackets' inner pockets.

"Will there be anything else?" Henry asked.

"No," Noah said. "I think you've met our needs quite nicely. We'll be in touch if we need anything else in the future." He shook hands with the Englishman and they made their way back out to the taxi.

Ernesto was smart enough not to ask any questions, but only smiled as they climbed back inside. The car took off and the four of them enjoyed looking at the old city. Established more than a thousand years ago, Madrid had served as the capital of Spain since the early sixteen hundreds. During its long history, it had transformed from a Muslim community to a Christian one, and though there were few signs of its Muslim heritage still around, the city managed to maintain an atmosphere of diverse cultures all trying to fit together.

Ernesto told them some of the history as he drove, and was delighted when Noah invited him to join them on a tour through the Palace. Covering more than 1,400,000 square feet, and with more than three thousand rooms, there was no possibility of seeing the whole thing. Much of the edifice, however, served as a museum and was open to the public.

In a tour that lasted more than two hours, they saw incredible works of art by Caravaggio, Velasquez and even Francisco de Goya. There were smaller areas devoted to particular arts, including porcelain, watches, silverware and furniture, and gift shops permitted tourists to buy replicas of some of the rarest pieces. Sarah fell in love with a tea set, so Noah bought her one that was almost identical.

From the palace, they went to the famous monastery, San Lorenzo del Escorial. The monastery had become a major cultural and heritage location, seated in a town of the same name nearly 30 miles from downtown Madrid. Many Spanish kings were interred there in the mausoleum, and Noah and the team were awed by the architecture and grandeur of the Royal Library.

"I never would have believed that Madrid was so beautiful," Sarah said. "I mean, all I really know about it is the stuff I learned in school, and that wasn't much. I'm really glad we got to see this place."

"I've been here once before," Moose said. "Back in my college days, a couple of friends and I spent a summer tooling around Europe. I think we were only here for a couple of days, and I didn't get to see nearly as many things as I wanted to."

Noah looked at him. "Well, we may get some time to just play tourist..."

He was cut off when the burner phone in his pocket vibrated. Noah excused himself and walked away from the group for a moment to answer.

"Yes?"

"You placed an advertisement," a female voice said. "You are available to discuss business?"

"My advertisement has not yet been published," Noah said.

"Not in print, but we were notified that it had appeared on the website of the newspaper. Are you available to discuss business?"

"That will depend entirely on the nature of the business to be discussed," Noah replied. "I am a cautious man."

"We are looking for a man who is experienced in the removal of certain problems. We have been anticipating the arrival of such a man who would place an advertisement such as you have done."

"Then perhaps it is fortunate that I have chosen to visit Madrid at this time," Noah said, maintaining character. "I might have gone to Geneva or Marseilles in my search for opportunities." Geneva and Marseilles were two of the other cities where IAR suggested Adrian might place the ad, so mentioning them confirmed that he was responding to their attempts to reach him.

"Then I am certain you are the man we are seeking," the woman said. "Are you willing to meet?"

"I prefer to conduct my business at a distance. My line is secure, is yours?"

There was silence on the line for a moment, but then the woman cleared her throat. "The business we wish to discuss is very sensitive. The principal would prefer to discuss it face-to-face."

"Then I'm afraid we have reached an impasse. I never show my face to my employers."

Another silence that lasted for half a minute. "The business we wish to discuss will impact the entire world. The compensation will be greater than any you've ever received in the past. Is there no possibility that we can arrange a meeting between yourself and our principal?"

Noah hesitated, trying to give the impression that he

was considering her request. "A meeting would have to be on my terms, and with no others present. Call this number again in four hours, and I will give you the details. If they are acceptable, then the meeting will take place."

He ended the call and slipped the phone back into his pocket, then rejoined the others.

Moose caught his eye. "That was awfully quick," he said softly.

"Welcome to the age of the internet," Noah said. "Apparently my ad was posted on the newspaper's website and spotted there."

Moose nodded. "So, what's next?"

"They'll call me back in four hours. I need to set up a meeting with their representatives. To stay in character, it needs to be a very private meeting where I can keep my face concealed. I think we'll do it late tonight, somewhere with lots of shadow."

"Then maybe we should get Ernesto to show us where some of the nightlife can be found. Look for a spot you can use that's somewhere around there."

They conferred with Ernesto and took a two-hour tour through parts of the city best experienced after dark. Noah chose a blues bar called La Coquette to set up his meeting, because of several dark alleyways close by.

They said goodbye to Ernesto and entered the bar, where they were quickly escorted to a large, private table. A waitress took their food and drink orders and then hurried away. She was back in what seemed like only moments with their drinks.

"Interesting," Neil said. "I don't think I've ever heard blues played with a flamenco flair."

"It is an unusual sound," Moose said. "Not bad, though."

Noah nodded. "It has an unusual beat, not like the blues back in America. Still, you can tell the relation is there."

The bar was entirely different from others the team had been in, and the music, while somewhat loud, was comfortable and enjoyable. They enjoyed their dinner, occasionally talking with other patrons, and then relaxed with bottles of San Miguel beer. Neil couldn't help grinning, since the drinking age in Spain was only eighteen.

"A guy could get used to this," Moose said. "Kinda makes you understand why a lot of Americans choose Spain when they decide to leave the country."

"It is pretty nice here," Sarah said. "Of course, it would be even nicer if we were really on vacation."

"Yeah, well, some of us have to work," Neil said. The look on his face said he was trying to cover her slip, but Sarah only laughed.

"Yes, but at least we get to enjoy a day off now and then. Let's let work wait for tomorrow, there's plenty of time for that. Tonight I just want to relax and have fun." She cast a sidelong glance at Noah, fully aware that he was on the job twenty-four hours a day.

"For now, in any case," Noah said.

It was slightly more than an hour later when Noah's burner phone rang again. He excused himself from the group and walked outside to answer.

"Yes," he said.

The same female voice came back to him. "Are you ready to meet?"

"I am," Noah said. "There is a small group of trees near the intersection of Calle de las Hileras and Calle de las Fuentes, just in front of the Infinity Comics building. Tell your principal to be standing there in one hour, and to come alone." He ended the call and then immediately took the SIM card out of the phone and used a lighter from his pocket to burn it. The phone went into a nearby trashcan as he walked back into the bar.

SIX

Noah sat down at the table and looked at Moose. "I set the meeting up for an hour from now, under the trees in front of the comic shop. Go on out and find a spot where you can keep me covered. Neil and Sarah can stay here in the bar."

Moose nodded once and then got up and walked out of the building. Noah sat with Sarah and Neil for another twenty minutes, then walked outside and found a dark spot to wait.

A half-hour later, a car turned onto the street and parked 50 yards away from the front door of the comic shop. There was one man inside, Noah could see, and a moment later that man stepped out of the car and walked toward the trees that stood near the entrance. Noah waited until he was under the trees and then stepped out of hiding and walked toward him.

The light jacket he wore had a hood, and he had flipped it up when he had come outside. By keeping his head tilted down, the hood concealed his hair and face fairly well. He walked directly toward the man under the tree and stopped eight feet from him.

"You want to talk business?" Noah asked.

The man was watching Noah's feet intently and swallowed nervously. "I have a job for you," he said, his accent seeming Middle Eastern and thick; Noah placed it as Iraqi, probably from the Kirkuk area. "It involves the removal of someone who is preventing my employers from accomplishing things they want to do. I have been sent to discuss this with you."

"You are not the principal? I was told I would be meeting with the principal."

"I—I am the principal for this job," the fellow said anxiously. "If you agree, you will deal only with me."

Noah studied him for a moment. "It is very fortunate that you are an intelligent man," he said, "which is obvious since you have not tried to look at my face. However, I do not deal with underlings. You may go and tell your employers that I am not interested in whatever work they want to offer."

The man jerked and for a split second his eyes almost rose to Noah's face, but he caught himself and looked down again. "Please, I—I cannot do that. How can I satisfy you so that you will accept this employment?"

Noah spat on the ground in front of the man's feet. "You cannot," he said. "If I do not speak with your employer directly, I will not consider any employment you offer."

The man kept his eyes on the ground, but nodded slowly. "I can arrange for you to—to speak with him. Should he contact you on the same number?"

"That number is no longer functioning. Can you not call him at this moment?"

The man stood silent for a moment, then carefully withdrew a cell phone from his pocket. "One moment, please," he said. He dialed a number and put the phone on speaker. A man's voice answered a moment later.

"Hello?"

"This is Mustapha. I am with the man I was sent to meet, but he will not speak to anyone but you. I have the phone on speaker, so that he can hear you."

There was silence on the line for twenty seconds, and then the voice, which had a mild French accent, said, "Am I speaking with Adrian?"

"I am he," Noah said. "I do not appreciate this game you're playing."

"Then, please forgive me, but it was necessary to ensure that we were speaking with the right person. Has Mustapha told you what we want you to do?"

"In only the vaguest of terms," Noah said. "However, I do not discuss such business with anyone other than my actual employer."

"Nor can I discuss it over a telephone. I know that you are very secretive, but if you wish to discuss this matter with me, it must be in person. Are you willing to do so?"

Noah waited for ten seconds before answering. "No one who knows what I do has ever seen my face and lived. That has kept me free and safe for these last four years. Why should I change that practice for you?"

"Because I can provide you with a great deal of employment in your specialty. No one but myself would ever have to know who you are, and you would be able to reach me at any time. I have spent the past few years dealing with this type of work, and have never allowed anyone to know anything about my contacts. Since I would not know your true name, nor anything about your private life, there would be nothing I could use to betray you."

Noah hesitated a few more seconds, trying to give

the impression that he was considering the proposal. "I would meet with you, and you alone. If there is any sign that others are watching, I will simply walk away and within three days you would be dead. Is that acceptable?"

"Perfectly," the man said. "We can meet two days from now, wherever you choose. Only tell me when and where."

"Then let it be in London, the day after tomorrow. Take a room at the Elizabeth Hotel under the name of William Sykes. Be completely alone, and I will come to you at three in the afternoon. Trust me to know if you have anyone watching. Do you understand?"

"William Sykes, Elizabeth Hotel, three o'clock on the day after tomorrow. I will be alone."

"Very well. I will come to you. Tell this man to leave and never approach me again."

"Mustapha," the voice said. "Ring off the call and leave immediately. Report to your superior at once, and forget this conversation ever happened."

"Yes, Sir," Mustapha said, and then he ended the call and turned away. He walked quickly to his car and got in, then drove away, keeping his face averted from Noah the whole time.

Noah stood and waited for Moose, who appeared a minute later. "Get Neil and Sarah, while I find a taxi," Noah said to him. Moose turned and headed into the bar while Noah took out his phone and dialed a number from memory.

A woman answered. "Hello?"

"Catherine?"

"Yes, this is Catherine Potts. I believe I recognize the

voice, is this Mr. Colson?"

"Yes, it is. You have an excellent memory."

"I'm told it comes with the job. How can I help you, Mr. Colson?"

"Are you aware of Pierre Broussard?"

"Oh, indeed I am."

"I need surveillance on the Elizabeth Hotel. I believe Monsieur Broussard will be checking in there under the name of William Sykes the day after tomorrow, but I'd like to be sure that none of his associates are checking in between now and then."

"I can arrange that," Catherine said. "Will he be enjoying the pleasure of your company?"

"I'll be paying him a visit, yes. Whether he enjoys it or not is entirely up to him. I'll check in with you the day after tomorrow, just let me know if there's anyone else staying there I should be suspicious of."

"I'll have it all under control, Mr. Colson. Just let me know if there's anything else I can do for you."

"I'll be sure to do so. Have a good night." He ended the call and slipped the phone back into his pocket.

A lone taxi was coming down the street from the opposite end, and Noah flagged it down just as Moose, Neil and Sarah appeared. It was a small car, and Noah had Moose sit in the front while he joined Sarah and Neil in the backseat. The four of them laughed and talked about the fun they had in the bar all the way back to their hotel.

They gathered in Noah's room and he quietly explained what was going on. They would fly to London the following day and begin preparing for the meeting on Sunday.

"Neil, I want you to book a private plane first thing in the morning, as early as possible. I want to be there by early afternoon if we can. Everybody get some sleep, tomorrow could turn out to be a long day."

Neil and Moose said goodnight and left the room, heading for their own. Sarah looked at Noah with a grin.

"If you want to get any sleep tonight, then let's go to bed now." She giggled. "I'm just a little bit tipsy and you know how I get when I'm tipsy."

Noah raised his eyebrows and reached out to pull her into an embrace. "Yes, I do," he said. He kissed her, and then began undressing her.

Sarah giggled again. "Mmmm, I love it when you take charge."

* * *

The four of them packed their things the next morning before heading down to breakfast. Noah and Sarah got there first, with Moose and then Neil arriving only moments later.

"I found a guy with a private Cessna jet," Neil said, "all ready to go as soon as we can get to the airport. I told him it would probably be around nine, so we got time to eat."

"Well done," Noah said. "That should put us in London around one o'clock at the latest. When we get there, we'll get a car and look the situation over. I'm fairly sure it was Broussard I spoke to last night, but I have no idea if he's in London at the moment or not. I asked Catherine Potts last night to set up surveillance on the hotel, watching for any of his associates or anyone else we ought to be wary of."

"That's our lady in London, right?" Moose asked. "She

sounds like she's a pretty tough gal."

"She's efficient, and that's what I'm counting on," Noah said. "With her double connection to both our outfit and MI6, she's got the resources we need right now. If there's anybody around that hotel we need to know about, I'm pretty sure she'll be able to fill us in."

"Are we going to stay in the hotel?" Sarah asked. "I mean, would it be a good idea for us to just be there when he arrives?"

"Not all of us, no. I'm going to have Moose take a room there tonight, so he can have his eyes on the situation as well. The rest of us will go somewhere else."

"How did you pick the Elizabeth Hotel for the meeting?" Neil asked. "We never stayed there when we were in London."

"No, but it's on a list of places I saw once, places where you can stay cheap and still get a decent room. I remember thinking it looked interesting, so when I needed to pick a spot in London in a hurry, it came to mind. Hopefully it gave the impression that I know London a lot better than I do."

They ate their breakfasts when they came and then checked out of the hotel and caught a taxi to the airport. The pilot was waiting with the little jet fueled and ready for the three-hour flight, and his copilot helped them stow their bags in the small luggage compartment. Less than fifteen minutes after their arrival, the plane was moving into position for takeoff.

The plane hesitated at the start of the runway for a moment, and then the pilot shoved the throttles forward and they began moving. All of them were shoved back into their seats as their velocity rapidly climbed to the point that the wings grabbed the air and lifted them away from the earth.

The copilot, who doubled as flight attendant, leaned out of the cockpit to ask if they wanted anything to drink, but they all shook their heads so he settled back into his seat. The team sat and looked out the windows, not bothering to try to talk over the loud roar of the engines.

Sarah managed to doze off, but the three men stayed awake throughout the flight. Noah was trying to anticipate what the meeting with Broussard would tell him, planning for every contingency he could imagine, but Moose and Neil were only watching the earth pass along below them. When the pilot announced their descent, Sarah finally stirred and awoke, and then they were making their final approach to the London City Airport.

"We're here," Neil said as the engines began winding down.

SEVEN

Getting through customs from a private flight was pretty easy. The bored inspectors asked them if they had anything to declare, then waved them along to passport control and immigration. No one bothered to look into their bags, so the guns they'd picked up in Spain were safely carried through.

Finishing up with immigration took almost an hour and then they walked to the Avis counter and rented a Jaguar sedan. Sarah smiled as she slid behind the wheel and adjusted the seat for her short frame. "Oh, yeah, back in the saddle again!"

"Just remember to drive on the right side of the road," Neil said.

"No, this is England," Moose said, "she has to drive on the wrong side."

"Whatever! I just figure I've got enough chances to get killed on this mission without worrying about getting hit head-on by some giant truck!"

"Oh, chill out, Neil," Sarah said, "I haven't wrecked yet with you in the car." She put the car in gear and drove out onto the street.

"Did anyone but me notice that she said 'yet' in that

sentence?" Neil whined. "It's like she's warning me that it's coming."

Moose looked at him and then reached for his cell-phone. "Hang on a minute, I want to record this and post it to Facebook…."

"Don't you dare!" Neil said, and then the two of them were fighting over the phone in the back seat. Moose was laughing like a teenager as he tried to keep it out of Neil's reach.

Noah looked at them and then turned back to face the road ahead. "Let's go and find Broussard's place," he said. "I'd like to get a feel for the guy."

"You got it," Sarah said. She reached into her purse and brought out her own phone, then called up its navigation app. "I programmed his address in before we even left home, just in case." The computerized voice began giving her directions, and she had to turn the car around at the next intersection.

The ride to Broussard's large estate near Basildon took almost an hour, most of which was spent in finding their way out of the city itself. The big house sat in the midst of a twenty-acre wooded lot, and could barely be seen from the highway that ran along in front of it.

"That place would make a pretty fair fortress," Moose said. "Think we'll have to force our way in there, Boss?"

"Not if I can avoid it," Noah said. "Those trees are thick enough to hide a small army, I'd hate to try to infil-trate the place."

"It wouldn't be that bad," Moose said. "We could come at it from the east, they're a little less dense there. We could move low, keep some of the brush between us and anyone inside that perimeter until we got to the fence line."

Noah nodded. "We'll keep that in mind, but I doubt we'll be coming here. If Broussard is the one we want I should be able to take him down without having to try invading his little private country." He turned to Sarah. "Okay, now let's go look at the Elizabeth."

"Aye, aye, Skipper." She turned the car at the next crossroad and stopped, then entered the hotel into the car's GPS. Once it began talking she followed its directions onto another highway, the A127, that led them back to London.

"Boss," Neil asked, "how do you intend to find out if this is the right guy or not? I mean, the mission is to cut off the IAR's head, right? What if you take out Broussard and he ain't it?"

"Remember that satellite phone?" Noah asked in return. "If he can meet my demands without calling someone above his pay grade, then he's the guy. If he uses that phone to call someone else for approval, then the job just gets extended. I've got to be certain I'm cutting off the head before I take anyone out. Once I take the first one, they'll be on alert and I won't have a chance to take anyone else by surprise."

"Okay," Neil said. "Then the only problem is how do we identify whoever he calls?"

"That's why I've got you. I need you to come up with a way to tag that phone so we can monitor or trace its calls. Got any ideas?"

Neil snorted a laugh. "It's actually pretty easy. Sat phones use a pretty heavy radio signal, and their encryption has been broken so that there are commercial devices available that can monitor and track them, even get their GPS location. I'll get one and be ready if your pigeon uses his, and that'll let me get the location of the phone he calls. Most people seem to think sat phones are safe, so they don't even bother to move after using one. We could pinpoint the bastard in no time flat."

"You'll know where the other phone is?" Moose asked. "Boss, should we go for a double whammy? Take out both ends at once? If the other phone is close enough, I could go and take a shot at whoever has it."

"I can do it even easier than that," Neil said. "Get me a decent programmable drone that can carry some weight, and I can send it straight to the spot with a bomb."

Noah shook his head. "At this point, we won't know enough to make the call, I don't believe. It will be best to wait and analyze the information we get. I'd rather let Broussard have an extra few days of life than make a mistake and hit the wrong guy." He turned to look back at Neil. "Can you lock onto the signal and monitor calls made by the other phone, as well?"

Neil nodded his head. "Shouldn't be a problem. I just need to get some equipment. Make a stop at a decent electronics store and I can get what I need to make one, or if you can find a sat phone store they probably sell one."

"See if you can find one," Noah said. "I'd rather you just buy one that's ready to go than try to make one yourself."

Neil nodded. "No problem," he said as he started punching buttons on his phone. A moment later he said, "There's a Satphone Store at 2007 Hornton Street, not far from Kensington Palace. They've got the Delma MMS Satphone Tracker. With one of those, I can listen in on any sat phone call within a mile."

"All right. Sarah, let's go by there after we look at the

hotel. Neil, I've changed the plan. You'll be staying at the Elizabeth with Moose after all. If Broussard uses his sat phone, I want you close enough to pick it up."

"What about you and Goldilocks, here?" Moose asked. "Where will you be staying?"

"We'll go to the Cavendish," Noah said, "where we stayed before in London."

"Ooh, good, can we get the honeymoon suite this time?" Sarah asked with a grin.

"No, and we can't even stay in the same room. Adrian never had a woman with him, as far as we know, and I can't break character now that we're getting close."

Sarah scowled at him. "Well, this mission is gonna suck!"

"You'll survive," Neil said. "Look at Moose and me, we don't get to be with our girlfriends and we make it through."

"Shut up, Neil," she growled. "You're not helping."

They drove along in silence for a few minutes, and then Sarah pointed at a large building ahead. "That's the Elizabeth," she said. "Place looks like it must be pretty old, but it's in good shape."

"It's nineteenth century," Noah said, "but that's all I know. I think it'll work fine for what we're doing."

They drove past it and then Sarah asked Neil to get directions to the Satphone Store he wanted to visit. He pressed a button on his phone and its navigation started reading off directions.

"There are too many GPS direction devices in this car," Sarah said as she turned where the directions indicated. "Just when I get used to one electronic voice, another one pops up and starts telling me where to go."

"That's what they're for," Moose said. "Cause girls get lost so easy."

"I'm gonna lose you," Sarah grumbled. "First chance I get, trust me."

They arrived at the Satphone Store a few minutes later, and Neil hurried inside. Moose waited in the car with Noah and Sarah, listening to Sarah singing softly along with John Legend. Neil was back in less than ten minutes, holding something that looked a lot like an old brick phone.

"This thing will do the job," he said. "I can lock onto the signal of a phone and use this device to get its ESN so I can find it again and listen to any calls made to or from it, and I can grab its GPS location at the same time. I can even pinpoint a location on whoever Broussard might call."

"Good," Noah said. "It's almost five o'clock; we're going to drop you guys off at the Elizabeth and let you get settled in for the night. You can go out and relax a bit this evening if you want, but be in your rooms tomorrow. Neil, I want you to monitor for any satellite phone usage in the hotel tomorrow, okay? If you find any, see if you can tell who it is and what the call is about."

"No problem, Boss. Want me to record the calls? This unit has a record feature."

"Yes," Noah said. "That way I can compare it to the voice I heard on Mustapha's phone last night. Assuming that was Broussard, I'll recognize his voice. We'll check in with you tomorrow around noon."

"Sounds good," Moose said as Sarah pulled up in front of the old hotel's entrance. He and Neil climbed out and got their bags out of the trunk, then walked inside without saying another word. Sarah put the car back in gear and drove out of the entryway and onto the street.

"Are you getting hungry?" Noah asked.

Sarah nodded and grinned. "Starving. We seem to have skipped right over lunch, and breakfast was a long time ago as far as my stomach is concerned."

"Yes, it was. Let's go find some dinner." He took out his own phone and told Google Now to find restaurants near their location, then looked at Sarah again. "Greek food okay? The Santorini is over on Moscow Road, off Queensway."

"Just hit the direction button," Sarah said. "Might as well have one more gadget telling me where to go today."

Noah did so, and they got to the restaurant in less than fifteen minutes. The food and service were both excellent, and they managed to enjoy dinner without thinking much about the mission.

"I've got a little surprise for you," Sarah said. "I was supposed to wait 'til tonight, but since we can't stay in the same room, I want to go ahead and tell you now."

Noah narrowed his eyes. "Surprise? What kind of surprise?"

"Well, while we were getting our ID kits, Allison took me aside. She wanted to tell me something and let me be the one to share it with you."

"I noticed you seemed surprised about something," Noah said. "What is it?"

"Remember your old friend Molly? She's transferring to E & E, coming in to work directly with Allison and Mr. J in the planning department." She watched his face closely as she finished speaking.

Noah's expression didn't change. "I shouldn't be surprised," he said. "Now that she knows I'm with the agency, it would make sense for her to want to be part of it, too." He cocked his head slightly and looked into her eyes. "Is this going to make you uncomfortable?"

Sarah kept her face as expressionless as she could. "Should it?" she asked.

"No," Noah said. "I have no feelings for Molly, but I do seem to have some for you, even if I don't quite know how to classify them. I can assure you that I won't be with anyone but you, unless the mission forces a situation I can't avoid."

Sarah rolled her eyes. "I know that," she said. "Trust me, I haven't forgotten about little Felicita! I just want to know I don't have to worry that Molly might come between us."

"I can't see how she could," Noah said. "I don't want to go back to pretending to be her boyfriend, and she already knows I have some kind of real attachment to you. She wouldn't want to interfere with that; she'd be more likely to try to hang out with us and observe it, so she can figure out more about what makes me tick."

Sarah blinked. "Well—I guess I could handle that, as long as it wasn't all the time, y'know?"

Noah nodded. "I understand. And I don't want you to worry about it. You're the only girl I want, Sarah."

She smiled, and they finished eating. An hour later, they had checked into the Cavendish and gone to their rooms, and Sarah lay in her bed and cried silently.

EIGHT

Noah was already up, showered and dressed when Sarah called him at seven the next morning.

"Hello," he said.

"Hey, there," Sarah said sleepily. "Did I wake you?"

"No, I've been up for a while. I was about to call you and see if you're ready for breakfast."

"Hmmf. Can you give me ten minutes? Okay, make that twenty minutes?"

"I want to go on down. Why don't you meet me in the restaurant when you get ready. I can just drink some coffee until you get there."

"Aw, that's sweet," Sarah said with a chuckle. "Okay, I'll be there as fast as I can."

Noah ended the call and left the room, following the hall to the elevator. An older couple was waiting and he rode down with them, but they headed for the exit while he walked into the restaurant that was off the lobby. There were very few people there, so he asked the hostess who greeted him to show him to a table for two. He ordered coffee and said a guest would be joining him, then settled in to wait for Sarah.

She arrived fifteen minutes later and Noah stood to

hold her chair for her. "Wow," she said, "aren't we a gentleman today."

A couple at a nearby table was smiling at them, so Noah gave her a grin. "Just being the new me," he said as he took his own seat again. "Judging from what I've seen and heard, I'm something of a gentleman when I'm not performing my usual services."

Sarah's eyes went wide for a moment, but she couldn't quite stifle the smile that escaped onto her face. "And here I thought you were just trying to be sweet," she said. "Oh, well, I guess I'd better take what I can get."

The waitress came back and handed the menus to them, and they both chose folded eggs with treacle bacon and Boston beans, with a fresh cup of coffee for Sarah and a refill for Noah. The waitress drifted away to put in their order and the two of them sat and chatted as they waited.

"So, where do we start today?" Sarah asked.

"I need to check in with our local lady," Noah said, "see if anyone has checked into the Elizabeth that we need to pay attention to. I'll check with her now and then, all the way up to time for my meeting. I'm going to let you check in with the guys after we leave here. I don't want to take any chance that someone could over-hear me talking to them, or them talking to me. Don't let them use any names during the call."

Sarah nodded. "Okay," she said. "Any particular in-struction you want me to give them?"

"I think they know what to do. I just want to give them the opportunity to let us know if there's anything I need to watch out for."

"Okay, so what's on our agenda for this morning?

Anything special or unusual?"

"I think not," Noah said. "We can probably go drive around the city for a while, just to keep moving. I don't see any point in sitting still."

Their breakfast came a few moments later and they dug in. "I think one of the best parts about being an international traveler is that we get to try so many different kinds of food," Sarah said. "If anyone had ever told me I would be having baked beans and eggs for breakfast right now, I probably would've said they were crazy, but this is really good."

"I've always enjoyed trying different fare in my travels. Of course, sometimes that means trusting someone else to order for you, if you don't speak the language. I went to some kind of a restaurant with some men from my unit once, and ended up eating some little pieces of red meat on a skewer. It was really good, but when I asked what it was they told me I was eating rat."

"Eww! That's disgusting! People actually eat rat?"

"I understand it's quite a delicacy in some places. It actually was very good."

Sarah shuddered and refused to look at him for a minute, then shoved her plate away. "Okay, you have officially ruined my appetite this morning. That's rotten, I was really enjoying that until you opened your big mouth."

Noah looked at her for a few seconds, then went on eating his own breakfast. After a minute she pulled her plate back over and continued eating.

When they were finished with breakfast, they got into the Jaguar and drove into the city. Noah waited until they were some distance from the hotel, then had Sarah pull the car over and park. He took out his cell phone and dialed the number for Catherine Potts.

"Catherine, it's Alex Colson," Noah said. "Anything going on I should know about?"

"Not much of anything, actually," Catherine said. "Your bird landed, checked into the hotel under the name you gave me late last night, in room 303. There are also a couple of young American men staying there, and I get the distinct impression they might be yours. I understand one of them has walked past Mr. Sykes's room a few times this morning. He's on a different floor, so it appears he might be keeping some surveillance of his own?"

"Probably a big guy?" Noah asked. "Lots of muscle?"

"That would be the one. I thought I smelled a bit of our outfit around them. Do you want me to keep my people on station? I've got two watching from outside and one of the maids is actually with SIS."

"It wouldn't break my heart if you keep them on their toes. Mr. Sykes can be pretty slippery, from what I understand. As long as he doesn't have anyone else around there shouldn't be a problem."

"All right. When will you be making your appearance?"

"I'll be there at around three. You can reach me on this number if anything changes."

"Very good, Sir," Catherine said. "I'll let you know if anything comes up. Ta-ta for now."

The line went dead and Noah slipped the phone back into his pocket. "When you talk to Moose, tell him he's being too obvious. Catherine's people spotted him and she figured out he was with me."

"Good," Sarah said. "He's been getting pretty cocky

lately, maybe it'll take him down a notch or two. When do you want me to call them?"

"I suppose now is as good a time as any."

Sarah glanced at him. "You know, it's really weird how you can drop in and out of character so easily. Right now you sound like Adrian again, but when you were talking to Catherine Potts, you sounded like you did when we were here before."

Noah shrugged. "She only knows me as Alex Colson," he said. "I thought it would be a good idea to keep that identity going for her, at least for now."

Sarah grinned and took out her own phone. She tapped an icon and put it on speaker so Noah could hear the conversation.

"Roadkill Café," they heard Neil say. "Can I take your order?"

"Hey," Sarah said, "it's me, but no names, okay? Boss wanted me to check in and see if you guys have spotted anything he needs to know about."

"Nope. I've been checking off and on, and haven't heard a peep. The lunkhead's been prowling around for a little bit, he said he hasn't seen anything to worry about. He saw you-know-who check in last night, but the guy hasn't even come out for breakfast yet this morning."

"Yeah, we heard the quarterback was watching him pretty closely," Sarah said. "Tell him to back it down a notch, Catherine's people spotted him, and she knows he's with us. Call me if anything comes up, all right?"

"You got it, Sis. Tell the boss I said howdy."

Sarah turned to Noah with a grin. "Sure will," she said, and the line went dead. "How was that?" she asked.

"Very good. Of course, this means that we have nothing to do for the next couple of hours. Perhaps we might do a little sightseeing?"

Her eyebrows raised slightly. "Okay," she said. "Anything in particular you want to see?"

Noah nodded. "Yes. Let's go and see Westminster Cathedral. I've long admired the architecture there but I've never gotten to see it up close. It shouldn't be too far away."

Sarah smiled and turned back to face the road, put the car in gear and pulled out. She pushed a button on the dash and told the car's "Intelligent GPS" to give her the best route to the Cathedral. A feminine voice with a crisp British lilt began speaking only seconds later, and Sarah had to turn around and go back the way they had come.

NINE

The alarm went off beside Sam's bed and he flung out an arm to silence the horrible thing. His palm hit the reset and killed the noise, but he was already awake. He tried to lay there for a few more minutes but there was no hope of getting back to sleep, so he tossed off the blanket and rolled so that his feet hit the floor.

Belinda stirred beside him. "Do you have to go so early?"

Sam gave a sigh. "Afraid so," he said. "That lot at the office can't seem to do much without me there." He turned and patted her rump, then got to his feet and padded into the loo. After eight years of marriage, he knew that she would be back to sleep before he even got the shower started.

Belinda was a good wife, and Sam knew that he was a lucky man, but she had made it clear early on that she was not the kind of wife who got up and made breakfast every morning. When he considered all of the other wonderful things about her, he was able to accept that, but it meant either making his own breakfast or running through a drive-up somewhere on his way to work. He'd become rather fond of Egg McMuffins, and it was beginning to show around his middle.

He stopped in his office when he got to Vauxhall Cross and found a note on his desk telling him to report to Mr. Simmons. Simmons was the actual head of the FEG, but Sam thought the man to be a complete idiot. Occasionally he insisted on sitting in on Sam's interviews with Adrian, and if Sam didn't know better he'd think the man idolized the assassin.

It was Simmons who had agreed to provide Adrian with books to read in his cell. None of the other secret prisoners got such relief from the terminal boredom, but Simmons had authorized it. Sam wanted to take the books away and burn the bloody things, let Adrian sit in that cell with absolutely nothing to do, as was intended. That boredom was often enough to break the subject, but Simmons had thwarted him on this case.

He sighed and made his way down the hall to Simmons's office. "You wanted to see me, sir?"

Simmons looked up at him and Sam realized the man's eyes were bloodshot. "You might want to sit," he said. "There's been something of an event here, this morning."

Sam narrowed his eyes and took the chair in front of Simmons' desk. "An event? Something to do with Adrian?"

Simmons swallowed and looked at the top of his desk. "Yes, actually. At just after one this morning, one of the security men heard some odd sounds coming from Adrian's cell. He opened the window and looked inside and saw Adrian hanging by a twisted bedsheet from the vent in his ceiling. His face was blue but his legs were still kicking a bit against the wall, so he opened the cell and rushed inside. He grabbed Adrian and lifted him to try to take the pressure off his throat, and that's the last thing he remembers."

Sam's eyes had grown wider as Simmons spoke, and he leaned forward to stare at his superior. "Last thing he remembers?" Suddenly he gasped. "Dear God in Heaven, are you telling me Adrian has escaped?"

Simmons refused to raise his eyes to meet Sam's face. "He struck our man and rendered him unconscious, then changed clothing with him and took his keys and radio. The guard in the booth saw what he thought was our man in the monitor, and the voice that came through the radio sounded right, so he buzzed the cell block door open. Adrian stepped through and rushed the booth." He coughed. "The guard was not as lucky. Adrian snapped his neck, and then made his way to the supplies exit. By the time one of the other security men discovered the guard in the booth, he was gone. He took our supply van. It was found a few blocks away; he appears to have managed to catch a ride with someone, because there are no reports of stolen cars in that area."

Sam's mind was racing. "What about cameras in the area? Traffic cameras, security cameras, anything?"

Simmons shook his head. "As far as we can tell, there was nothing. We've got our own people and the Royal Police going round, trying to find any trace."

Sam leaned back into his chair and rubbed a hand over his face. "They'll not find it," he said. "I searched after him for two years, and even then I'd not have found him if it weren't for stumbling across him." He let his eyes meet Simmons's own. "Why was there only one man on duty in the block? We were holding one of the most deadly assassins who ever lived, for God's sake, normal protocol says the security guards always work in pairs."

Simmons nodded. "Yes, yes, I know," he said. "Unfortunately, his shift-mate called off ill last night. Since Adrian had not caused any problems, the super on duty didn't feel it necessary to call anyone else in. He's been reprimanded already, for what it's worth."

"It's worth *shite!*" Sam shouted. "We've got a man dead and our biggest capture ever just waltzed out of here like he owned the bloody place! We'll never find him again, you can bet on that. What the bloody hell is the PM going to say?"

Simmons cleared his throat. "Yes, well, I'm being called onto that carpet this morning. Don't suppose you'd care to go with me?"

Sam's head reared back and his eyes shot open. "Are you bloody daft? Take the sodding super with you, he's the plonker that left one guard on the most dangerous prisoner we've ever had. Jesus bloody Christ, has everyone over me lost their bloody minds?"

Simmons slapped the desk. "I think that's enough," he said. "I fully understand your position, you don't have to keep going over it. What I need you to do right now is start putting together a team to go after the bloke. You literally know him better than anyone else alive, so Younger wants you heading up the hunt. You're to choose the team, anyone you want, and start planning how you're going to catch this bastard a second time." Alex Younger was the man in charge of MI6, and answered directly to the Foreign Minister.

"Oh, really? Does he want me to resurrect my mates who helped me the first time? Or do some other miracle, perhaps?"

Simmons came up out of his chair, both fists planted

firmly on the desk as he glared at Sam. "That's enough! You've got your orders, Agent Little, I suggest you get on with them."

Sam jumped to his feet, and for just a moment he thought about hanging a mouse on his boss, but common sense and years of dealing with the eejit got him through. He stood there for only a couple of seconds, then turned and walked out of the office.

"Younger wants me to bring Adrian in again, does he?" Sam muttered to himself. "All bloody right, then, and he wants me to put together a team? That I'll bloody do, all right!" He began going over names in his mind, trying to decide just who would be most likely to be beneficial in this new mission. By the time he got back to his office, he had a list to start with and began calling them.

Forty minutes later, Sam made his way to the unit conference room and found all but one of them waiting for him. Terry Stamper had been number four on the team that brought Adrian in; he, along with Lloyd Bonner, Nick Stratton and Harry Wessex, was sitting at the table when Sam entered and took the lead seat.

"In case you haven't heard yet," Sam said, "Adrian has escaped. Our bloody superiors have cocked up as they usually do and the result was a single guard on duty in K block last night. Adrian faked an attempted suicide, and the stupid bloke on duty tried to save him. It was a ruse, of course; he's lucky Adrian only knocked him cold. The man in the booth wasn't so fortunate, probably tried to put up a fight and got his neck broken."

"We heard," Stamper said coldly. "Jerry Guinan was in the booth. Me and him, we was mates."

"Well, it's falling to us..." Sam cut off as the fifth team

member he requested walked into the room.

"Sorry I'm late," Catherine Potts said. "What have I missed?"

"Morning, Catherine," Sam said, and the other men echoed him. "I imagine you've heard our distinguished guest decided to fly the coop last night. Younger and Simmons have ordered me to assemble a new team and try to do the impossible once again. Terry was with me on the last operation, but the rest of you will need to study up on Adrian." He tossed file folders to each of them. "Lucky for you, I've compiled quite a dossier on the son-of-a-bitch."

Catherine opened the folder and began scanning its contents. "This says you interrupted him as he was preparing for a hit. Any idea who the target was? He may try to complete it, now that he's loose again."

Sam shook his head. "No, that was one of the things I couldn't get out of him. There were rumors floating round that he was hired to kill the PM, but nothing substantial ever came up, and he laughed when I asked about it. He did tell me, however, that he was working on a deadline, and since he didn't get it done in time the contract probably wouldn't happen. I would guess he's going to have to tell someone that we had him, but I've no idea who."

"You know," Lloyd said, "the biggest problem is that he's always in demand. There's always someone out there willing to pay for his level of skill, but until you got lucky, we never had anyone who could even get close to him."

"Yes," Sam agreed, "but at least now we know what the bloke looks like. We took enough photos of him that I can paper my bedroom with them, and the bobbies all know who they're looking for, now. Security on all the railways, tubes, coach lines and airports is tight, and they've all been given photographs, as well. Same for car rentals and taxis; every possible way he could get out of the city has been put on alert."

"The man's been selling his services as a contract killer," Catherine said, "for quite a number of years. Do you think he wouldn't know how to change his appearance? A man's hair color takes only a few minutes and can be applied in a public toilet. Add a pair of spectacles and any kind of uniform, you've got an invisible man."

"She's right," Harry said. "Cor, we've all done such at one time or another. Disguise is part of the toolbox of anyone involved in espionage."

"Nevertheless," Sam said, "we're going on the assumption that he's still in London until we know differently, but I will see to it that police throughout the UK and Europe get his photos. He can change his looks, but I want the bastard to have to do it every time he rolls out of bed."

"What about any other leads?" Catherine asked. "You've been talking to him every day for nigh on a month, now. Do we have any known associates? Favorite places? Anything we can go on to give us hints of where to look?"

Sam shook his head. "Not a lot, there, I'm afraid," he said. "We talked a lot about his activities over the last few years, but he's not one to give up any personal details. I know a couple of pubs that he used to visit, but there's no doubt in my mind he'll avoid those. I'd like to believe he's out there with nothing, but this is one smart bloke; he'll have cash, maybe clothes and weapons stashed somewhere, and if he hasn't gotten to them already I'd be shocked."

"True," Terry said. "He might have kept a car stored somewhere. The truth is, he could be anywhere by now, even on the continent."

Sam leaned back and rubbed the bridge of his nose with his fingers. "All I've got is my gut," he said, "but it's telling me he's not gone far. As I said, we're going to operate on the assumption that he's still within the city. Toward that end, I'm looking for suggestions. Think before you speak, please, I want the ideas that are not obvious."

Several ideas were tossed out, and Sam made notes of those he thought had merit. It made a short list, because he scrapped most without even discussing them.

"All right, we've got some notions to start with," he said at last. "One last thing, people: we keep this under wraps. Nobody outside this section knows who it is we're looking for, not even the Royal Police. I want it to stay that way. We don't tell anyone, not anyone at all. Understood?"

Catherine looked at him. "You know the Yanks have some sort of interest in Adrian, right? I don't know the details, but I saw a memo that said they were getting copies of all your interrogations. Should we notify them that he's on the loose?"

Sam looked at her, and his eyes were cold. "I said no one, and no one I meant. I don't want the knowledge that Adrian is back on the streets going anywhere, is that clear?"

Catherine met his gaze evenly. "Perfectly clear, sir," she said.

TEN

Sightseeing took up the morning, and Noah took the opportunity to look over not just the Cathedral, but several other historical old buildings. "Architecture is always logical," he said during one tour. "No matter how crazy it might look, like one of Frank Lloyd Wright's clever designs, the limitations of materials and physics force the creation to follow rules that cannot be broken. This is undoubtedly why it appeals to me so strongly."

"I can see that," Sarah said, "since you think in terms of what's logical, what makes sense at the moment. Maybe that's why it's so hard for me to get used to you talking the way you're doing now, it just doesn't seem like you. It's kind of creepy, to tell the truth. I listen to you talking and I expect to see someone else when I turn to look at you."

Noah's face softened slightly. "I'm sorry," he said, "I know it must be weird. I'm just trying to stay in character, so there won't be any problems when I meet with Broussard."

"So, it's really him, then? Since he checked in like you said to, I'm guessing that means he really is the guy you're supposed to...."

"It's too soon to know. Until I actually speak to him and find out what the assignment is the IAR wants me to take on, we can't be sure whether he's pulling the strings, or someone is pulling his. The only way to take down a big tree properly is from the top, cutting off a section at a time until all that's left is the stump. That's what we need to do with IAR, cut off the top. That may be enough to make it wither and die."

She smiled at him. "Thank you," she said. "You sound a lot more like yourself at the moment. I was missing you, even though you're right here."

"You're welcome. I figured you needed a break from Adrian for a few minutes. I'll go back into character when we head for the meeting."

They decided to stop for lunch at a little after one, and Sarah spotted a chip shop. They pulled in and sat at one of the outdoor tables, despite the somewhat cool air. Noah held her chair for her as she sat, and an elderly couple seated nearby smiled at them.

"You look like young lovebirds," the old woman said, and Sarah smiled back at her. "Does my old heart good to see young love, it does."

"Thank you," Sarah said. "And it does mine good to see that love can last a long time."

"A long time?" the old man asked. "Oh, d'ye mean Alice and me? Don't let our old age fool you, luv, we've only just met two weeks past. This is but our third date, don't you know?"

Sarah's mouth dropped open. "Oh, I'm so sorry, I just...."

"Ignore the old fool Willie, dear," Alice said. "He's only playing the jokester. We've been wed nigh sixty years, now. If that young man is worth your love, dear, don't you let him get away! 'Tis a great comfort, to love one man for so many years. You'll see." She winked, and Sarah blushed prettily.

"I promise you, I'm doing my best," Sarah said. "Sometimes I just want to strangle him, but most of the time he's a keeper."

"Aren't they all that way? I think," Alice said, dropping to a stage whisper, "it comes along with his tally-whacker!"

Noah turned to look at Willie, who winked at him, then turned back to Sarah, who was choking on a piece of cod. He opened his mouth and started to say something, but then shoved a piece of fish into it instead.

Sarah chatted with Alice as they ate, and Noah and Willie shared a few winks and sly looks. They visited and joked for an hour, but finally the older couple announced an appointment and said goodbye. Noah rose as they walked away and was rewarded with a hug from Alice. Willie contented himself with kissing Sarah's hand, keeping one eye on the large and muscular young man with her as he did so.

"That was delightful," Sarah said. "Do you think there's any chance we'll still be together when we get old?"

"That would mean assuming we'll get old, and I have to say that's probably not the most likely fate for me. I hope you'll live a long time, though. And if I manage not to get killed, I wouldn't mind being with you."

Sarah narrowed her eyes at him, but a moment later she chuckled. "You wouldn't mind? Gee, you make it sound like an unpleasant prospect. Don't worry, Babe, I know you. That's probably as close to a compliment as you can manage for me."

"Did it not sound like one? I think I meant it to be. Frankly, I could think of many worse fates than being your old Willie."

She stopped grinning. "Oh, God, you're back in character. Is it getting close to that time?"

"It is, yes. We've less than an hour before I should be at the Elizabeth, but I want to make a quick stop on the way, so we'd best be going." He stood and reached for her chair, sliding it back as she rose from it.

"Yeah, okay," Sarah said. "So, what do you think, will it be over today? Do you think you can take him out during this meeting and be done with it?"

"I actually doubt that," Noah replied. He led the way to the car and opened her door for her. "If Broussard is wanting to employ Adrian, I'll need to know for certain that he's the top of the chain before I kill him. We can't risk the chance that there is another above him who will only continue. It's always possible that he's merely a figurehead, that there is another above him who is willing to sacrifice him as nothing but a pawn. I have to be sure that I'm eliminating the leader, not just one of his underlings."

"And you will," she said as she slid into the driver's seat. "You will, because you're the best. They want Adrian because they think he was the best out there, but that's only because they never even knew about you."

Noah got in and Sarah started the engine, then moved smoothly into traffic as Noah directed her to a small store he had found on a Google search. She parked in front and kept the car idling while he went inside, and then headed for the Elizabeth Hotel as soon as he came out and got back into his seat. They were only a few minutes away, so she drove by a circuitous route as

Noah took out his phone once again.

"Catherine, this is Colson," he said into the phone. "Have there been any developments?"

"Nothing new or exciting, I'm afraid. I've just had a report from my sources not ten minutes past, and other than your lad being a bit less noticeable, not much has changed. Your pigeon is holed up in his room, and no one else has gone in or out. Should I have anyone standing by to back your people up?"

"No, we've got it. If everything goes according to plan, this is just a meeting, with a possibly unhappy ending for the pigeon. All depends on what I learn inside."

Catherine Potts was quiet for a moment, but then Noah could hear the smile in her voice. "Mr. Colson," she said, "I do believe the world is a lot safer with you doing your job. You need to know, though, my cover assignment has been pulled in on something, so it's possible I might be a bit hard-to-reach. I can still get reports from my people on this, though, so I'll let you know of anything I hear that might be important."

The phone went dead, and Noah blinked once as he put it back into his pocket. He turned to Sarah. "Your turn," he said. "Tell the boys I'm on the way and to be ready. If I kill Broussard, I may need them to cover me as I make my way out."

"Okay," she said, reaching for her phone. She was about to dial but Noah put his hand over the phone.

"Wait 'til you drop me off, and then call them. I want to be inside the building before then."

Sarah nodded and set the phone on the console between the seats, then switched lanes to get into position for the driveway to the hotel. She whipped into it and stopped smoothly.

A doorman opened Noah's door and he stepped out, then leaned back inside. "I'll see you later, Honey. I'll call when I need a ride." He closed the door and turned to go inside as Sarah gave him a finger wave and drove off down the street. She had her phone in her hand before she even left the driveway, and Moose answered as she passed the next building.

Noah rode the elevator to the third floor and reached into his pocket as it rose. He took out the rubber mask of Donald Trump that he'd bought at the little costume shop and slipped it over his head, then exited the lift and turned right to enter the main hallway. Room 303 was the second door on the left, and he stepped up to it and knocked sharply twice.

Broussard's voice came from inside the room. "Yes?"

"We have an engagement this afternoon, Mr. Sykes."

The door opened and Pierre Broussard stood there, his eyes wide at the sight of the mask. Noah stepped forward so quickly that the man took a step back on instinct, and then closed the door behind them.

"You wanted to speak to me in person, Monsieur Broussard?" Noah asked.

Broussard stared at the Trump mask for a moment, then swallowed once before speaking.

"Indeed I do, my friend," he said. "There is a situation I feel needs to be resolved, and it will take a man of your special talents." He looked around for a moment as if disoriented and then motioned to a chair. "Would you care to sit while we discuss it?"

Noah reached out and took Broussard by his arms and shoved him roughly into the chair. The man yelped but didn't try to fight, and then Noah sat on the edge of the one bed.

"We are sitting," he said. "Who is the target?"

Broussard swallowed again and then smiled. "Someone you would know well, at least academically. My organization would like to have you eliminate a particular actor from the stage of the world, someone so well known that the task is said to be impossible."

"There is no impossible target," Noah said. "There may be some that are not worth the fee, however."

"This fee is quite high, I assure you, my friend," Broussard said, "because there are special conditions. The job must be done in such a way as to make it appear that someone else has done it, and no one can ever learn that it was actually your work. Is that agreeable?"

"Again, that would depend on the target and the fee. Tell me both, and if I do not leave, we may come to an agreement."

Broussard nodded nervously. "Yes, yes, of course," he said. "The fee will be three million US dollars, my friend, and the target—the target is the future king of England."

ELEVEN

"**W**hich one?" Noah asked. "If you pay attention to the various news sources, you could be talking about either Prince Charles or Prince William. There are consistent rumors that the Queen will bypass her son and abdicate at some point in favor of the Duke of Cambridge."

Broussard scoffed. "Those reports are ridiculous," he said. "Elizabeth may well disapprove of Charles, but she would not alter the line of succession. Unfortunately, Charles has too many outspoken views that will cause problems for the EU, even after the departure of the UK. Some of those views will make it difficult for certain people to operate in the European Union, and they would prefer to see William take the throne. If there were any validity to the reports you mention, we would not be having this discussion."

Noah nodded slowly. "I suspected as much, especially considering some of the news sources that were actively promoting such stories. However, when discussing a potential engagement, I want to be absolutely certain as to the identity of my target."

"Well, then you can rest assured that we are speaking of Charles. Do you have any questions?"

"I have no specific questions at this time," Noah said. "However, I shall be frank. What you're proposing would be an extremely difficult assignment. I am afraid the fee is not sufficient."

"Ah," Broussard said. "I see. And what would be more equitable, do you think?"

"For an assignment of this magnitude? Three million dollars US is not even close. For the removal of an ambassador, perhaps, but not for such a task as you propose. Perhaps you should discuss the matter with your superiors and learn whether they are willing to be more realistic on this matter."

Broussard shook his head. "Not yet," he said. "Tell me what fee you would demand. Perhaps we can reach an agreement today, after all."

Noah cocked his head to the right and looked at Broussard through the eyeholes in the mask. "Not yet?" he asked. "Did I not tell you that I deal only with the principal? If your superior wishes to engage my services, he should have been here in your place." Noah rose from the bed and started toward the door.

"No, wait," Broussard called out. "I do not have a superior to call, I am the one you will deal with. However, I answer to a council. They have given me authority to negotiate on their behalf, but if your fee is greater than the limit they have imposed on me, it will be necessary for me to go back to them for approval."

Noah had reached the door and had his hand on the doorknob, but now he stopped and turned back to face Broussard. "Then you are nothing but a middleman," he said, "and I do not deal with middlemen." He took a step back toward Broussard. "My fee for this assignment would be twenty million dollars USD. This is due not only to the difficulty it will present, but also due to the requirement you have imposed that I must make it appear to have been the work of someone else. Can you authorize that fee?"

Broussard seemed to sag a bit in his chair. "Not without the approval of the Council," he said. "If you will give me just a few moments, however, I believe they would agree."

"And so you wish me to simply stand here while you call your masters and ask for their approval?"

"The call will take only moments, I assure you. This assignment is of such importance that I'm certain they will agree. I do not believe anyone else could accomplish it, nor do they. This is why they specifically wanted to engage you."

Noah stood stock-still and stared at Broussard for a moment. Suddenly he nodded and went back to sit on the bed once more. "Call them, then," he said. "Make it clear to them that this is my only offer. There is no room for negotiation, and if they do not accept, they need not ever contact me again."

Broussard nodded vigorously and rose from his chair. He stepped carefully around Noah to the nightstand beside the bed, opened the drawer and withdrew a satellite phone. With his back to Noah, he punched in a number and then turned and faced Noah as he held the phone to his ear. He seemed to be listening to the ringing on the other end of the line for a moment, and then his face snapped to attention as the call was answered.

"Hello, this is B," he said. "I am with the man we discussed for the special assignment, and he is not comfortable with the fee we had offered." He listened for a moment, and then said, "Yes, he says the fee would be twenty."

Noah watched Broussard's face for reactions, and saw only a momentary grimace as the person on the other end of the line seemed to be surprised at the figure. The expression passed instantly and was then replaced with a smile.

"Yes, one moment and I will ask," he said, and then held the phone against his chest as he looked at Noah. "There is a meeting scheduled in three weeks," he said. "Can the assignment be completed before that time?"

"Three weeks?" Noah asked, putting surprise into his voice. "That is not a lot of time. I normally require at least twice that much time to prepare and execute such an assignment."

"Nevertheless, it is necessary that the assignment be completed prior to that meeting. Several EU member nations will be gathered to discuss future relations with the United Kingdom, and the impact of this assignment will greatly affect the outcome of that discussion."

Noah hunched over as if deep in thought and folded his hands together in front of him. He stayed that way for several seconds, and then looked up at Broussard once again.

"I can accomplish it, if my fee is met," he said. "However, for something of this magnitude, I must insist on meeting with your council."

Broussard's eyes went wide. "The Council is comprised of individuals whose identities cannot be compromised," he said. "They have never agreed to a meeting with anyone."

Noah shrugged his shoulders. "Then we have nothing more to discuss. I'm certain you realize that my own identity is something I protect very jealously, so there should be no doubt of my intention to protect those of my employers. If you know anything about me whatsoever, you should be aware that no one has ever been charged with the crime of employing me, nor even implicated beyond simple rumor. To accept this assignment, I would insist on meeting with your council, at which time I would receive one half of the fee into an account I will provide. The balance would be payable once the assignment is completed."

Broussard looked like he wanted to say something, but instead he put the phone back to his ear. "The contractor will not agree to complete the assignment by that deadline without meeting with the Council. Yes, yes, I explained, but those are his terms." He listened for a moment, and then his eyes widened once again in surprise. "Very well," he said, "I shall tell him."

Once again he put the phone against his chest and looked at Noah. "The Council will meet with you, but only if it can be done tonight. You and I would meet again here tonight at ten, and will be taken by limousine to the meeting place sometime after that." He hesitated for a moment, then shrugged. "I am afraid your current appearance would not be acceptable to them. The mask, you would not be able to wear it."

Noah nodded. "I would expect as much." He reached up and removed the mask suddenly, and Broussard quickly averted his eyes. "You may relax," Noah said. "Considering the circumstances of our meeting, I believe I can trust you not to ever reveal any details of my appearance. If I am wrong, of course, you and I will meet again with a much more unfavorable ending to that meeting."

Still keeping his eyes on the floor, Broussard nodded.

"I understand completely," he said. "Shall we conclude our meeting for now, then, and resume again tonight as scheduled?"

Noah nodded, dropping the mask onto the floor. "That will be fine," he said. "I shall see you then." He rose from the bed and walked directly out the door, then took out his phone and called Sarah. "I shall be needing a ride," he said, remaining in character.

"Be right there," she replied. Noah hung up the phone and rode the elevator down to the lobby. He stepped out the front door and Sarah drove up only seconds later. Noah slid into the passenger seat and she drove back out onto the street, turning right.

"Call Neil" Noah said, "and make sure he got a recording of the call Broussard made while I was with him."

Sarah nodded and picked up her phone from her lap, dialing the number and putting the phone on speaker. A moment later, Neil answered her call.

"Joe's Mortuary, you stab 'em, we slab 'em."

"Very funny," Sarah said. "Did you happen to get the call that was made a few minutes ago?"

"I sure did," Neil said. "Boss want to hear the recording?"

Noah reached over and hit the mute button. "Tell him to get a taxi and bring it over to the Cavendish. We'll listen to it there."

Sarah nodded and unmuted the phone. "Why don't you guys grab a cab and meet us at our place. Bring your gizmos along and we can check it out there."

"You got it, sis," Neil replied. "Mind if we grab some lunch along the way? Lug nuts didn't want to take a break until this was over."

Noah nodded, so Sarah said, "Okay, that's fine. We'll see you in an hour or so." She ended the call and looked at Noah. "Back to our hotel?"

"Yes," Noah said, "but make absolutely certain that no one follows us. I don't think Broussard would risk it, but let's not take any chances. Hopefully the guys won't take too long."

"I'll make sure," Sarah said, and then she grinned. "As for the guys, it all depends on where they stop for lunch. If they have to go inside to eat, we won't see them for a couple of hours." She reached over and took Noah's hand into her own. "So, how did it go?"

"Broussard is not the top man," Noah said. "There is apparently a council of some sort running the organization, and that's who he answers to. I insisted on meeting with them and it's set up for tonight. The most important thing I learned is who their target is. They want Adrian to kill Prince Charles of England."

Sarah's eyes bugged out. "Are you serious? Has anyone actually ever tried to assassinate a member of the royal family?"

"Of course they have," Noah said. "Royals have been assassinated at different times in the past, and I remember reading once there was even one botched assassination attempt on Queen Elizabeth. Someone stepped out of the crowd and pointed a gun at her, but it was only loaded with blanks. Her security took him down and that was pretty much the end of it. It was just a teenager trying to make a big name for himself, but he spent several years in jail for it."

"But they want you to kill Prince Charles," Sarah said. "Any idea why?"

"Broussard said it's because he holds views that are

unpopular in the European Union, so I'm assuming there is some concern that his attitude would cause them problems once he becomes King. He's been rather outspoken about a number of things going on in the world, but my guess would be his opposition to Muslim immigration. He's made some pretty bold statements about Muslim leaders radicalizing immigrants, and has bluntly told Muslims in the UK that they need to abide by British law and custom, rather than those of their own culture."

"But that would only affect England, right?"

"From the standpoint of Royal influence, yes," Noah said. "However, and especially after Brexit, it's likely the EU's policies that are already getting pretty strict about Muslim immigrants would cause them to rally behind that attitude. They would point to England as setting a standard they should follow. That might cause problems for organizations like IAR that use Islamic extremists as pawns in their own political games."

Sarah waggled her head and grimaced. "Okay, I guess that makes sense. But if he gets taken out, who would take his place?"

"Prince William would be the next in the line of succession. There have even been rumors for the last year or two that the Queen wanted him to be next in line, anyway. He's a little more liberal than his father, so I'm assuming they think they'd have fewer problems out of him. It's likely that IAR is using terrorism to advance some sort of agendas that are more about manipulating markets than politics; if that's true, then all they're really after is keeping the immigration routes open, so they have plenty of willing pawns to sacrifice."

"So now what do you do?"

Noah shrugged. "I go to this meeting tomorrow and try to figure out who sits on this council so I can take them out. I doubt I'm going to get the opportunity while we're there, so we need to identify them. After that, I can start making plans on how to eliminate them."

Sarah rolled her eyes. "Oh, is that all? Gee, I thought it was going to be something difficult."

TWELVE

They got back to the hotel—with Sarah certain that they weren't being followed—at just before four thirty, and Moose and Neil arrived a half-hour later. Moose dropped a big bucket of fried chicken onto the table in Noah's room while Neil set up his computer.

"Broussard called another sat phone in Italy," he said. "I managed to get its ESN as well, so I've got a little surprise for you. The woman he called started making calls of her own as soon as she hung up from talking to him, and I've got those for you, too. Here, listen to his call while I stuff some chicken down my throat." He tapped a key on the computer and the reporting began to play.

There was ringing, and then a woman's voice, with a slight Italian accent, could be heard: *Hello?*

Broussard: *Hello, this is B. I am with the man we discussed for the special assignment, and he is not comfortable with the fee we had offered.*

Woman: *And I presume he has made a counteroffer?*

Broussard: *Yes, he says the fee would be twenty.*

Woman (apparently shocked): *Twenty million dollars? And if we agree, can it be done by the deadline?*

Broussard: *Yes, one moment and I will ask.* There was

a rustling noise and then his voice came through somewhat muffled. *There is a meeting scheduled in three weeks. Can the assignment be completed before that time?*

Noah could hear his own voice in the background, but could not make out the words.

Broussard: *Nevertheless, it is necessary that the assignment be completed prior to that meeting. Several EU member nations will be gathered to discuss future relations with the United Kingdom, and the impact of this assignment will greatly affect the outcome of that discussion.*

There was silence on the line for a moment, and then Broussard's muffled voice went on: *The Council is comprised of individuals whose identities cannot be compromised. They have never agreed to a meeting with anyone.*

Once again Noah could hear his own voice muffled in the background, and then Broussard continued. *The contractor will not agree to complete the assignment by that deadline without meeting with the Council.*

Woman: *Meeting? We have never revealed ourselves before.*

Broussard: *Yes, yes, I explained, but those are his terms.*

Woman: *Unfortunately, he is probably the only one who could accomplish it. We will agree to a meeting, but it shall be on our terms, and only if he will agree to a meeting this very night. Have him with you tonight at ten and we will arrange to bring you both to the place of meeting. If he objects, simply allow him to leave and we will explore other options.*

Broussard: *Very well. I shall tell him.* There was another rustling and then Broussard's voice was muffled again. *The Council will meet with you, but only if it can be done tonight. You and I would meet again here tonight at ten, and will be taken by limousine to the meeting place sometime after that. I am afraid your current appearance would not be acceptable to them. The mask, you would not be able to wear it.*

Noah heard his own muffled voice again for a moment.

Broussard: *I understand completely. Shall we conclude our meeting for now, then, and meet again tonight as scheduled?*

More of Noah's muffled voice in the background, and then Broussard returned to the line. *He is gone. He agrees to your terms for the meeting.*

Woman: *Very good. He undoubtedly has you under some form of surveillance, so do nothing to draw any attention or arouse any suspicion. If it is possible to engage him for this assignment, we must do so. The money is of far less importance than the assignment itself.*

Broussard: *I understand. I shall remain in the room and use room service for dinner, rather than going out.*

The call ended then, and Noah looked at Neil. "Any idea who she is? The woman he called?"

Neil shook his head while he chewed and swallowed. "Not entirely," he said. "But she made three other calls right after that one, and I had already tagged her phone for recording by then. Listen to this one." He reached over and tapped another key.

There was ringing again, and then a man's voice answered: *This is François.*

Woman: *Broussard has met with Adrian, and you were right about the fee. He demands twenty million, but he also refuses to accept the assignment unless he meets with all of us. We are flying to London this evening. Be at the airport at six PM.*

François: *I expected as much. You don't suppose this is some sort of trap, do you?*

Woman: *Of course not. Adrian is undoubtedly the best, and he would never have gained that reputation if he ever betrayed a client.*

François: *I suppose that is true. Mais oui, I shall be there. Are you arranging security?*

Woman: *Yes, I will have security in place when we arrive. I will see you at the plane.*

The call ended, and Neil reached over and tapped a key again. "Next!"

The familiar ringing sounded three times, and then another man's voice answered. "Yes?"

Woman: *We are meeting with Adrian tomorrow in London. He requires it as part of his agreement to take on the contract. I shall have the airplane ready at six o'clock tonight.*

The man grunted and hung up the phone. The woman's voice could be heard muttering for a moment and then her line went dead, as well.

Noah looked at Neil, who only reached over and tapped the key again.

This time the call was answered on the first ring.

Man: *Hello?*

Woman: *James, this is Deanna. Broussard met with Adrian, but he insists on meeting with all of us on the Council before he agrees to the contract. I've set the meeting for tonight, in London. We'll be flying out tonight at six.*

James: *Do you think that's wise? We have never exposed ourselves before.*

Deanna: *The Muslim immigration conference is in only three weeks. We can achieve the outcome we want, but only if the members are certain they will never have to deal with Charles on the throne of England. As unpopular as he has become in his own country, his security is heightened to the point of making him almost invincible. We all agreed that Adrian is the only one who could possibly accomplish this task, so if meeting him is the only obstacle in the way, we must accommodate him.*

James: *I suppose so. All right, I'll be at the airport.*

The line went dead and Neil swallowed. "That was it," he said. "Just those four calls. All of them went to sat phones in Rome, which is where she was at, too, by the way."

"So there are apparently only four on this council: this woman Deanna, François, James and one other man we have no name for. Are there any clues that can help us identify them further?"

Neil shook his head. "There are more guys named Francois and James in the world than I could possibly ever go through, and there are enough women named Deanna that it would take months to figure out which one she might be."

"What about tracking them when they fly here? The way Deanna talked, they've got a plane of their own. How hard would it be to figure out what private jets are flying out of Rome this evening?"

"Already thought of it, Boss. There are only two air-ports in Rome, Leonardo da Vinci and Ciampino, but both of them handle an awful lot of private plane traffic. By the time I started checking, there were already half a dozen flight plans filed for London, and I don't even know if their flight is one of them. It's not terribly likely that I could spot the right one in time to get any kind of finger on who would be on the plane."

Noah sucked in his cheek and chewed on it for a second, then took out his phone. He hit a couple of buttons and then put it on speaker.

"Brigadoon investments," said a feminine voice. "How may I direct your call?"

"Allison, please," Noah said.

The line was put on hold, and they listened to some old pop tunes for a few seconds. The music ended suddenly, and Allison Peterson's voice came on the line. "This is Allison."

"Camelot," Noah said. "I'm wondering if we have any assets in Rome at the moment."

"Rome?" Allison asked. "What do you need?"

"There are two airports in Rome, and one of them is launching a flight toward London tonight. There will be four people on the flight, although I expect more because they'll be bringing security with them. Those four people comprise some sort of Executive Council that runs IAR."

"Seriously? An Executive Council? Organizations like this are usually run by one person, a sort of dictator. Do we have any names?"

"There's a woman named Deanna, speaks with an Italian accent, who may be the main person in charge. Everybody else seems to jump when she yells frog. Then there are three men, one whose name we don't have, another who calls himself François, and one more named James. All four of them are currently in Rome, apparently, since they are meeting at the plane at six o'clock. Neil checked on flight plans, and there are already several of them aimed at London. Just thought maybe you could get someone to those airports to try to get a lead on who we're dealing with."

"I can call in a few favors, get some eyes out there. So why are they coming to London?"

"To meet with me, or rather, with Adrian. Their target is the Prince of Wales. Apparently they want to make sure he's not going to ascend to the throne when his mother finally retires or dies."

"Prince Charles? Holy crap, I didn't see that one coming. Kind of makes sense, I guess, if you think about how hard he's hammered the Muslim countries in his speeches about immigration and cross-culturalism."

"Right. They say the EU might follow his lead, even after Brexit, and they want him out of the way before some big meeting scheduled in three weeks."

"Okay, okay, that makes even more sense. The next big meeting in the EU is the Muslim immigration conference in Vienna. Even with the UK out of the EU, they'll still have some influence over a lot of political issues. Charles is dead set against allowing any kind of Muslim culture to take root in the UK, and while his own people don't think much of him, a lot of European leaders admire the man."

"That's the way these people see it," Noah said. "They want him shut down before he can exert any influence over this meeting, or maybe just to make sure his ascension to the throne is off the table. I pleaded out the way Adrian would, demanding a lot more money than they were offering and insisting on meeting with the principals involved. Because they want this done before that meeting, they wanted to set our face-to-face up as quickly as possible. It'll happen sometime tomorrow, but I don't have a specific time or place."

Allison grunted. "That's a little unsettling," she said. "I'm guessing they're going to take you somewhere to meet with these people?"

"Yep. I'm meeting with Broussard again tonight at ten, and they'll apparently send a car after us sometime during or after that."

"That means you'll be going in unarmed. Camelot, I want you to understand something. You have my approval if you decide to call off this mission. If anything smells funny to you, I want you to get yourself and your team out of there."

"I'm probably going to go ahead and ride this out," Noah said. "I could have tapped Broussard today, but we need to know who's behind him. These four people seem to be the top level, so my goal tomorrow is simply to find enough identifying information to let us track them down. Once I get that, I can take them out quickly, before they have time to react. If we can take out everyone from Broussard up, IAR might self-destruct. Isn't that the objective?"

"Of course it is, but that doesn't mean I want to risk my own best asset. I'm telling you, if anything smells fishy, don't go. Be ready to get yourself out of that situation, by whatever means necessary. Meanwhile, I'll get CIA checking into private flights out of Rome tonight. Maybe we'll get lucky and get an ID on these people without you having to go nose-to-nose with them."

"All right. I'm planning to leave my phone in the car with Sarah tomorrow morning, so you won't be able to reach me after about nine forty-five my time. Let me know if you want me to abort, but my gut says we need to ride this one out."

"Your call," Allison said. "What do you think would be the chance that your team could follow you?"

"Pretty slim, probably. They'll be looking for any kind

of tail, I'm sure. If I had a half-dozen more people we might pull it off, but not with just Moose and Sarah."

"What about one of those camera drones, like the Delta force guys were using?" Neil asked. "Any way we can get our hands on one of those?"

"Camera drone?" Allison asked. "Oh, I know what you mean. Delta used one on your last mission, right, to keep track of you? I can make some calls, see if there's one available in England somewhere. Neil, would you know how to use it?"

Neil snorted loudly. "Does a fish know how to swim? It's an electronic gizmo, of course I know how to use it."

"All right, then, let me see what I can do. I'll get back to you as quickly as I can." The line went dead.

"I'm with Allison," Sarah said. "I don't like the idea of you going off with them all by yourself, with no kind of backup. If anything goes wrong, they could blow your head off and we'd never know what happened."

"I don't expect anything to go wrong," Noah said. "I'm pretty sure the way they see it is that Adrian simply wants a little insurance. They'll figure that by meeting him face-to-face, he could always track them down if he needed to. Their goal is to convince him to do the job and that he'll get paid for it, so there won't ever be any reason for him to want to. I seriously doubt they would actually try to eliminate him, even if their business doesn't turn out the way they wanted to."

"I don't care, I still don't like it. It's bad enough I know you walk into life-threatening situations all the time, but at least I'm usually close enough to know what's going on. This time I won't have any idea where you are or what's happening."

"She's got a good point, Boss," Moose said. "You know,

if we round me up a motorcycle, I could probably keep whatever vehicle they use in sight."

Noah shook his head. "No, I don't want to give them any reason to wonder who's following them. If Allison can find Neil one of the drones, then he might be able to use it to keep track of me, but nothing else."

Sarah, sitting on the bed, crossed her arms over her chest and glared at him. "What about a bug? Something Neil can track, so we know where you are all the time?"

"No, they'll almost certainly check me for any kind of signal transmission. I think that Adrian, if he found himself in this position, would simply go along with it. That's what I'm gonna have to do."

Sarah closed her eyes. "Fine," she said angrily, "but if you die in there I'm going to kill you!"

"Then I'll do my best not to get killed." He turned to Neil. "If everything goes well with this meeting, they're going to be giving me ten million dollars, and I'll need an account to have it transferred into. What can we set up in a hurry?"

Neil leaned toward the computer and began tapping the keys. "We've got access to an account in Panama that passes any transfers straight out to the Cayman Islands. That's the kind of thing they'll be expecting, so let me give you the transfer instructions for it."

"Ten million dollars?" Moose asked. "What happens to that money after it gets transferred?"

"It goes from the Caymans to another account somewhere in the US, one that becomes part of E&E's funding. Kind of ironic that the money they pay you to kill for them ends up helping us take them out, right?"

THIRTEEN

T he four of them gathered around the table and ate chicken, with Noah vetoing different ideas they each presented on how to keep track of him while he was with the IAR Council later that night. No matter what they suggested, he saw a flaw in it that made him refuse to agree. They had been at it for nearly an hour, and Sarah was getting even more upset with him.

"If you'd only..." she began, but Noah's phone suddenly rang. He pulled it out and looked at it, then answered and hit speaker.

"Camelot," he said.

"Camelot," came a familiar voice. "This is Wally. How's it hanging?"

Noah's eyebrows went up just a bit. "I suppose it's hanging the way it's supposed to," he said. "What's up, Wally?"

"The boss lady called and told me to find a way for your team to keep track of you while you're out of touch. She wanted to know if there was any way I could set you up with some kind of a remote drone, something with enough range that it could follow you wherever you go and let us see where you're at. I talked to some of my whiz kids and we came up with an idea. Is Neil handy?"

"I'm right here, Wally," Neil said. "What you got?"

"Boss lady says you're in London," Wally said. "Get your tail end in gear and head down to the Quadcopter store. What you want is the new DJI Phantom Five, and you want the spare battery pack. That little drone has enough lift that you can wire the spare battery in, and if you add on a FLIR Vue Pro camera and plug it in, it will transmit both HD and Infrared video and its own GPS coordinates back to your phone from up to three miles away. Tacking on the spare battery will give you about an hour of flight time, so hopefully that will last long enough for you to keep track of where Camelot goes. If you hang back a mile or so, no one should notice you're following them. Think you can handle that?"

Neil's face was glowing with excitement. "Hell yes," he said. "No problem at all. This'll work."

"Okay, then, call me if you have any problems. Hope it works out."

"I'm sure it will, Wally, and thank you," Noah said. "We'll call if we need anything." He ended the call and looked at Neil, who was already on his computer looking up the location of the store. "It's almost five-thirty," he said. "Do you have time to get it tonight?"

"Yeah, the store's only about fifteen minutes away, and they're open until nine." Neal looked up at Sarah. "Hey, Sis, can I borrow the car?"

"Are you crazy?" Sarah asked. "Come on," she said, "I'll drive you." She grabbed her purse off the bed and the two of them headed out the door.

Moose looked at Noah. "You okay with this plan?" he asked.

Noah nodded. "It's the only one I've heard yet that

makes any sense. With the drone, Neil can keep track of where I'm at without us giving away that I'm being tracked. The only question is whether he can control it well enough to keep it focused on me."

Moose had pulled the computer over and was looking at the monitor. "DJI Phantom five," he said. "He won't have to. With this thing, he can simply tell it to follow whatever car you get into, and it will stay on you no matter what. Even dodges obstacles in its way."

Noah blinked. "That sounds even better than the one the Delta force guys were using. They had to follow me manually with that one."

"Yeah, well, what can you say?" Moose asked. "They don't have Wally, and they don't have Neil. Between those two, I think they could just about figure out a way to put us on the moon if they had to."

Noah simply nodded.

Neil and Sarah returned an hour later, with Neil even more excited than before. He climbed onto Noah's bed and spread out a set of tools, then began disassembling the drone so that he could add the spare battery to it.

"Ever seen a kid in a candy store?" Sarah asked. "That's Neil, any time he gets near new gadgets. I had to keep reminding him of what we were there to get, or he would've bought out the store."

Noah nodded. "That's one of the reasons he's so valuable to the team. He's always got his eye on the latest technology, anything that might help us complete a mission."

"So how are we going to do this, then?" Moose asked.

Noah reached over and grabbed the chicken bucket, fishing out the last wing. "I'll take a taxi to the Elizabeth for the appointment, but I want you guys all in the car with Sarah and parked close by before then. You'll need to be able to watch the door for when I come out, so Neil can get the drone in the air in a hurry. If it can follow a car, then hopefully it'll be able to stay on whatever car they take me in to wherever we're going. At that point, assuming you can find a spot that works, I want you to deploy yourself into position to cover me. If I come out in one piece, don't worry about following me back. That will mean the meeting went well, so at that point I want you and the team to try to track where the councilmembers go."

"Gotcha," Moose said. "If we can figure out where they're staying, you have a shot at taking them out right away, right?"

"That would be ideal," Noah said. "At the very least, though, I want some way to start tracking these people. Maybe Neil can get photos of them as they leave the place, something we can run through facial recognition. Anything that helps us identify them is a mission goal at this point."

Sarah leaned close to Noah. "But you're not going to try taking them down during this meeting, right?"

"I sincerely doubt any opportunity will present itself. You heard the phone calls; Deanna plans to have security in place, and that means security that can protect them from me, I'm sure."

"Good," Sarah said. "Allison said this could turn into a suicide mission, but I don't want to see that happen."

"Don't worry, Sarah, neither do I. I'm not going to sacrifice myself if I can possibly avoid it."

Neil tinkered with his new toy for about half an hour, then began mounting the camera on it. "This thing is awesome," he said. "With this, we shouldn't have any trouble at all keeping track of where they take you. I'm gonna hang onto this puppy when we're done here, I can think of a million ways it could come in handy in the future."

"Just as long as it does what it's supposed to do tomorrow," Sarah said.

"It will. All I got to do is tap the car on the screen once we spot it, and this thing will follow it until its battery gives out. Somehow, I don't think they're going to take you that far away from where they pick you up. Considering they think their meeting is with the most dangerous assassin in the world, I think they're going to want to get it over with as quickly as they can."

Moose suddenly burst out laughing, and Sarah looked at him. "What's so funny?"

"It just hit me," Moose said between bouts of laughter. "They're right, about meeting with the most dangerous assassin, but they aren't meeting the guy they think they are. Adrian might have been good, but I think Noah could take him any day."

"I appreciate the vote of confidence," Noah said, "but the thing we always have to remember is that anyone, no matter how professional he may be, can make a mistake. Sooner or later, Adrian would have made one, too. I just have to hope I don't make my big mistake during this mission. Something tells me we'll never get another chance at these people if I botch it tomorrow."

"So, don't botch it," Moose said. "You go in, you get out, and then we go after the bodies."

"That's exactly the way I've got it planned," Noah said.

"Hey," Sarah said, "I just had a thought. Do you think there's any chance one of their people might have seen you getting out of the Jaguar yesterday? Or getting in it when I picked you up?"

"According to Catherine, Broussard didn't have any accomplices with him, but you make a good point. For all we know, it's possible he had someone out on the street, watching for my arrival and departure. Go back to the rental company tonight and tell them the car's giving you some kind of problem, that you need to switch it out. Try to get something completely different, not another Jag. Maybe a Land Rover, something like that."

"That's what I was wondering. It wouldn't do for someone to notice the same car sitting there close by, somewhere. I've got a red wig in my bag; I think I'll wear that, too, cover up this blonde hair."

"That's another good idea," Noah said. "The only drawback to having you as my driver is that you do attract a lot of attention. If Broussard or anyone else had a man watching, he probably would've noticed you."

Sarah stuck her tongue out at him. "Come on, I'm not all that," she said. "I just figured the blonde hair might be recognizable, that's all."

Neal looked up at her and grinned. "Blondes are a dime a dozen," he said. "Blondes that look like you, on the other hand, are pretty rare. Any man who didn't notice you would probably be halfway to being gay."

Sarah blushed, but didn't say anything.

Noah picked up his phone and glanced at it. "It's almost seven," he said. "Anybody hungry?"

"Not after all that chicken," Moose said. "Neil?"

"There's a snack machine down by the lobby," Neil said. "I can run down and grab some chips later if I get the munchies."

"Somebody mark today on the calendar," Sarah said. "I think it's the first time I've ever heard Neil say he wasn't hungry."

"Oh, I'm hungry," Neil said. "I just don't feel like going out for dinner or anything. Besides, we've got to leave pretty soon, if we're going to go and switch cars."

"True," Noah said. "You should probably get started now, in fact."

FOURTEEN

Neil collected his computer and the drone, then he and Moose walked out the door. Sarah looked at Noah for a moment, then kissed him passionately. "That's to remind you that you want to come back alive," she said. Noah held her for a moment, then let go and watched her walk out before settling in to watch television until it was time to go.

He was watching a local newscast when his telephone rang. He recognized the number as coming from Allison's office.

"Camelot," he said.

"It's Allison. I just got the report from the people we put on the airports in Rome. The plane you were talking about left from Leonardo da Vinci airport at about six-thirty local time there. It will land at Heathrow in a little over an hour. There were eight people on board, all men except for one woman. She's the only one that could be identified. Her name is Deanna DiPrizio, and she has no known political affiliations. She's the CEO of Florentine Global, an export company that sends shiploads of containers all over the world."

"Interesting," Noah said. "Has the company ever been implicated in anything?"

"No, it never has. That may change in the near future, because CIA is opening a case file on them. If I learn anything more, I'll do my best to let you know." The line went dead.

At just after nine, Noah went down to the lobby, stepped outside and hailed a taxi. He had left his gun and cell phone in the room, knowing that there was no way he would be allowed to take anything with him to the meeting. He told the driver to take him to the Elizabeth Hotel and settled back to enjoy the ride.

The cab pulled up at the hotel at just ten minutes before ten. Noah paid the driver and slid out, then entered the hotel and went directly up the elevator. It was still five minutes before ten when he knocked on Broussard's door. It opened only a few seconds later and Broussard, with his eyes on the floor, stepped aside to let Noah come in.

"I am supposed to frisk you and be sure that you have no weapons or tracking devices on you," Broussard said nervously.

Noah turned to face him and nodded. "I expected no less," he said. "Please do so." He took off his jacket and tossed it on the bed.

Broussard patted him down efficiently, then went through the jacket as well. "You seem to be clean," he said. "If I missed anything, our escorts will be certain to find it."

"There was nothing to miss. I have brought nothing with me except the clothing I wear, and a little cash just in case I need to hire a taxi to get back to where I'm staying." He sat down in one of the two chairs in the room and let himself relax. "Have you any idea when we'll be leaving here?"

Broussard shook his head in the negative. "No. Only that someone will come for us sometime tonight." He pointed to a tea service sitting on a sideboard. "Would you care for tea? Or we can order something from room service, if you prefer."

Noah smiled. "No thank you," he said. "I need nothing."

Broussard sat in the other chair, and continued to avoid letting his gaze rest on Noah. "I want to ask," he said, "will I find myself in danger, after this meeting?"

Noah cocked his head slightly to the left and looked at him. "I have taken a calculated risk," he said. "The very magnitude of the assignment you proposed leads me to believe that there may be additional opportunities for me with your, shall we say, organization. You may find this hard to believe, but I do not wish to remain in this occupation for many years. I simply determined that my skills are the thing that will allow me to become wealthy, and I have been putting them to that use for some time. I have a financial goal set, and a few assignments such as this one could allow me to achieve it relatively soon. I am confident that I can compose enough safeguards to ensure that you and your superiors will not pose any danger to me in the future, one of those being that you don't want me to pose a danger to you. With those assumptions in place, I feel that I can allow such a limited number of people to know my face."

Broussard swallowed. "I assure you, you will have nothing to worry about with me. I hope to continue enjoying my life for some years to come, and I avoid situations that can put it at risk."

Noah watched him for a moment, noting that he occasionally glanced up, almost as if it were involuntary.

"So you're part of this council?"

Broussard nodded his head once. "I am its most junior member. I only became involved with this organization about a year ago. Inadvertently, I might add."

"Inadvertently?" Noah asked.

Broussard cleared his throat and then nodded again. "I was approached around that time to facilitate the sale of some arms. When the terms of the sale were presented to me, I realized that the weapons would be used in acts of terror, and stated that I wanted no part of it. My associates, however, can be extremely persuasive, and I found it necessary to reconsider my position."

"Necessary? Or only prudent?"

Broussard looked around the room for a moment before he responded. "I would have to say necessary. I have a daughter, you see, the product of an indiscretion about ten years ago. It was not possible for me to be fully a part of her life—her mother, I'm afraid, was already married to someone else at the time—but I am permitted visitation and I contribute to her upbringing. All of this is done secretly, of course, in order to avoid any embarrassment to her mother's husband. I am 'Uncle Pierre,' as far as she knows, but the other members of the Council somehow learned about her. When I attempted to avoid doing business with them, I was shown several photos of my daughter, all of them with crosshairs drawn over her face. The implication was clear; if I did not cooperate, she would be killed."

Noah looked at him for a long moment and then nodded. "Necessary. Yes. However, this makes me wonder whether you believe in the ideals of the organization."

Broussard turned and faced him squarely for the first time. "Some of their goals are good ones. Some of their actions are designed to make parts of the world a better place, at least for some people. I have learned, however, that there is no way to make all of the world better for all of the people. There are too many differences among us, too many cultures that simply cannot coexist in the same place." He let out a deep sigh. "Then there is the problem of motivation. Even the loftiest of goals is tainted when it is motivated by lust for power or wealth."

Noah shrugged. "The lust for power is a universal human trait. The same can be said of the lust for wealth, but it is a given that they come hand-in-hand. He that is wealthy will find that he has power; he who has power will find wealth coming to him. Do you not lust for them yourself?"

Broussard grinned sadly. "There was a time when I did," he said, "but I have learned that financial wealth carries with it certain burdens. True wealth is not found in banks, but in the heart. Oh, sure, having financial wealth can make life better in some ways, but the burdens that come with it—the weight of responsibility, the necessity of constant effort to maintain that wealth —they drain the joy from life. As for power, the man who has it is as much its slave as its master. The use of that power imposes obligations upon the one who uses it, and failure to meet those obligations will result in feelings of guilt and despair."

Noah chuckled. "My friend Broussard, you are a philosopher."

Broussard shook his head. "No. I am no philosopher. I am merely a man who has learned that every good thing has its dark side."

* * *

Two blocks away from the hotel, Sarah, Moose and Neil sat in the Land Rover they had acquired two hours earlier. Moose was watching the front of the Elizabeth Hotel through binoculars, ready to signal Neil the moment Noah appeared at the exit. He had watched as Noah had left the taxi and entered the building, and now they were simply waiting for their team leader to be escorted to the place where the meeting would be held.

"How long has he been in there now?" Sarah asked.

"Not even half an hour," Neil replied. "You might as well relax, Sis, he could be in there for hours yet."

Sarah grunted as she adjusted herself in her seat. "I'm relaxed," she said. "I just want to get this meeting over with. I don't know what it is, but something about it has got me worried. I mean, come on, we're supposed to just sit back while he walks into a meeting with some of the most dangerous people in the world. Where was that in the training manual?"

"Chapter 7," Neil said, "section B. 'Operations Procedures.' That's the part where it says when the boss has to enter a mission theater alone, the team has to stay ready for anything, but just wait for the outcome."

"Well, it's a stupid, sucky rule. What did you do, memorize the whole damn thing?"

Neil, in the backseat, stuck his tongue out at her in her rearview mirror. "Up yours. It's not my fault I have an eidetic memory."

"Knock it off, Neil," Moose growled. "You know damn well why she's worried. That's not just her boss in there, that's her boyfriend. Are you gonna try to tell me you wouldn't be just as worried if that was Lacey going into this meeting?"

"I never said I didn't understand," Neil said. "I was just answering her question. She wanted to know where the rule was that said we have to wait, so I told her."

"Yeah? And where's the rule that says team members have to work together to help make the mission a success?"

"Hey, I'm doing my part. Are you trying to say I'm not doing my part?"

"No, I'm just saying you're being a pain in Sarah's ass. Stop doing that."

Sarah gave a sigh. "He can't," she said, "I already figured that out. I never should've adopted him for a little brother because this is exactly the kind of thing little brothers do."

"Heads up," Moose said suddenly. "Limousine just pulled in, and the guy in the shotgun seat is going inside. This could be it. Got your sky copter ready?"

"It's ready," Neil said. "Just give me the word and I'll set it loose."

* * *

There was a knock on the door, and Broussard and Noah looked at each other. Noah nodded, and Broussard rose and went to open the door. A large man stood there, and a quick glance told Noah that he was carrying a large sidearm, probably a full auto machine pistol.

"Gentlemen," he said, his British accent thick. "My name is Gerald, and I'm here to escort you to the conference."

Noah got to his feet. "Mr. Broussard has already inspected me," he said. "Would you like to confirm his findings?"

Gerald smiled and stepped inside. "I'm supposed to do just that, actually." He stepped behind Noah and frisked him thoroughly, a search so thorough that it bordered on the obscene. "No problem, mate, ain't nothing on you."

Gerald turned to Broussard. "Now you, mate," he said. "Just to be sure this bloke hasn't turned you to his man."

Broussard's eyebrows went up, but he turned his back and spread his arms to submit to the search. Gerald was just as thorough with him, but pronounced him clean as well.

"Let's be off, then, right?" Gerald asked, and they followed him out of the room. A quick ride down the elevator and stroll across the lobby led them to the front entrance, where Gerald opened the back door of a Bentley limousine. Noah climbed in first and slid across the big backseat, followed by Broussard.

The windows in the back were completely blacked out, making it impossible to see where they were going. They heard Gerald climb into the front passenger seat and the car began moving. It turned right, taking them directly past the Land Rover.

* * *

"Okay, they're coming our way," Moose said. "Don't let the bird go until they go past us."

They were parked on a side street, where they would be blocked from view by a building once the limousine passed them. Sarah started the Land Rover and put on the right turn signal. As soon as the limousine went past, Neil would launch the drone and send it out over the buildings to where he could see the car, and Sarah would make the turn and pull out a short distance behind the limo.

The limousine went by with the driver paying no attention to them. Neil quickly opened his door and held the drone out, then tapped his phone to launch it. He sent it straight up over the three-story building beside them, then concentrated on guiding it remotely until he had the limousine in its camera view. As soon as the car was acquired, Neil tapped it twice on the screen, telling the drone to follow it wherever it went.

Sarah made the turn and saw the limousine almost two blocks ahead already. She followed leisurely, letting the distance between them grow in order to avoid attracting attention.

"Neil, you got it?" she asked.

"I got it," he said. "I can keep it in sight on my phone, so hang back as much as you want. I'll let you know if they turn."

"Okay, I'm hanging back. Just don't lose them, Neil, please." She sounded worried. "If they spot that drone..."

"I keep telling you to chill, don't I? They're not going to spot it, I disabled its navigation lights. That baby's invisible in the night sky."

Sarah swallowed hard. "That's good, I guess. Now, as long as no big bird runs into it, we can at least know where they take him."

FIFTEEN

Noah set part of his mind to counting seconds, something he had discovered he could do when he was a teenager. It was actually a technique used by many commandos, something that anyone could learn, and which didn't require them to maintain conscious thought. The seconds ticked by and were automatically added up into minutes and hours, so that Noah would be able to tell almost exactly how long the trip took.

Just under two minutes into the ride, the car made a turn and he could tell that it was descending, probably on a ramp of some sort. When it gained speed, he concluded that they were on one of the main highways that cut through London.

Eleven minutes later, an ascending ramp and decreasing speed told him they were getting off again, and then the car turned left at an intersection. It wound its way through city traffic for seven minutes more, then slowed and turned down a much steeper ramp.

We've entered a parking garage, Noah thought. *The meeting is probably going to be in the building above us.*

The car made another turn a few seconds later and stopped. The engine was cut, and a moment later Gerald opened the rear door.

"All right, gents," he said. "If you'll just follow me, please."

Noah and Broussard followed him through the dimly lit garage to an elevator. Gerald pressed a button and it opened almost instantly, allowing them to step inside. The lights in the elevator were much brighter, and Noah noticed that Gerald pressed the button for the sixth floor. They rode up in silence, and Gerald led them directly across the hallway when the elevator opened. He knocked on the door, and a woman opened it.

She looked Noah directly in the eyes. "Welcome," she said. "It is truly a pleasure to get to meet you. My name is Deanna DiPrizio, and you, of course, are the famous Adrian."

Noah smiled at her. "The pleasure is mine," he said, taking the hand she offered. He bent down quickly and gently brushed her hand with his lips.

Deanna smiled and blushed slightly. "Please come in and meet the others," she said.

Noah stepped inside and followed her around a cabinet to where a conference table was set up. Three men sat at the table, while two others stood looking out a window at the skyline with their backs toward the table. Gerald took a position by the door as if standing guard.

"Adrian, I'd like you to meet François Devereaux, James Millington and Roberto Cannellini. Gentlemen, this is Adrian."

All three of the men rose and offered their hands, and Noah shook each one. There were six chairs around the table, and Deanna pointed to the one beside her own for Noah. Broussard took the last empty chair and they all

DAVID ARCHER

sat down.

"I'd like to begin..." Deanna said, but François cut her off.

"So you know what it is we wish you to do, yes?"

Noah looked him in the eye. "I'm told you wish me to eliminate the Prince of Wales."

"That's correct," James said, his accent marking him as British. "However, we have a very short window. The elimination must be completed within the next nineteen days. Can you do that?"

Noah turned to face him when he began speaking. "I have never failed to complete a contract that I have taken," he said. "If I were not certain I could accomplish what you want me to do, I would not be here."

Roberto suddenly began drumming his fingers on the table. Noah looked at him, and found the man staring directly into his face. "Here is my concern," he said, his own accent marking him as Sicilian. "We must be certain that there will be no connection to our organization when this assassination takes place. In fact, it would be best if responsibility for it could be placed on some group from within the UK itself."

"And do you have such a group in mind? Perhaps the IRA?"

Roberto nodded once. "They would certainly be viable as suspects. They have a long history of rejecting the royalty and British domination. Some of their more radical elements might consider a strike against the royal family to be a powerful statement."

"The problem," James said, "would be how to implicate them. They are best known for bombings, so if an explosive device could be used that contained certain signature elements from their previous attacks, that could work."

Deanna looked at Noah. "Perhaps Adrian has a suggestion along this line."

"The most incriminating evidence would be a body," Noah said without hesitation. "I'm certain MI5 has a list of IRA members within Great Britain itself. I can arrange for one of them to be present when the event occurs, his body found shortly afterward. His death would be due to a gunshot from a Security Service weapon, allowing MI5 to take credit. Of course, there would be some circumstantial evidence arranged to tie him to the assassination."

"And you're certain you could arrange that in the timeframe we have set?" François asked.

Noah allowed a slight grin to appear on his face. "I have certain contacts that could provide me with an appropriate name and his location. The rest is simply a matter of logistics. I have no doubt that I can accomplish the effect you desire."

"You'd use a bomb, then?" asked James.

"For the outcome you desire, I believe it would be appropriate. Something primitive, such as IRA has used before. Remote detonation by use of a cellular telephone would suffice."

James nodded his head. "Be even better if the body you leave behind had a phone on him, perhaps with the detonator number in its history."

"That is exactly my thought," Noah said. "As I said, I can create circumstantial evidence that will lead MI5 to the conclusion you desire."

"Then let's discuss the fee," James said. "Twenty bloody million? Has anyone ever paid that much for an assignment such as this?"

Noah smiled coldly. "Has anyone ever demanded the political assassination of the Crown Prince? Leaving aside the difficulty in accomplishing the assignment, considering the security around the target, you have set conditions that make it far more involved than a simple elimination. Tying this assassination to the IRA, accomplishing it in a timeframe much shorter than I normally work with and generating the particular political impact that you want requires me to take unprecedented steps. I can do what you wish, but my fee is nonnegotiable. Twenty million US dollars, and I will not even begin to plan the event until I have received half of it, transferred to an account I will provide you."

James looked at the others, and a moment later Roberto nodded his head. François followed after another moment, then Broussard and finally Deanna. James looked at her. "Would you make the call, my dear lady?"

Deanna swallowed, then picked up a satellite phone and pressed some buttons. She held it to her ear and appeared to be waiting for someone to answer. Noah watched in silence, noting that her face seemed stressed even though she was obviously trying to conceal that fact. Her eyes widened slightly when the call was answered.

"This is Deanna," she said. "We have met with Adrian and reached a tentative agreement. He will do what we want within the timeframe we require, under the price and terms I sent to you earlier. Do we have your approval to complete this arrangement?"

She pressed the phone to her ear as if she was having trouble hearing whoever was on the other end. She started to speak a couple of times, but each time closed her mouth again. After more than a minute, she finally said, "Yes, sir, I understand. I assure you, we have impressed upon him just how critical this assignment is. I will finalize it and speak with you again tomorrow."

She ended the call and turned to Noah. "It appears," she said nervously, "that we have reached an agreement. Do you have the transfer codes with you?"

Noah reached into his shirt pocket and withdrew a slip of paper, which he passed to her. She reached down beside her chair and picked up a tablet computer. She began tapping on it as François leaned toward Noah.

"A question," he said. "We will have sometimes more need for your specialty. Will you be available to us for future assignments of this nature?"

Noah looked at him coldly. "I am a contractor, so I am always interested in working. I will look at each opportunity on a case-by-case basis, of course. I am now concerned, however, because I thought I was already dealing with the decision-makers of this organization. From the call the lovely Deanna has just made, I see that I was mistaken."

"The call I made," Deanna said softly, pausing in what she was doing, "was to our Executive Director. Every decision we make is finalized by seeking his approval. In all the years I have known him, he has never shown himself. None of us has ever met him, but his leadership and guidance has been invaluable to us. If you cannot accept that, I must respectfully withdraw the offer."

Noah turned his eyes to her and sat silently for a moment. His eyes bored into her own, and then he spoke. "There are those who would speak of me the same way. I will not object, as long as this assignment and my final payment are both completed successfully."

Deanna resumed what she was doing.

"How can we reach you?" James asked, and Noah turned to him.

"Once we have successfully concluded this contract," he said, "I will provide you with a way to message me securely. I have someone who is very good at secure communications."

"Hmpf," James said. "The way ours gets buggered about, perhaps we should employ you to set something up for us. Bloody ragheads we use now seem to think email is perfectly safe."

Deanna held up a finger to get their attention. "The transfer is done," she said. "I'm sure you won't want to use my computer to check, but you'll see the money in your account when you do." She looked around at the three men. "I believe that concludes our business tonight, unless someone has any other questions?"

All three shook their heads, so Deanna turned back to Noah. "Is there anything else we need to do at this point?"

Noah smiled at her. "Just prepare to send the rest of my payment when this assignment is complete." He stood, and the others all did likewise. "Until then, I believe I have everything I need." He turned to Gerald, who was standing beside the door. "Shall we go?"

* * *

"Okay," Neil said when the limousine had turned into the parking garage. "I had to stop the drone from following it inside, now what do I do?"

"God, I don't know," Sarah said. "What if there's a back exit out of that place? Maybe they're just trying to be sure no one is following."

Neil tapped the screen of his phone. "I'm taking the

drone all the way around the building," he said. "We're on the east side, going around on the north—nothing there, checking the west side—no, no exits there, I'm going around to the south. Nothing there either, that entrance is the only way in or out."

"Park where we can keep an eye on it," Moose said, "but try not to be too obvious about it."

"Don't be obvious, he says," Sarah muttered. "This is a wide-open street, there isn't anywhere to hide."

Neil suddenly leaned over the back of the front seat and pointed through the windshield. "There's a UPS truck over there. Get behind it. You should still be able to see the exit for the garage."

Sarah shook her head but did as he suggested. "Good grief, we're supposed to be part of some super espionage outfit and the best we can do is hide behind delivery trucks. If they spot this Land Rover and recognize it from back by the hotel, we're nailed and Noah is probably dead."

"Oh, chill," Neil said. "This is a silver Land Rover, that's the most common color there is. You take off that red wig and we won't look anything like the same vehicle."

Sarah flipped him a bird over her shoulder as she parked behind the truck. "Can you find out what building that is?"

"Sure, give me a minute." He pulled his computer onto his lap and started tapping keys. A moment later he said, "Belongs to an export company, Florentine Global out of Italy. These people all came here from Rome, I'd take bets they're all connected to this outfit."

"Ya think? Okay, Moose, you're on," she said.

Moose nodded, then opened his door and stepped out

onto the sidewalk. He flipped the hood of his jacket up and stood there for a moment as if deciding which way to go, then began walking nonchalantly toward the garage entrance. The garage had a single security guard on duty in the attendant's booth, a man who was staring at a video on the cell phone in his hand and paying no attention to pedestrian traffic. Moose watched him for a moment as he approached the entrance, then quickly slipped inside and made his way soundlessly into a darkened corner.

There were a few cars parked in the garage, but he spotted Noah in the dim light and was able to keep an eye on him until he and his escorts entered the elevator. He stepped out of his concealment and continued walking until he got to the elevator itself, noticing that it stopped on the sixth floor. He pushed the up button for the elevator beside it, stepped inside when it opened a moment later, and pressed six.

When it opened again, he poked his head out and looked up and down the hall, but saw no one. He walked briskly along the hallway, listening and looking for any sign of Noah, but to no avail. He spotted an open closet and slipped inside, closed the door and took out his cell phone. He hit a button and Neil answered almost instantly.

"He's on the sixth floor," Moose said, "but I have no idea where. This is pretty obviously some kind of office building, but I think most of the offices on this floor are empty, this time of night. Any ideas?"

"Yeah," Neil said. "Hang tight a minute."

Neil had landed the drone on top of a nearby single-story building, but now he tapped his phone and let it rise into the air. He watched the image on the phone as the drone climbed up to the sixth floor, staying a couple of hundred feet away, then maneuvered it slowly around the building once more. He zoomed in the image so that he could see into the rooms that had lights on, and spotted Noah sitting at a table with several other people in a conference-style room on the west side of the building. Two men were standing at the window and looking out, but neither seemed to notice the drone.

"Okay, he's in a conference room on the back," he said. "It would be just about the middle of the building. Some of the other rooms on that floor look like they might be apartments, maybe guestrooms of some kind."

"Middle of the building? That's about where the elevator is, it must be that room straight across from it. Can you see what's going on in there?"

"Just talking, from what I can see. Boss man looks relaxed. I've got about thirty-five minutes of battery life left; want me to keep an eye on him?"

Moose was quiet for a few seconds. "Nobody inside can see that thing, right?"

"No," Neil said. "It's painted black, so without the navigation lights it's absolutely invisible. There's a couple of guys standing at the window looking out, but there's no way they would notice it unless I cut across something brightly lit in the background. Most of the skyline is too low for that to happen, and I'm not going to be zipping around, anyway."

"No, I don't think you need to watch all the time. If you pull it back in and turn it off, will that extend the battery life any?"

"Of course," Neil said.

"Then I think you should. Remember, you're supposed to try to see where the Council people go when this meeting is over. Better save it for that."

"Roger Wilco," Neil said. "Bringing the baby home now."

Back at the Land Rover, Neil watched as the drone came into view and settled into the back of the pickup, then turned off both the drone and the camera. "And now the waiting begins," he said.

Sarah leaned her head back against the headrest. "We should have bought more batteries for that thing," she said. "I'd feel a lot better if you could keep it up there watching over him."

Neil nodded. "You're probably right. I'm sorry, I should've thought of that."

"Not your fault. None of us was thinking about trying to watch what went on in the meeting. Besides, it's not like we can hear what they're talking about."

Neil reached up and laid a hand on her shoulder. "Sarah, come on, relax and have faith in the boss. He's the best, you know that. He'll come through this okay, just wait and you'll see."

Sarah chuckled mirthlessly. "Wait? Yeah, that's exactly what I'm doing. Just waiting."

SIXTEEN

Gerald nodded and turned to open the door. Noah and Broussard followed him through it and into the elevator across the hall. As he entered, Noah instinctively looked up and down the hall, and so only he noticed the closet door was open about an inch.

As soon as the elevator doors closed, Moose took out his phone again. "Okay, he's out of there. He and Broussard and their shadow are headed down to the garage. He didn't seem to be under any kind of duress, so I'm going to stay here and watch for the others. I'll let you know when they get into the elevator. They'll probably be headed for the garage, but God only knows what cars they might be in. There's quite a few down there."

"Watch yourself," Neil said in reply. "Like I told you, some of the other rooms on that floor look like living quarters. Those people might be staying there tonight, so be careful they don't spot you."

The conference room door open suddenly, and Moose ended the call instantly. A woman stepped out followed by five men.

"I'll see you all in the morning," the woman said. "We're due at the plane just before noon, so we'll have time to stop for breakfast somewhere along the way."

She turned and walked into the room that was closest to the conference room and closed the door behind her. The men moved along the hallway, each of them entering one of the other rooms.

Moose waited until they were all inside and then slowly pulled the closet door open. He listened for any sound but heard nothing, then slipped out and went to the elevator. He pushed the down button and wasn't surprised when the elevator he'd ridden up in opened instantly.

He pressed the button for the garage level and breathed a sigh of relief when the doors closed. A moment later, he stepped out into the garage and made his way toward the exit, staying in darkness whenever possible. When he came into view of the attendant's booth, he froze. The security guard was standing just outside the booth smoking a cigarette.

Moose stayed in the shadows and watched silently as the man puffed away. He still had the cell phone in his hand, and seemed to be engrossed in whatever he was watching. From the weak sounds that reached Moose's ears, he guessed the man was watching a pornographic video.

Finally the guard dropped the cigarette and ground it under his foot, then stepped back into the booth. He sat down in a chair and leaned back, his eyes still fixed on the screen in his hand. Moose moved slowly toward the exit, but whatever the guard was watching had claimed all of his attention. He never even noticed the man in dark clothing who stepped out onto the sidewalk just a few feet from where he sat. Moose shoved his hands in his pockets and walked calmly back toward the Land Rover.

Sarah looked over at him as he climbed inside. "So what now?"

"Neil was right, those are guestrooms up there. These must be bigwigs with the company that owns the building. I heard the woman say they're headed back to the airport before noon, but they want to stop and get some breakfast somewhere on the way."

"So we know where they're going to be for the rest of the night," Neil said. "That's what the boss wants to know. What should we do now?"

"Noah's supposed to ride back to the Elizabeth," Moose said, "and then make his own way back to the Cavendish. I guess we should go back and wait for him there."

Sarah looked at him for a moment, then started the truck and put it in gear. She pulled out around the UPS delivery truck and headed toward the Cavendish Hotel once again. "He looked okay when he left?"

"He looked fine. No sign of stress that I could see. If I had to guess, he probably left everybody else in that room more stressed than he was."

Sarah didn't respond and they rode the rest of the way back to the hotel in silence. She parked the truck and led the two guys up to her room, with a couple of people pointing at the drone that Neil carried. She unlocked the door and they stepped into the room, then she turned on the television and flopped onto the bed.

"So, we know where Broussard is staying, and now we know where the rest of this council will be. Maybe Noah can finish this thing tonight."

* * *

"You are troubled," Broussard said in the backseat of

the limousine. "You are annoyed that no one told you about the Executive Director."

Noah turned and looked at him. "When we spoke on the phone the night before last, I told you that I do not deal with middlemen. Tonight, it seems I did so anyway. Am I annoyed? Yes. However, what I said earlier is still true. This organization can offer me opportunities to achieve my financial goals very quickly, so I have decided that I must be ready to bend at least slightly. I will reserve judgment on this matter for now, and wait to see how this arrangement concludes."

Broussard let out a long, ragged breath. "I was afraid," he said softly. "I feared that you might feel that I had misled you and decide to punish me. I swear to you that was not my intent. If I had known that they had not cleared this arrangement before our meeting, I would have told you."

"We need not speak of it again," Noah said. "We are now in business together, so put your fears at rest." He turned his head and looked at the black glass beside him, watching Broussard in the reflection.

The limousine arrived at the Elizabeth a short time later, and Gerald stepped out to open the back door. Noah slid out of the car as Broussard followed.

"If you need a ride somewhere else, mate," Gerald said, "we'd be happy to take you wherever you need to go."

Noah smiled at him. "No, I prefer to make my own way. I thank you, but it will not be necessary."

Gerald grinned and chuckled. "Thought you might feel that way, but I was told to ask. Cheerio, then, mate." He closed the door and got back into the front passenger seat. The car drove away only a few seconds later.

Broussard stood there looking at Noah. "Is there anything more I can do for you tonight?" he asked.

"No," Noah said. "I'm certain we will meet again at some point, but not tonight. I shall go back to my own accommodations, so that you might go and get some sleep." He turned and began walking down the street as Broussard stared after him.

Three blocks later, certain that he was not being followed, Noah caught a passing tram and slid onto a bench inside. His route would take him to the Cavendish, and so he sat back to think about who this unknown Executive Director might be, and how to find and kill him.

The ride took almost an hour, but finally he stepped off a block from his hotel and strolled briskly up the street. The night desk clerks were bending over some paperwork as he entered, and paid no attention to him walking through. He pressed the button for the elevator and rode it up to his floor, then bypassed his own room and tapped on the door to Sarah's.

Moose opened the door carefully, then stepped aside to let him into the room. Sarah bounced up off of the bed, where she had been sitting, and threw both arms around his neck. She kissed him once, quickly, then let go and looked up at him. "Took you long enough to get back here," she said. "Everything okay?"

"Not particularly," Noah said. "I went into this meeting expecting to come out with a clear idea of who the targets are, but things just got a little screwy. This so-called 'Executive Council' had to call somebody higher up to authorize the fee I demanded." He looked at Neil. "Deanna made the call and she used a sat phone. Any chance you can find out who it was she called?"

Neil's mouth fell open. "Oh, shit," he said. "Noah, I'm sorry, it never occurred to me to keep the system on. I thought we were done with sat phones for now."

Noah laid a hand on his shoulder. "Yeah, I thought so too. This messes me up, though, because I'm not supposed to make any further contact until I pull off the assignment. If I go back to them now, the best I can hope for is to take out the Council itself. Problem with that is that it leaves the Executive Director in place, and he can probably replace them with a couple of phone calls. I don't think it would do a lot of good." He pulled the extra chair from the table in the room and sat down. "What about the Council? Do we know where they're at?"

"Right where you left them," Moose said. "I was hiding in the closet down the hall from the room you were in, and I saw them come out before I could slip away. They're all staying in guestrooms right there on that same floor. I had to wait until they all went into their rooms before I could get out, and by that time you were already gone and out of sight."

"There were guestrooms on that floor? Neil, can you find out who owns that building?"

"I already thought of that," Sarah said. "It belongs to a company called Florentine Global Export. Why?"

"Okay, that makes sense," Noah said. "Allison called me earlier and told me that Deanna DiPrizio is the CEO of Florentine. She actually set up a meeting with a professional assassin in one of her own office buildings. If she's using the company as a front for the IAR, that could explain why there would be guestrooms in an office building."

"No kidding," Moose said, "but don't get too cocky

yet. I heard her say that they're flying out again around noon, so they aren't planning to stay in town."

"That's okay. I know who they are, now, and we can put somebody back in Rome on tailing them. I can reach out and touch them whenever I need to, but what I've got to do is have a really good reason to contact them again."

"Well, they wanted you to kill Prince Charles, right?" Sarah asked. "What if you call them up and say it's too difficult, you can't get to him."

Noah shook his head. "I already assured them that I can get the job done," he said. "If I go back now and say I can't, they'll probably cut me off and might even go into hiding. They've seen what they believe is Adrian's face; saying I couldn't complete the mission would make them nervous about whether I might want to eliminate them for my own protection."

"Then what do you do?" Neil asked.

Noah sighed. "I start making preparations to kill the Prince of Wales."

"Boss," Moose said, "you're not serious, are you? You're not really going to do it?"

"Of course not, but the preparations I'm referring to are things they would hear about. They'll be able to convince themselves I'm really working on carrying out the assignment they gave me, and that will buy me time to come up with a reason I need to speak with them again. When I do, I'll make sure I demand something they'll need approval for, and then Neil can work his magic when she calls the big guy."

Moose, Neil and Sarah looked at each other, then all three of them turned their eyes to Noah.

"So what's next?" Moose asked.

Noah pointed at Neil. "First thing in the morning, I want you to get on your computer and track some things down for me. Number one, I need a place to work out of, somewhere I can hold a prisoner if I need to. Then, I need to locate a local member of the IRA, someone with definite connections who's living in England, and preferably single. You can probably find an MI6 watch list you can hack into, that would probably be the easiest way to find the guy I'm looking for. Then, I need to know about every appearance Prince Charles is going to make between seven and fifteen days from now. I need to leave a trail those people can follow, so they're convinced I'm going through with it."

He turned to Moose. "I think you should go ahead and check out of the Elizabeth and come on over here for tonight. It'll be easier for us to work on this if we're all together, and there's no telling what we may have to do suddenly. Get the keys from Sarah, and you guys can go on and get checked out now and bring all your stuff over here. You can use Sarah's room for tonight, and she can sleep with me."

Sarah broke into a big smile. Moose nodded, and accepted the keys that Sarah passed to him. "You got it, Boss." He and Neil got up and walked out the door, leaving Noah and Sarah alone.

"So you've got to keep looking like him for a while, yet, right?" Sarah asked.

Noah looked at her and shrugged. "I guess so," he said.

She shook her head. "Okay. I guess if I have to put up with it, there's nothing I can do. I'll just be so glad when this is over and I can have the real Noah back."

* * *

The brown-haired man in the Derby hat and wire-rimmed spectacles sat down at the table in his flat and pulled the cell phone out of his pocket. He quickly dialed the number without looking at the keypad and put the phone to his ear, keeping one eye on the other patrons and staff as he did so. He listened to the ringing on the other hand and smiled when a man's half-awake voice came on the line.

"It is three o'clock in the morning," the voice said crisply.

"You recently contracted my services," he said softly. "Were you aware that I was taken into custody?"

There was silence on the other end for a few seconds, but then the man sounded wide awake. "There were rumors, yes," he said. "I trust you kept our names out of it?"

"Of course I did, or you would have undoubtedly joined me in my cell. They know nothing of the contract, nor of who had employed me. The frustrating thing was that I had all of my preparations in place when I was taken. One day more and the contract would have been fulfilled. I am calling to determine whether you would like me to proceed."

"Is that even possible?" the other man asked. "Are you not compromised?"

"Not at all. They now know the face I was wearing when I was arrested, but I have many faces. They have nothing that can lead them to me again. In this case, an old and trusted source of materials in London had apparently been turned into an informant. The case officer was kind enough to let his name slip, so I have already rewarded him for his faithlessness. I have other sources, and will take all necessary precautions when I use them."

The man on the other end cleared his throat. "I'm concerned," he said. "The fact that you were caught at all suggests that you may be losing your touch, as it were. I had contacted you because I was assured that you could handle a task of this magnitude, but now I'm in doubt as to whether that is true."

"There are perhaps three of us in all the world who would be capable of assassinating your Prime Minister. I am the only one who would be willing to do so. You've already paid the required deposit. While I'm aware that your timeframe has been inconvenienced by my untimely detention, I think the outcome you desire can still be manifested if I proceed."

The hesitation on the other end lasted a few seconds longer this time. "I'll need a little time to think about this. Can you call me again tomorrow, preferably during the day?"

The man in the Derby smiled. "Of course," he said. "Shall we say two o'clock?"

"Yes, that will be fine. I will have an answer for you by then." The line went dead.

The man in the Derby put a finger to his chin as he thought through the conversation. He had been honest in the call, insofar as his claim that preparations for the PM's assassination were all in place. He hoped to be able to complete the assignment, simply because he was going to need the money, but he would never presume to proceed with an assassination if the client disapproved for any reason. The man he had just spoken to was not actually the client, but could almost certainly make the decision in this case without having to seek the approval of the Baroness.

Oh, well, he would know in a few hours. Now, however, he had another call to make. He dialed a number and put the phone back to his ear. The line rang twice, and a woman answered.

"Hey, gorgeous," he said, this time with a Western American accent. "Are you keeping dinner for me?"

The woman on the other end of the line was silent for just a moment, and then she took a deep breath. "Henry? Is it really you?"

"Sure is. I got a little tangled up over here for a while, hope you weren't too worried."

"I've been a wreck," she said. "I kept checking all the news websites, looking for anything that might explain why you disappeared. I haven't been sleeping, that's why I was sitting here awake when you called. Are you all right?"

"I'm fine, Rachel," he said. "Had to put in a little extra work to get out of a mess, but it's all over now. I just wanted to check in and make sure you're okay."

"I will be," Rachel said. "You'll be coming home soon, right?"

He frowned. This was the part of the call he was dreading. "Not quite yet," he said softly. "That last contract may have gone bad on me, so I need to go ahead and make some money pretty quick. There was another company looking to hire me just before everything got screwed up, and I need to make contact with them."

"Oh, God, Henry," the woman said softly. "I get so worried." He heard her sniffle, but then she pulled herself together. "All right, then, what can I do to help?"

"That's my girl," he said. "Remember I emailed you an ad I ran across? It listed a few different cities, can you take a look and see if London was one of them. I'm pretty sure it was."

"All right," Rachel said. "Give me a couple of moments." She was quiet for nearly half a minute, and then she said, "I found it. Yes, London is in the list. You are supposed to place an ad in the newspapers saying that you want to discuss business, and use the code AD229."

Henry smiled. "That's great," he said. "Okay, sweetheart, just give me a few days to look into what they want, and I'll call you again. Don't worry, everything's going to be fine. If this is too big a job, I might be home by the end of the week."

He heard a sob escape her. "I hope so, Henry," she said. "I really hope so."

He ended the call and looked at the time display on the phone. It was well after three AM, and there was no possibility that he could place the ad before eight. He wandered off to his bed and set the alarm on his phone to rouse him at seven.

He woke on schedule, went to his little kitchen and made himself some breakfast. At just after eight, he took out his phone and dialed another number.

"London telegraph," the receptionist answered. "How might I direct your call?"

"I'd like to place a classified ad, please," Henry said. The receptionist put him on hold for a moment and then another young woman came on the line. Henry explained to her that he wanted to place an ad, dictated it to her perfectly and then gave her a credit card number from memory.

"Thank you," the girl said. "Your advertisement will

appear in this evening's paper, as well as appearing on our website right away."

"Well, thank you," Henry said. "You were a great help."

SEVENTEEN

Noah woke five minutes before the alarm he had set for six AM, and roused Sarah so that they could get their showers out of the way. He wanted to be ready for anything by the time Neil and Moose were up, but they surprised him by knocking on his door while he and Sarah were drying off. He left her in the bathroom and went to the door with just a towel around his waist.

"About time," Neil said as he pushed past Noah into the room. "We've been up for an hour already, working our butts off while you two were probably playing kissy-face."

"Ignore him," Moose said. "He's just jealous."

"I am not jealous, I am just impatient. The boss man said he wanted me working on some things first thing this morning, so I got up and worked on them. You want to hear what I found, Boss?"

Noah had closed the door and dropped his towel, and slid into his slacks as he nodded. "Of course," he said. "Go ahead."

Neil had already set his computer on the table and opened it. "First item you asked for was a house, right? I found one in East Kensington that ought to be ideal.

Fully furnished, fully stocked pantry, five bedrooms, a two-car garage attached to the house and almost two full acres of yard that's surrounded by a 10-foot-high brick wall. It's available for only 900 pounds per week. The estate agent will be open at seven thirty, if you want to grab it, but I didn't see anything else that was half as likely to work."

Noah nodded. "Go ahead and get it when they open," he said. "We can move over there later today."

"Okay, now the second thing." He pulled up a photo on the monitor and pointed at it. "Patrick Iverson," Neil said. "Forty-eight years old. Known member of the off-shoot organization known as the Real Irish Republican Army. SIS has been keeping tabs on him for almost a year, now, and he's been hauled in for questioning about IRA activities in the country on four different occasions. So far, there's been no evidence linking him to any actual events, but circumstantial evidence against him is mounting. He's had direct contact with bad actors in at least two of those attacks, and he's suspected of helping to set them up. He lives in the London Borough of Hackney, in northeast London. It's not quite a slum, but the area has seen a lot of poverty and some increase in crime over the last few years. Single with no known family anywhere in the area, and he seems to be a loner. Works in a factory, and doesn't seem to have any friends."

"What about skills? Has he had any kind of military training?"

Neil nodded. "Yep, served four years in the Royal Navy. Never saw combat, but his specialty was underwater demolitions. Sounds like a guy who would know how to rig up a bomb, don't you think?"

"Any general criminal history?" Noah asked.

"Minor stuff, mostly," Neil said. "like traffic tickets, public intoxication. In nineteen ninety-nine, he was accused of rape by a young woman who lived in the same apartment building he did at the time. Police investigated, he was arrested but then was released only a couple days later with the charges all dismissed. Apparently the girl had made the exact same accusations about a couple of other men in recent months, identical all the way down to descriptive details of the event. She ended up being sent to counseling."

Noah was leaning over his shoulder, studying the photos of the man that were displayed on the monitor. "Okay, he looks like our guy. Moose and I will go round him up within the next couple of days."

"Cool," Neil said. "Now, as for Prince Charles; he's only got five appearances scheduled in that time frame, and three of them all next Thursday. All three of those will be in connection with schools and teachers charity, at three different primary schools scattered around London. He'll be accompanied by the Prime Minister, and they'll be surrounded by kids the majority of the time in each one, so I'm guessing you wouldn't want to have them on the list?"

"You guessed right," Noah said. "We're not going through with it in any case, but I don't even want to plan a dummy operation that would involve killing innocent kids."

Neil nodded and snapped his fingers. "Way cool," he said. "Okay, next Wednesday, the Prince will be hosting a meeting of business leaders from around the city. There will be about two hundred in a conference room set up like a theater, and he'll be addressing them from the stage. Then, on Friday, he's attending the opening, like a ribbon-cutting, of a hospice in Tower Hamlets. That one is open to the public, so it's likely to be pretty packed around it."

"Where is the conference room for the business meeting?" Noah asked.

"It's in the Canary Wharf building, One Canada Square in the Canary Wharf Borough. The meeting will be on the forty-seventh floor."

"That would make it tough to get out of, Boss," Moose said. "I'm assuming you're going to want to plan this all the way out, with escape routes and everything?"

Noah nodded. "You're right," he said. "Still, it's probably the most likely situation where anyone would have a chance to make the hit. I think we'll have to take it."

"Okay, does anybody but me think this is getting to be a little scary?" Sarah asked. "Noah, what are you going to do if you haven't identified the Executive Director by the time you're supposed to make this hit?"

"I've thought of that, and there are couple of possibilities. First, it could simply be a failed assassination attempt. I could miss, in other words. Second, and this one might be a little trickier, we could call in our girl Catherine and let her know what's going on. She could probably manage to make contact with the Prince and get his schedule changed at the very last possible second. That would naturally make it impossible to complete the assignment as planned, and I'd have to go into sudden-death overtime. It might even give me the reason I'm looking for to make Deanna call the top man again."

"I don't see why you can't just call them in a week or so and make up an excuse," Sarah said. "Why go to all this trouble for an assassination you aren't really going to do?"

"That group of people organizes assassinations and terrorist attacks all over the world," Noah said. "You can bet they'll be watching closely, checking every news story and looking for signs that I'm actually setting this up. If they don't find any, they're going to start wondering whether they wasted their money on me. There's got to be enough convincing clues or they won't even take a call from me again."

"That's your logic talking," she said. "Only problem there is that I can't argue with it."

* * *

The cell phone on the table rang suddenly, and the man who called himself Henry snatched it up. "Hello," he said, his American accent completely gone.

"You want to discuss something?" a woman asked.

"Yes," he said. "I am responding to your attempts to contact me."

The woman was silent for a moment, and when she spoke again, Henry could hear confusion in her voice. "Is there a problem with the arrangement?"

It was Henry's turn to be confused. "Arrangement? We have not even begun to discuss it yet."

Another moment of silence passed. "You placed a code in your advertisement. How did you come by that code?"

Henry scowled. "Dear lady," he said, "that code was listed in advertisements placed by you and your people, advertisements that were obviously intended to get my attention and elicit a response. I regret that it has taken me some time to respond, but I have been unavoidably detained. I have now overcome that detention, and am willing to discuss whatever work you might have for me."

"I'm afraid I don't know what to say," the woman said. "That work is already assigned to the person we were trying to reach."

Henry's eyebrows rose half an inch. "I find that to be quite startling," he said, "since I'm quite certain I am the person you are seeking. If you have made an arrangement with someone using my name, then you have been seriously misled. Let me suggest that you notify those above you of this fact, and tell them how they can contact me at this number. I shall keep it for no more than two hours, and if I have not heard from them by that time it will be destroyed."

He pressed the end button on the phone and set it down on the table once again.

So, he thought, *someone is trying to impersonate me? The only possible reason for such an impersonation is an attempt to infiltrate the organization that wishes to employ me. That would mean that we are dealing with a government agent, but from which government?*

Henry lay back on his bed and stared at the ceiling. This was troubling, and he needed to be certain of how he wanted to proceed. He could conceivably walk away, let IAR—he was certain that was who he was dealing with—find themselves rounded up and held accountable for their crimes, but he had been hoping that the employment they were offering would lead to more.

It wasn't that he needed the money so much; the fact was that he needed to work. He had learned early on that the only thing that satisfied the "itch" inside him was to take a life. As a child and teenager, he had contented himself with animals, spending every possible moment hunting in the fields. By the time he was fifteen, he knew that killing deer and bulls and the occasional bear was not enough, anymore, but he didn't find an opportunity to discover the solution until he was almost 17.

He had been out on a hunt one day, and was moving as quietly and stealthily as he could, following fairly recent spoor of a bear. The animal had passed that way only a few hours before, and he was hoping to come across it when it settled down to rest.

A sound caught his ear, a sound that was out of place in that part of the forest. It was the sound of laughter, the sound a woman might make when she was in the company of a man she fancied. He had turned aside in curiosity, finding the young couple only 100 yards off the trail he was following. They were lying on a blanket, and the young man was pretending to hold the girl down.

Or was he? The laughter he had heard a few moments before was gone, and the girl was protesting and demanding to be released. The young man was not cooperating, insisting to her that she lay still and enjoy what he was planning to do.

"You know you want it," the man said. "You may have everyone else believing in your innocence, but we both know what you truly desire."

"No," she protested again. "I do not do that, I have never..."

The man thrust his face downward and forced a kiss upon the girl. She struggled beneath him, trying to get loose, and then suddenly he pulled back. She had bitten his lower lip, and it was bleeding. He raised a hand to his mouth for a second, then slapped her violently across the face.

"Bitch," he said. "I don't care if you want to be coy, but be careful. Look what you've done!"

The girl was sobbing at that point, and the man lowered his hand to caress her breast. She shook her head vigorously, again pleading with him to stop, but then the sound of tearing fabric could be heard.

That was enough, Henry decided. Without even thinking about what he was doing, he raised his rifle to his shoulder and centered the sights on the man's face, then squeezed the trigger. The bullet entered through the young man's left eye and blew out the entire back of his skull.

Henry felt a thrill run through him. He had toyed with the thought of killing a human a few times, but had never actually believed he would do it. Now, feeling justified by the circumstances, he allowed himself to enjoy the rush that came, the "itch" suddenly replaced with an excitement he had not known since the first time he had killed a neighbor's dog. It felt like waves of pure energy washing through him, and only the screams of the young woman made him pull himself out of it.

The body had collapsed on top of her, and she was in complete panic. She was screaming, terrified and horrified at what she had just seen, and it took her a moment to gather her wits enough to push the body off herself. She scrambled to her feet and looked down at the blood covering the bodice of her dress, then turned her eyes to stare at the dead man's broken, destroyed face as she continued screaming.

Henry watched her, and suddenly the itch began

again. Without even giving any thought to what he was doing, he worked the bolt and chambered another round, then raised the gun to his shoulder and aimed at the center of her chest. For just a moment there was a voice inside his head insisting he not squeeze the trigger, but the itch was too strong. The first kill, the man, had only teased it; now it was awake, and knew what it wanted.

The bullet passed through the center of her chest, entering just below the breastbone and blowing out two vertebrae as it exited through her back. She fell instantly, but the bullet had not come near her heart, so she continued screaming even louder.

Fascinated, Henry stepped out from behind the tree he was using for cover and walked toward her. She had fallen onto her back, and though she was bleeding profusely, she was still alive and conscious. She looked up at him in terror, tears flooding from her eyes as she used her arms to try to drag herself backward and away from him. Amazingly, she moved her limp, useless body a good six feet in the time it took him to reach her.

She stopped moving as he stared down at her, her eyes flicking from the gun in his hands to his face. She was trying to speak, but every time she opened her mouth only garbled sounds and bloody spittle came out. Henry stood and looked down at her, and the thrill washed over him with incredible intensity.

He glanced at the body of the man and felt nothing. That one had deserved what happened to him, so it wasn't as satisfying. The girl, though, had been innocent. Henry looked down at her face and saw even more blood coming out of her mouth. There was no way she could survive, her wound was definitely mortal. Surely it wouldn't take long, he thought, so he simply stood there and watched.

It took almost a half-dozen minutes for her to bleed out, and Henry stared at her face the whole time. When her eyes finally went dim and he knew that death had claimed her, he finally sat down and leaned against a nearby tree. He still felt the waves of excitement and pleasure rolling through him, and knew that he would never hunt animals again.

Henrik Schultz had discovered his true passion. From that moment on, he would hunt and kill human beings. It took him only two years to graduate from choosing and stalking his own victims to accepting payment to stalk someone else's.

His reverie ended as the phone rang again, and he realized that only fifteen minutes had passed since he spoke to the woman who replied to his advertisement. That old memory often took him for a detour, and it had done so again. He rose hurriedly and snatched up the phone.

"Hello?"

"I understand there may be some confusion regarding a recent employment contract?" The voice that came to the line was now that of a man, and Henry recognized it as the voice of Pierre Broussard.

"There is no confusion, Monsieur Broussard," he said. "You have been duped into hiring the wrong man."

Broussard hesitated for a couple of seconds. "How can that be possible?" he asked. "And how do you know..."

"I know who you are because I have been present during some of your arms negotiations, though you would not have seen me. As for your first question, it is possible because I have been held in a cellar dungeon at Vauxhall Cross for several weeks. The man you hired is almost certainly a law enforcement agent, probably from either the UK or the United States. His purpose, I am sure, was to ferret out the identities of those in your organization. Did you make such an error as to allow that to happen?"

Henry could hear the nervousness in Broussard's voice. "He said—he said he would not accept the employment if he did not meet with those who actually made the decisions."

Henry chuckled. "Then you have undoubtedly given him exactly what he wants. I am sorry for this, for I would have liked working with you, but as I am certain you know, I never meet with my employers. All transactions are completed through secure communications, but no one ever sees my face, and I do not care who is paying me."

"No, no," Broussard said quickly. "If you are telling the truth, what can we do?"

Henry smiled as he leaned back again on the bed. "Well, if you are wise, you will employ me to find and eliminate the imposter. It is even possible I can do so in time to save all of your lives, and perhaps even complete the assignment you gave to him."

Broussard closed his eyes and pinched the bridge of his nose. "Tell me how we can do that, please, and I shall immediately attempt to arrange it."

EIGHTEEN

Broussard hung up the phone and realized that he was trembling. In hindsight, he realized that they had all fallen for a ruse that should have set off alarms. Adrian's reputation was based on the fact that no one ever met him face-to-face, nor did he ever meet with those who hired him. The entire situation was so far out of character for the legendary Adrian that they should have known there was something wrong, they should have seen it.

He took a deep breath and picked up the handset again. He dialed in his security code, which would reroute the call through untraceable circuitry, and then entered the number for Deanna's sat phone. It rang three times before she answered. "Yes?"

"This is B," he said. "We have a complication. One of our agents here in London was notified a few hours ago that an advertisement had been placed with our signal code. She called the number and found herself speaking with a man who claims to be the real gentleman that we thought we had met with earlier."

There was a gasp on Deanna's end of the line. "B, are you serious?"

"I'm afraid I am deadly serious," Broussard said. "I

called the man and spoke with him, and I believe he is telling me the truth. He suspects that the man we met is an agent of one of the major governments, and that his purpose is to identify all of us so that we can be arrested."

Deanna thought furiously for a few seconds, and then said, "Holy Mary, mother of God, what do we do?"

Broussard swallowed. "He suggests that we employ him immediately to find and terminate the imposter. I have the information necessary to wire a deposit of three million dollars to his account. He says the total fee will be ten million, and for that he will even complete the assignment we awarded to the imposter. I—I took the liberty of explaining to him just what that assignment would entail."

"Then let us hope beyond hope that the imposter is not the one you have just spoken to," Deanna said. "I presume he wishes to meet? Fortunately, we are still in London and I can delay our return flight."

"No, he does not want to meet. He reminded me that he has never met with any employer, nor ever let anyone see his face and live. If we had only been wise enough to remember that about him, we would not be in this position today."

Deanna was quiet for a few seconds. "The Director will be furious," she said. "Have you told anyone else about this yet?"

"Of course not," Broussard said. "I never call anyone else, only you."

"I want you to keep it that way. All right, all right, there is only one thing to do. I shall transfer the money from my own accounts. If this is true, and he completes the other assignment, I can recover it from the final payment that would have gone to the first man. Give me the information, and I will transfer the money immediately. Do you have a way to contact him again?"

"Yes, I have a number that will remain good for another hour. After that, I will have to wait for him to contact me." He gave her the financial transfer instructions.

"Ring him back immediately, and tell him that I am transferring the funds now. Give him any additional information he might need and make it clear that he can contact you at any time. I am going to have to trust you on this, B, so you can make any decision necessary from this point out. Whatever you do, do not allow the others to find out about this. If we handle it properly they will never know, and that will undoubtedly lead to longer lives for both of us."

Broussard swallowed again. "I completely understand," he said. "I will ring him right now."

He held down the cradle on the old French-style phone for a second, then dialed his security code and the number to reach Adrian. The call was answered halfway through the first ring.

"Do we have an agreement?" Adrian asked.

"We do," Broussard said. "My contact is wiring the money right now. Is there any other way I can assist you?"

"Can you describe the imposter to me? Be as detailed as possible."

"He is about six-foot-two, with red hair and green eyes. He is stockily built, like an athlete. I suppose his most notable feature would be his nose, which is rather large and bulbous."

Adrian chuckled. "Really? That is very interesting. Do you have any idea where he might be staying?"

"No, I am afraid we do not. Please remember that we thought we were dealing with you. Would anyone dare to try to follow you, assuming they knew who you were? We did not even attempt it."

"I suppose I can understand," Adrian said. "No matter, I'm fairly sure the fellow won't be a problem much longer." *Particularly since he is now wearing the most wanted face in all of the UK,* Adrian thought. *Whoever he is, his agency has gone to a great deal of difficulty to put him in place. He has apparently agreed to assassinate the Prince, though I doubt he would actually do so. Why would his superiors allow him to go to such lengths, when they could undoubtedly have simply followed him and arrested these people when he met with them?*

The answer came to him suddenly, and he almost laughed again. The imposter was not an undercover policeman; he had to be one of the special agents whose purpose was to eliminate threats to the security of nations. He had no intention of arresting anyone; at some point, he would be going back to kill them. His problem was that there was someone involved that he had not yet identified. Otherwise, Broussard and his associates would already be dead.

Adrian's own comment earlier about saving their lives suddenly took on new importance.

"I suspect," he said into the phone, "that this imposter will contact you again at some point. He will want another meeting, and I want to know when you get that call. You will schedule a meeting with him, and I want the details of that meeting, as well."

"You want us to meet with him again?" Broussard sounded incredulous.

"I most certainly do not," Adrian said. "I said I want

you to schedule a meeting; when the time comes, it will not be any of you that is waiting for him. It shall be me. Naturally, I do not want any of you to be anywhere near that location at that time."

Broussard breathed a sign of relief. "Very well," he said. "How shall I notify you of that meeting?"

"I have another phone, and I shall give you its number. You and you alone will have it, so if anyone else calls me, it will be you that I shall visit next. Do you understand?"

"Yes, yes, of course. I shall give it to no one."

"That would be wise. Do you have a pen?"

* * *

It was almost 10:30 by the time Deanna completed the transfer. The others would be ready to go to the airport, but she suddenly wondered if they might be wise to remain in London. It was highly likely that the imposter now knew who they were and where they lived, but she was doubtful that he had been able to determine where their meeting the night before had taken place, nor that they had rooms there. Staying in the building was probably safe, especially with the security team they had brought along. Their men might not be professional assassins, but every one of them had served as a commando in one military organization or another.

The only problem was how to justify it to the others. She did not want to tell them the truth, that they had been duped by some sort of undercover agent. Far better to let them think that there was some other reason to remain.

It was a Machiavellian idea, she thought. If the imposter were from the British Military Intelligence, they would undoubtedly expect the Council to return to Rome immediately. By staying in London, directly under the noses of those who might be hunting them, they stood a chance of making it through this. Once the imposter was dead, his identification of them would be useless in any sort of prosecution. Yes, it was a great idea.

There was a knock on her door, and she rose from the chair to open it. James and François stood there, and she invited them inside.

"Where is Roberto?" she asked.

"He should be here in a moment," James said. "Are we ready to go? I confess to being a bit famished, so looking forward to stopping for breakfast on the way."

"We can go out for breakfast," Deanna said, "but I've been thinking. Perhaps we should remain in London for a couple of days. We need to monitor the situation, watch for progress toward the completion of the assignment. While we have people in place to do that, we can react more quickly, if necessary, if we are still here to do so."

James shrugged, but François scowled. "Do you believe it to be necessary? I have plans with my family this weekend. Will we be back by then?"

Deanna forced a smile onto her face. "Oh, I certainly hope so. I just think it would be wise to keep an eye on the situation for a couple of days more."

Roberto knocked at that moment, and Deanna let him in. She quickly explained the situation to him as well, but he had no objection.

"Good," she said, "that's settled, then. Let's gather our security and go have a bit of breakfast, shall we?"

* * *

"Has anyone but me noticed it's getting close to lunchtime?" Neil asked. "We skipped breakfast so we could get to work, but now my belly is starting to think my throat's been cut."

Noah looked over at Sarah and raised one eyebrow.

"I'm a little hungry myself," she said.

"Okay, I guess we can take a break. We need to check out of here anyway. Let's go down to the restaurant and get a bite to eat first. We can tell them we're checking out when we finish, then get all our stuff and head out to the house."

The four of them walked out of Noah's room and rode the elevator down to the lobby. The restaurant, which was just off the lobby, was relatively busy but the maître d' found them a table for four. They placed their orders and were waiting for them when two policemen walked into the establishment.

The two officers glanced around as they were being seated, and one of them let his gaze rest on Noah for a moment. Noah noticed, but kept his face turned so that it was facing Sarah, beside him. It gave the officers his profile, and allowed Noah to watch with his peripheral vision.

The policeman took out a phone and punched a couple of icons. He looked at the display on his screen and then looked at Noah again, just before passing the phone to his partner. The second policeman glanced at it, then casually let his eyes roam around the room until they found Noah.

The two of them looked at one another, and the first one got up and left the restaurant for a moment. He returned a couple of minutes later and took his seat, pointedly ignoring Noah as he did so.

"Heads up," Noah whispered. "The bobbies over there are paying some serious attention to me, and I suspect they're waiting for backup. Not sure what's going on, but let's play it cool."

"You're right," Moose said. "A patrol car just pulled into the parking lot. No resistance?"

"No," Noah said. "If they run me in for something, I want you guys to just continue working on the project. I'm pretty sure I can talk my way out of anything that may be going on, and I can always call Catherine if I need help. Just play it cool."

A second pair of policemen entered the restaurant, and the first officer rose from his seat. His partner followed a moment later and all four of them approached Noah's table.

"Pardon me, sir," the first officer said. "Might I trouble you to show us your identification?"

Noah looked up and feigned surprise. "My ID," he said in his own distinctly American accent. "Um, sure." He reached carefully and slowly for his wallet, then took out his driver's license and handed it to the policeman. While they looked that over, he looked over at Sarah. "Baby, let me have my passport, okay?"

Sarah had put on her best "puzzled kitten" look, and wore it while she slowly picked up her purse and fished out Noah's passport. She handed it to him, and he passed it to the second officer.

"You're an American, are you?" asked the first officer.

"Yes, sir," Noah said. "We came over on vacation, me and my girlfriend and these two moochers. Is something wrong?"

"Not necessarily, sir," the officer said. He was studying both the driver's license and the passport, both of which were in the name of Michael Jamison. "May I ask what you do for a living, Mr. Jamison?"

"Oh, sure," Noah said. "I'm a counselor. I work with troubled youth back home, in Springfield, Illinois." This was part of the cover story he'd been given for the ID he was using. A search of national records would find a complete history for Michael Jamison, including an office address for a licensed private clinic.

All of the officers looked over the documents, and then looked at each other. The first one turned back to Noah. "Mr. Jamison," he said, "are you planning to leave this restaurant in the next few minutes?"

Noah glanced at Sarah and then back to the officer. He shrugged. "No, not really," he said. "We just placed our orders a few minutes ago, we haven't even gotten our food yet."

The officer nodded and handed back his ID and passport. "Very good, sir," he said. "I'm afraid you strongly resemble someone we're looking for, but as your paperwork seems to be in order, I need to call in someone who will know for sure." He hesitated for just a moment. "I must advise you, sir, that if you attempt to leave before they arrive, we will be forced to detain you."

Noah grinned. "No chance of that," he said. "If I tried to drag these guys out here without feeding them, they'd probably do worse to me than just detain me."

Moose and Neil chuckled, and Moose said, "Hear, hear! He laid in bed so long this morning we missed breakfast. We're not going anywhere until I get some food in my belly."

The officers grinned despite themselves, and visibly

relaxed. "I'm sure it's just a coincidental resemblance, sir," one of the other officers said. "We can get it all cleared up as soon as the others arrive."

"No problem, officers," Noah said. "I promise you, we'll be sitting right here."

The policemen all sat down at the table the first two had been using, and one of them made a phone call. Noah noticed that at least two of them had eyes on him all the time. He turned back to his team and they made public small talk and jokes while they continued to wait for their food to arrive.

The waiter was coming with a tray filled with their plates as five other people entered the restaurant. Noah glanced up at them and instantly recognized Catherine Potts. The five spotted him just as quickly, and made their way directly to his table.

Sam Little looked at Noah directly in the eye. "You're Mr. Jamison?" Noah noticed that the man was staring hard at his face, as if trying to convince himself he wasn't seeing what he was. He rose slowly to his feet and extended a hand.

"Yes, sir, that's me," he said. Through the corner of his eye, he saw Catherine Potts staring at Moose, but when he spoke her eyes jerked back to his own face. They narrowed for a second and then went wide.

"Mr. Jamison," Sam began, but then he seemed to hesitate. "I'm afraid I'm going to have to apologize. You bear a startling resemblance to someone we're trying to locate, and I'm afraid you may run into this again during your stay here. Every policeman in the country has been provided a photograph of the man we are seeking, so it's likely every single one of them is going to think you're him."

Noah let his eyes go a little wider and smiled. "But you know I'm not, right? I mean, you checked out my ID and found out I'm for real, right?"

Sam returned the smile. "Bit better than that, I'd say," he said. "I actually know the blighter in question, and while the resemblance is uncanny, to my eye it's obvious you're not the same man. We'll circulate an alert to let all the policemen know that you've already been checked out, but I'm quite certain you are going to be asked to produce identification from time to time." He stared at Noah's face for a moment longer. "Absolutely uncanny resemblance."

He turned to those with him and motioned for them to follow him back to the policemen's table, but Catherine stood her ground as they walked away. As soon as they were out of earshot, she leaned down and looked into his face. "Mr. Colson," she whispered softly, "that's an amazing job of makeup. You do realize I'll be giving you a call shortly, right?" She stood straight, turned and walked away before Noah could answer.

Sam had noticed that she waited behind. "Something wrong, Catherine?" he asked her.

"Not a bit of it," she replied. "Didn't you know I've got a bit of a fancy for gingers? Just wanted to do a wee bit of flirting, nothing wrong with that now, is there?"

Sam looked at her for a moment, then smiled and shook his head. "I'm sure I want to know what's really going on," he said, "but I'm equally sure you're not going to tell me just yet. Just reassure me that it's nothing I need to know at this moment."

Catherine tried to look innocent. "Wot? Can't a girl fancy a sexy man like that? I work long hours, Sam, if I can get me a bit of something looks that good, I'm bloody well going to take it."

Sam shook his head again, turned to the officers and assured them that Noah wasn't the man they were looking for. All four of them looked over at Noah, smiled and waved. He waved back with an equal smile and then gave them a thumbs up.

"Good to see the London police are doing their job," he called loudly. "Makes us all feel safer while we're visiting."

When Sam and his crew were gone, Sarah looked at Noah. "What on earth do you think that was all about?" she whispered.

"I'm afraid it means there's a complication," he whispered back. "The only possible reason for them to be looking for someone with this face would be if Adrian is no longer in their custody. He's escaped."

Moose stared at him, but Neil muttered, "Shit!"

"Keep it together," Noah said. "It doesn't change anything as far as our orders go, but it means I need to make things happen quickly, before the real Adrian can make contact with the Council."

"Do you think he will?" Sarah asked.

"Almost certainly. If he's escaped, he's probably in disguise and trying to figure out a way to get back on his game. He would know they were trying to reach him before, and probably knows how to make contact. If he gets in touch with them, they're likely to vanish and we'll be back to square one."

"Maybe you should get hold of them first," Moose said. "Tell them somebody is running around pretending to be you."

Noah shook his head. "That would be too far-fetched," he said. "They would almost certainly decide they couldn't trust me, even if I convinced them not to trust him. They'd vanish into the woodwork like cockroaches when the light comes on."

They were eating as they talked, but the situation caused them to rush. Noah was glad Moose had complained about being hungry, because the four policemen seemed to be amused at how quickly they were shoving the food down. As soon as they were finished, they rose and headed back to the room. Noah made a point of stopping at the officers' table and shaking hands with all of them.

* * *

"It isn't two o'clock yet," the voice said when Adrian identified himself.

"Yes, but something has come up. I have an opportunity to complete your contract in conjunction with a new one."

The Assistant to the Home Secretary hesitated for only a couple of seconds. "You can finish the job? You're certain?"

"All I need is your approval," Adrian said. "The PM will be in a location soon with another target I've been employed to eliminate. Taking both at once would be very simple."

"Well, then," the Assistant said. "I only had a brief moment to speak with Her Ladyship, but she told me to use my own judgment. Very well, let's proceed, then. I trust there will be no change in the fee?"

Adrian smiled into the phone. "None at all," he said, and then the line went dead.

NINETEEN

As soon as they got back to the room, Noah looked at Neil. "Is there any way you can determine whether the Council left on schedule?"

Neil thought for a moment, then nodded. "I should be able to find out," he said. "We know what time their plane arrived last night, so I should be able to get their tail number. Then I can check flight plans to see if it's departed yet."

"Get on it. And if you can think of a way to delay them leaving, do it." He turned to Sarah. "I can't do anything about the nose, that has to wear off on its own," he said, "but I need you to go out and get me some other hair dye. I don't know if my own natural blonde will cover this red, so let's go with black."

Sarah grinned. "Sounds good," she said. "Anything but that god-awful red. I'll be back in an hour." She picked up her purse again from where she had just set it down and started out the door, but Noah told her to wait.

He turned to Moose. "Go with her," he said. "I don't want any of you going out alone until this mission is either over or aborted."

Moose nodded and slipped on his jacket, tucking his

pistol and its holster down his pants as he did so. He and Sarah walked out the door together and Noah went into the bathroom. "Give me a second, Neil, I want to get rid of these contacts now." Neil heard the water running, and then a blue-eyed, red-haired Noah came back and sat down in a chair near where Neil was working on his computer.

"Boss man," Neil said, "Moose said they were talking about leaving by noon, but there isn't even a flight plan filed for that plane. As far as I can tell, it's still sitting on the tarmac."

Noah narrowed his eyes, deep in thought. He wasn't paying any attention to the computer monitor, but suddenly looked at Neil as he mumbled, "Yes!"

"What?" Noah asked.

"Well, you know we found out that Florentine outfit owns that building, right? I did a search and located the security company they use. Like a lot of security companies, their video security is tied into a cloud server, and I managed to hack into it. Just for safety's sake, I went back to last night and found the bit where Moose was skulking about in their hallways and erased it, but now I'm looking at the live feed. Take a look, there goes Ms. Deanna what's-her-name back into her room right now. I think they're all still there."

Noah watched, and saw that Neil was correct. A moment later, François and James came into view and entered their own rooms. "The camera seems to be right near the elevator, am I right?"

Yeah, looks that way," Neil said. "They're not real serious about building security, though, cause there's only one camera on each floor, in the same position."

Two other men came out of a room, and Noah

pointed at them on the monitor. "Those guys are body-guards, I think. They were in the room when I met with the Council, but they kept their backs to us."

Neil nodded. "Yeah, I saw them with the drone. They were just standing there staring out into the darkness, like they were almost afraid to turn around."

Noah picked at his upper teeth with a thumbnail for a moment. "You've got Deanna's sat phone number, right? Can you tell if it's the same one she's got with her now?"

Neil blinked at him, then minimized the web browser he was using and called up another program, before reaching down into his computer bag to retrieve the Sat Phone Tracker he'd purchased the day before. He plugged it into the USB port on his laptop and then tapped some keys. "The tracker keeps a log of all the calls and phones it detects," he said a moment later. "I can get the Electronic Serial Number of her phone from the log, then run a GPS trace on it and see where it's located." The computer made a couple of soft sounds and the display changed. Neil copied a line of data and then entered it into another program, which brought up a map of London and put a Google-style marker on a point.

Neil turned and grinned at Noah. "Bingo!" he said. "That's the building we were looking at just a minute ago, so she's got it with her."

"What about getting into her call history? Can you do that?"

Neil shook his head. "Not without access to the phone itself. While they're fairly simple radio devices, that works against us when it comes to hacking them. A regular cell phone has encryption that regulates how you access different files inside, but a sat phone doesn't.

I can monitor the calls it makes, but I can't get into any of its background logs."

Noah nodded, chewing gently on his bottom lip. "What about the others? Do they have their phones with them, as well?"

Neal went back to the computer for a couple of minutes and then turned to Noah. "Only one of them is at the same location, the one that apparently belongs to James. The other two are still in Rome."

"Okay. Now check on Broussard. I want to know where he is."

Another moment passed and Neil grinned again. "At the moment, he's at home."

Noah leaned back in the chair and closed his eyes for a moment. "If Adrian contacts them, they're not going to trust me at all. What I need to do is get busy leaving the trail I want them to follow. That will at least give me some bargaining power, a way to convince them that I'm actually working on the assignment they gave me."

Neil leaned his chin on his fist and looked at Noah. "If Adrian wanted to contact them, wouldn't he have to do it the same way you did?" He turned back to the computer and called up a program, then began entering search parameters. Lines of data streamed across the screen for a couple of moments, and then there was a beep. "Well, there it is. He placed an ad in the London Telegraph this morning, and it's on their website now. Same code you used and everything."

Noah was looking at the ad on the screen. "Remember how quickly they got back to me? It's quite possible that they've already spoken to him. There's a phone number in the ad, can you find out where it is?"

Neil opened yet another program and entered the

number. A moment later he shook his head. "That number isn't showing up on the network," he said. "Somebody has destroyed the SIM card. No way to find it now, but cell tower logs might tell us something of its call history." He continued tapping the keys for a couple of moments more. "Okay, that phone was only activated less than twelve hours ago, so there isn't a lot of activity. Its first call was to a number right here in London, at about 2:45 this morning. It only lasted a few minutes, but then he made another call to a number in Vienna, Austria. That will last a little longer. The next call was to the Telegraph at just after eight this morning. After that, it's had only three other calls. The first was from a cell phone, only lasted a few minutes, and then the other two were both incoming calls from an encrypted number."

"Encrypted number?" Noah asked.

"Yeah, like rerouting a call through a dummy line. I can see the number the call came in from, but there is a suffix on it that tells me it was only a relay. I can't see the originating number."

Noah scowled and let out a sigh. "That would probably be from Pierre Broussard, then. I think we can safely say that Adrian has made contact with the Council. Now the question is how to convince them he's the phony and I'm the real one."

Neil shrugged. "What if you called to warn them that you heard there's someone out there trying to impersonate you?"

Noah shook his head. "I'm pretty sure that's exactly what they would expect," he said. "They probably think I'm an undercover agent trying to gather evidence against them. Trying to play myself off as the real guy being on their side would fit right into that sort of an undercover op."

Neil started to speak, but Noah's phone rang at that moment. He pulled it out of his pocket a glass of the display, then answered. "Hello," he said.

"Now, then, Mr. Colson," Catherine Potts's voice said through the line, "perhaps you can enlighten me on why you are wearing the most-wanted face in all of Europe?"

"I was actually hoping you might be able to clear that little mystery up for me," Noah said. "I take it Adrian is no longer the guest of the British government?"

"I'm afraid that's true," she said. "He escaped last night, and I've been called in to work the task force that's trying to locate him. Your turn."

"I was sent over here to impersonate him," Noah said. "My mission was to identify the top leadership of the IAR, and I was actually getting somewhere. Just last night, thinking that I was Adrian, they hired me for a spectacular assassination that I have no intention of going through with. Unfortunately, there is at least one man above the people I'm dealing with that I need to identify. If I can get to him and take him out along with the ones I've already met, IAR will probably be finished."

"Well, that would be a lovely boon to us all, wouldn't it, now?"

"I think it would have been, but this has thrown a problem into the situation. I'm about 99% certain that Adrian has already contacted IAR's ruling council. That means they probably know I'm an imposter, and he's aware that someone is impersonating him. It'll be almost impossible for me to complete the mission if I don't have their trust."

"Yes, I can see that would be a problem. Is there anything I can do to help?"

"Well, if you can round him up in a hurry," Noah said. "That might help a bit, but I'm not sure the damage isn't already done. I'm trying to work out a plan of action right now."

"Hmm. What's this spectacular assassination you spoke of? Anything I need to be aware of?"

Noah thought for a second, then said, "Actually, you probably should. If the real Adrian has made contact with them and told them that I'm a fake, there's the possibility he might try to pull it off himself. The contract was to assassinate Prince Charles, and my plan was to make preparations as if I were really going to do it, which of course I'm not. I just wanted them to see certain things happening that would fit into the basic plan I outlined with them."

Catherine was quiet for several seconds. "Don't mistake my meaning, but there might be a lot of Brits who wouldn't be too upset if it happened. Charles has actually alienated an awful lot of our citizens, and there is a move in Parliament to actually bring the monarchy to an end, rather than see Charles take the throne. They want to let Elizabeth complete her reign, but with the understanding that she will be the last monarch." Noah heard her sigh. "But of course, we can't let that happen. I believe the majority of the people still revere the crown, no matter who wears it. On the other hand, if Adrian is going to try to accomplish it, it seems to me he's going to be even more interested in finding and putting a stop to you."

Noah nodded into the phone. "Yes, I've thought of that. The situation could conceivably pit the two of us against each other, and it's possible it could end with only one of us surviving." He paused for a second. "Catherine, tell me something. Are your people determined to get him back alive?"

"I'm sure Sam would love to," she said slowly, "but I think the best possible scenario would be the recovery of his dead body. Sam isn't aware of my double position, so I can't approach him about this. What I can do is go to Mrs. Wimbley—she's in the top administrative offices, has the ear of the director and knows about my special affiliation with your group—and let her know that one of our people is on the job and has a need for a free hand in the matter. Considering the damage Adrian has done in the past, I'm certain Mr. Younger will approve it."

"Okay, that would probably help. Can you tell me anything about what went on while your people had Adrian?"

"Days on bloody days of interrogation," Catherine said. "About the only thing we really gained was confirmation that some older assassinations were his work, things over the last three or four years. He was setting up an assassination that he referred to as some sort of magnum opus, but we never did find out who the target was or who hired him for it. Speculation was that it might have been the PM, but nobody knows for sure."

"The Prime Minister? Who would want to kill her?"

"Oh, it might be easier to ask who wouldn't! While the citizens may love her dearly, the same cannot be said of the House of Lords. She's thwarted a number of their attempts to circumvent her on different policies they want to implement. If they had their way, the people would have a much smaller voice in the goings-on of our country. Several of them, including a few cabinet members, have been overheard wishing something might happen to her. No evidence, you understand, just a lot of speculation."

"I can understand," Noah said. "I suspect the same thing goes on in our Senate and House sometimes, with respect to the president. Incidentally, the last I knew you were just a clerk in the British-American liaison office. I take it you got a promotion?"

She laughed. "Actually, I got in a spot of trouble a bit back, and being transferred to Foreign Espionage Group was my punishment. It doesn't affect the special affiliation, and frankly, it's a lot less boring than the old job. The only problem is having to keep Sam in the dark, but I think he has a wee fancy on for me so he doesn't get too upset when I have to make up a weak excuse for where I've been or what I've been up to."

"Whatever works," Noah said. "Listen, Catherine, if this comes down to the wire, I may need you to get one of Charles's appearances canceled. Hopefully I can track down Adrian and complete my own mission before that becomes necessary, but just be ready to call whoever you have to in a hurry if it comes down to it."

"I'll be ready," she said. "You just take care of yourself, Mr. Colson. I'd greatly prefer this not be the last time we work together."

"I couldn't agree more," Noah said. They added goodbyes and the call ended.

Noah looked up at Neil. "She gave me an idea," he said. "If Adrian has actually made contact with IAR, then he's fully aware I'm out here. He's going to want a confrontation, a chance to take me out. I think we should give it to him."

Neil's eyebrows rose halfway up his forehead. "Boss, are you insane? Don't get me wrong, I know how good you are, but this guy's been at it a lot longer than you have. Sarah would go through the roof if you suggested this in front of her."

Noah was nodding. "Which is why I'm discussing it privately with you. What I need to do is create a situation where he can expect to find me at a certain place and time. He'll want to set a trap for me, but I want to make sure it backfires on him." He leaned back and thought for a couple of minutes, then looked at Neil again. "They'll be expecting me to call and say I need to meet with them again. When I do, they'll agree to a meeting and set a time and place for it, which I'll be forced to agree to. They'll give that information to Adrian as soon as I'm off the phone, so that he can start making preparations, or he may have even proposed a place and time to them. We need every possible advantage when it comes to that meeting, because the Council won't be there; it will just be me and Adrian, and only one of us is likely to come out of it alive."

Neil stared at him for a moment, but Noah could tell the gears in his head were spinning at high speed. "I've got the drone," he said after a moment. "It's nearly silent, so I should be able to do a search of the location with it, maybe find Adrian for you that way. That would definitely be an advantage, if you knew where he was hiding."

"Yes. What else can you think of in that genius brain of yours?"

Neil bit his lower lip. "It'd be sweet if we had any idea what phone he's using now. I might be able to put a GPS lock on it, track wherever it goes."

Noah cocked his head to one side and looked at me. "So, if Broussard used his satellite phone to call Adrian, could you identify his phone that way?"

"Yeah, but I'd have to be within a mile of Broussard."

Noah nodded. "Okay, we can arrange that. Make sure everything is all charged up, we're going mobile as soon as I change my hair color."

* * *

Adrian entered the chip shop and looked around for only a moment before he saw the two men he had come to meet. He had added a false beard and mustache to his disguise, giving him the appearance they would remember from the last time they'd worked with him. He slid into the booth beside the smaller man.

"'So good to see you again, Arthur," the bigger man said. He was a handsome man, though he had a roguish look about him. He often used both gifts in order to charm his way into the affections of women who could help him accomplish his goals.

Adrian smiled and shook his hand, then patted the man beside him on the shoulder. "Likewise, Eddie. You been keeping Georgie, here, out of trouble since then?" His own accent was only slightly less cockney than Eddie's.

"Boys and toys," Eddie said. "You know Georgie, he loves to see things go boom." He looked at Georgie as he spoke. Georgie was a smaller man, and though he possessed a brilliant mind, his appearance tended to remind people of some sort of ape they had seen at a zoo. He was often ignored as he went about seemingly menial tasks, and witnesses never quite remembered him after his bombs exploded.

Georgie snickered, and Adrian grinned at him. "Don't worry, lad," he said, "I've got something up and needs your talents. Needs to be a bit bigger than last time, though, and you're gonna need to work fast. It's got to be ready in a week, and already in place."

Georgie grinned back. "Where's it got to go, then?" he asked.

Adrian looked him in the eye for a moment. "This one's going into Albemarle Primary School," he said. "We don't want to take out a lot of kiddies, though, so I want it to blast upward as much as possible. It's going in under a stage, to go off with a couple of special people standing on top of it."

Georgie nodded. "Shaped charges, then," he said. "I can do cones, launch your targets straight up to the moon, it will."

Adrian nodded. "That's the ticket," he said. "Needs to look like something that belongs there, though. Any thoughts on that?"

Eddie leaned forward. "Going under a stage, y'say? Right under the speaker's box?"

"Under the lectern, yes," Adrian said, "but it should blow the whole stage, just in case one of those special people is sitting down at the time."

"Easy peasy, then," Eddie said. "We get some lumber and build some new supports under it. Anybody looks at it will think there might be some weak boards and somebody shored it up. Put extra legs right in the middle and under where the blokes'll stand, with Georgie's toys hid inside. Oi?"

Adrian smiled. "That's why I like you lads," he said. "You both think like me." He reached into a pocket and took out an envelope. "10,000 pounds, all in tenners," he said, referring to 10-pound notes. "You get the other half after it comes off, right?"

"Chuffs me to bits," Eddie said. "We'll get it all sorted. Just a matter of getting into the school to fix the stage, oi?"

Adrian hissed. "Oi, there might be a rub there," he said. "It seems old Brian will be speaking there sometime soon," he finished, using the public nickname for Prince Charles that was made popular by the British satirical magazine, *Private Eye*.

Eddie and Georgie looked at one another, then both of them turned toward Adrian. "Cor Blimey," Eddie said, "are we blowin' up the bloody Prince of Wales?"

Adrian looked him in the eye and said nothing.

Georgie began to giggle. "Not that we give a fig," he said. "Sod me, not like we ain't thought about it before, right, Eddie?"

"Right," Eddie said. "Only I see what you mean about a rub. There's gonna be bloody bobbies all over, right?"

"Yeah," Adrian said, "there might be. That ain't never stopped you lads before. You can handle this, right?"

Eddie stared at him for a moment, and then smiled. "Oi, we can handle it," he said. "Ain't never seen a place we can't get into. There's bound to be a lonely bird there I can chat up."

Adrian smiled. Whenever Eddie "chatted up" a "lonely bird," it meant that he was seducing a woman who could get him access to whatever he wanted. Adrian had done his research and was fairly certain there were a number of eligible women for Eddie's purposes who worked in the administrative offices of the school.

"All set, then?" he asked, and both Eddie and Georgie nodded their heads. "Right, then, let me know when it's ready and where to pick up the signal device. Still got the number I called you from, right?"

"Saved in me phone," Eddie said. "Be hearing from us pretty soon."

Adrian smiled once more, then rose and left the shop. There was very little doubt in his mind that they would get the job done, but he had to prepare a backup plan, just in case. That meant a stop at Morrissey's.

TWENTY

Moose and Sarah had gotten back only a short time later, and Sarah went into the bathroom to help Noah recolor his hair. When they came out twenty minutes later, Noah still looked as much a stranger as before, but he didn't quite look like Adrian.

"Well?" Sarah asked Moose and Neil. "What do you think?"

"I'm gonna say it's an improvement," Neil said. Moose simply nodded his agreement and held up a thumb.

"Yeah," Sarah said. "I definitely agree. It's still not right, but at least it's better."

"Good," Noah said. "Now that we all agree I'm not quite as repulsive as before, it's time to get busy. Neil, you ready?"

"All set." Neil patted the computer case that was sitting closed on the table beside him.

"Okay, here's what we're going to do," Noah went on. "We need to get the number of the phone Adrian is using. The sooner we find him and put him down, the sooner I can start working on regaining IAR's trust. We're going out to Broussard's place, and then I'm going to give him a call and demand a meeting with the Council again. If we are right, he's going to call Adrian immediately, and Neil can get the number and even monitor the call. From that point on, we hope to keep a GPS lock on Adrian's phone so that we'll know where he is all the time."

"But why do you think Broussard is going to call him?" Sarah asked.

"Because he undoubtedly told them I'm an imposter, and to let him know if I asked for another meeting. His plan would be to set a trap for me; I intend to turn around and use it to trap and kill him."

Sarah stared at him for a moment, her face blank. "You're going to go up against him, one-on-one?"

"Not exactly," Noah said. "Neil is going to be monitoring that phone, and once we have a location for the meeting, he's going to use the drone to look for where Adrian will be hiding. Once we have that, Moose and I will hit him with everything we've got. Adrian is a mad dog, and we're going to treat him like one."

Sarah shook her head, still watching him. "I'm just worried something's gonna go wrong."

"I'm going to do everything possible to make sure it doesn't," Noah said. "Let's get moving. Take everything with us and we'll check out on the way out, then go by the agent and get the keys for the house. After that, I need to stop somewhere and pick up a couple of throw-away cell phones before we get to Broussard's."

They left the hotel and got into the Land Rover, and Sarah pointed it toward the estate agent that Neil had used to rent the house. They pulled up in front of the office and Neil went inside to sign the paperwork and pick up the keys, then came rushing back. Everything was set, so Sarah drove to an electronics shop that she called up on Google. It was only a few minutes away, and Noah sent Moose in to buy the burner phones. When he came back, Sarah called up Broussard's address on her phone again and started driving toward it. Neil opened his computer and verified that the man's satellite phone, which he doubtless would never leave home without, was still there.

An hour later, Sarah parked the Land Rover on a short, deserted side road that was overhung with trees. Noah waited for Neil to signal that he was ready, then took out one of the throwaway phones and dialed the number to Broussard's sat phone. It rang four times before the man answered.

"Yes?" Broussard said nervously.

"This is Adrian," Noah said. "Are you alone?"

"Y-yes," Broussard stammered. "How—how did you get this number?"

Noah chuckled into the phone. "Do you remember me telling you that I have people who are very good at secure communications? Did you think that routing your call through a firewall would stop me from getting the number? But enough of that, we need to talk. There is a complication, and I need to meet with your council once again."

In the house a half-mile away, Broussard's mind was reeling. This was exactly what the other Adrian—the *real* Adrian, apparently—had said would happen. He gathered himself quickly. "I—I don't know," he said. "I would have to call them and find out when they could meet with you again."

"Of course," Noah said. "Please do so immediately, and let me know as soon as you can. You see this number?"

"I—yes, I see it. I will ring you back in just a short while. Should I—is there anything else I need to do?"

"Just stress to them that it is urgent we meet as soon as possible. I can still complete the assignment, but there are a few things I must discuss with your entire council." Noah ended the call and turned in his seat to nod to Neil.

The tall, skinny young man was watching the monitor closely. After almost 30 seconds, he suddenly grinned and tapped a key. They could all hear ringing, and only a couple of seconds passed before the call was answered.

"Go ahead," came the voice that Noah recognized as Adrian's. He nodded twice to let the rest of them know that they were listening to the actual assassin himself.

"It was just as you said," Broussard blurted out. "He called, the other one, he called just a few moments ago and asked to meet with us all again. I told him I would have to call and find out when and where we could meet, so he is expecting me to ring him back in just a few minutes."

"Excellent," Adrian said. "Tell him that you will all meet tonight, at midnight, atop the multistory car park in Limehouse. Tell him that this is the only place everyone would agree on with such short notice. Ring him now, and when you have finished, ring me back."

"Yes, as you say." Broussard ended the call and immediately selected the number for Noah's phone and hit send. "I spoke with Deanna," he said when Noah answered. "The others were with her, and they have chosen the car park, the one with four floors in Limehouse. We shall all meet on the top floor at midnight tonight. She told me to say that they will be leaving the country very soon, and this is the only time they can meet so soon."

"Then I shall see you all at the car park tonight," Noah said, and then he ended the call immediately. He glanced over his shoulder at Neil, who was smiling from ear to ear. "I take it that means you got it?"

"I got it," Neil said. "I got a tracking program locked onto him right now. He's sitting in a restaurant called Holy Smoke in Wimbledon."

"Get directions," Noah said. "Let's go see if we can get him right now. Keep watching, Neil, let us know if he moves."

The GPS unit started spewing directions and Sarah put the truck in gear once again. According to the directions, they were almost 45 minutes away, but Sarah put her driving skills to work and managed to get them there in just over thirty.

"He's still in there," Neil said. Noah and Moose stepped out of the car and started toward the restaurant's front door while Sarah kept the engine running.

"Chicago-style hit?" Moose asked.

"Not if we can avoid it," Noah said. "If he's there, I'll make the contact while you hang back. I'm going to let him know he's covered and ask him to come out with me. If he puts up a fight, then take the shot if you can. Otherwise I'll go for it. If he comes out, we'll take him down the alley over there. Either way, if he's really here, he doesn't leave alive."

"Got it," Moose said. "How about I go inside first? He might recognize his own nose on your face."

Noah nodded once. "I doubt that, but go ahead. Remember that he won't be looking like his usual self, either. Considering that he's been running loose for less than twenty-four hours, I'm guessing he's using the same kind of cheap hair dye that I am. Might not be black, maybe a shade of brown."

"Okay. Give me twenty seconds."

Noah paused in his stride and let Moose go on ahead. Once the door closed behind him, Noah started counting seconds. At twenty, he resumed walking and stepped into the restaurant only ten seconds after that.

Moose was standing at the counter, looking around. Noah let his own eyes scan the interior of the restaurant and concluded that Adrian was not present. He thought for a moment, then walked up to the counter where a young woman was making eyes at Moose while she waited for him to decide if he wanted to order or not.

"Pardon me, Miss," Noah said with a Liverpool accent. "My brother was in here just a little while ago, and he thinks he left his telephone. Have you perhaps found one?"

The girl smiled at him brightly. "Why, yes," she said. "Looks to be a dear one, it does." She turned and hurried toward the back and into the kitchen, then came back just a moment later carrying a cheap cell phone. "Is this it?"

Noah smiled and held out his hand. "Thank you so much," he said. He took a five-pound note from his pocket and pressed it into her free hand as she gave him the phone.

She broke into a wide smile. "Oh, no, thank you!"

Noah turned and walked out of the restaurant, leaving Moose to extricate himself from the situation as best he could. Less than a minute later, Moose followed and climbed into the rear seat once again.

Noah passed the phone back to Neil. "He was expecting it," he said. "Ditched the phone and left it for us to find." He turned to Sarah. "Get us out of here, and look for anyone trying to follow us. He may have waited around to see who came looking for that."

Neil popped open the case of the phone and took out its battery and SIM card. "Just making sure he can't turn the tables. If he expected you to grab the phone, he might be tracking it himself."

Sarah blinked once and then the truck was moving. She made several turns in quick succession, then slid onto one of the major roads and drove at the speed limit. "Nobody on our tail," she said. "Damn it, Noah, he could have taken you out right then. If he'd been on top of one of the other buildings or…"

"He wasn't, so let's not worry about it. If he was watching at all, it was to find out whether we were on to him. It's possible he just ditched the phone automatically, assuming he wouldn't need it again. What we've got to do now is figure out how to beat him at his own game."

"Get me to that parking garage," Moose said. "He doesn't know me, so hopefully I can find a spot to hide and watch for him."

"He's had enough time to get there already," Noah said. "I'd say it's a safe bet that he deliberately walked away from the phone and is already in position to take me out when I get there. Neil, how close we have to be for your drone to work?"

"It's got a range of three miles," Neil said, "but remember that I don't know this building we're talking about. If we can drive by it once and park somewhere maybe a mile or so away, I can launch it and scan the entire garage. Only problem is the sun is still up, so he's likely to spot it. If we can wait until after dark there's a chance it can find him before he sees it."

Noah glanced at the time display on his own phone. "It's almost five," he said. "Waiting for darkness sounds like a pretty good idea. Meanwhile, we can work on plan A."

Sarah's eyes whipped around at him. "Plan A?"

"Yes, plan A. If I can't eliminate Adrian, I'll need to convince the Council that he's the fake and I'm the real one. I can do that best by going ahead with the planning for the assassination of Prince Charles. Tomorrow I'll ream Broussard's ass for setting me up tonight, and then we'll force a real meeting. For now, let's go unload everything into our new house, and then I need to get my hands on Patrick Iverson."

TWENTY-ONE

Noah and the rest walked through the house and chose their bedrooms, with Sarah pointedly dropping her own bags in the room Noah selected. Moose and Neil grinned but said nothing, and chose the two bedrooms that were furthest away from it.

"Okay," Noah said. "Let's go find Mr. Iverson, shall we?"

"Shouldn't be too hard," Neil said. "According to the MI6 reports, if he isn't at work he's either at home or at a pub called 'Mum's.' It's about half a mile from his apartment."

"How closely do they watch him?" Moose asked. "Are they going to notice us going to visit the guy? Or more importantly, are they gonna notice if we snatch him?"

"I doubt it. From what I read, they just tend to pay attention to him if they happen to be out his way for some other reason. I don't think he's considered important enough for regular surveillance."

"Then let's go," Noah said. "I've got another appointment later, and we need to work on prep for that one once the sun is all the way down."

Hackney was only about a half-hour's drive from the

house, and they were in luck: Iverson was at home when they got there. Noah and Moose went up to his flat on the second floor of his building. Noah knocked, and Iverson opened the door only a moment later.

The smell of ale was on his breath, but there was something else in the air, as well. "Yeah? What you want?" he asked when he didn't recognize his visitors. "You coppers, come round to gob me up again?"

"Not at all like that," Noah said, matching his Irish accent. "Just need you to come for a wee ride, is all."

Iverson's eyes narrowed. "Ride? Account o' what?"

Moose showed him the Glock he was hiding in his armpit. "We just think it might be a good idea." He pushed into the room a bit and Iverson, eyes on the large bore of the pistol, stepped back to let them enter. Noah shut the door behind them and then turned back to their host.

"'Fraid this is a bit of a siege, chum," Noah said, using Irish slang to let Iverson know he was in trouble. "Ya been muckin' about with our lads from back home, and the peelers're on ya. We been sent to get ya outa sight for a bit."

Iverson stared at him for a moment, then the alcohol in his blood seemed to reach his brain. "What? Aw, hump off wi' ya! What peelers? I ain't done nawtin!"

Noah looked at Moose and shrugged. "Well, I tried," he said. He turned back to Iverson and suddenly produced his own pistol, which he used to break Iverson's nose and knock him cold.

"That was subtle," Moose said with a grin. "Want me to lug him out to the truck?"

"Not yet," Noah said, shaking his head. "Did you catch the whiff that came past him when he opened the door?"

"Whiff? I smelled a lot of beer, maybe."

"No, something else. Bleach, for one thing, and a lot of it from how strong it was. I'd bet he wasn't doing any kind of laundry, so I'm wondering what else he might have been up to with it."

He left Moose to watch the unconscious Iverson and began walking through the four-room flat. He found the source of the bleach smell in the kitchen, where a large pan of it was heating on the stove. A bottle of potassium chloride was sitting open on the table, and there was a hydrometer, the kind used for testing car batteries, laying beside it. Noah turned off the heat under the bleach and continued looking around the flat.

He came to what looked like a bathroom door, shut tight, and turned the knob to open it. He was right about it being a bathroom, but that wasn't all it was used for. Stacked in the corner, beside the shower, were a half-dozen fairly new assault rifles, and there were four military-style boxes of ammunition for them, as well.

Noah went back to the front room and looked down at Iverson. "It might be a good thing we decided to snag this boy up," he said. "There's a small arsenal in the bathroom, and he was brewing up some homemade plastique in the kitchen. I don't know what he was planning, but it would have been nasty for someone." He pointed toward the bath. "Why don't you gather up the guns and ammo, wrap them in sheets or something, and take them out to the truck. I'll rouse our friend, here, and walk him out."

Moose nodded, and Noah reached down to haul Iverson up to a sitting position. He slapped him across the face a couple of times, and the man started to come around. When he was at least partly coherent, Noah said, "Here's the deal, Paddy. I'm taking you with me. Whether you go alive is up to you, understood?"

Iverson put a hand slowly to his broken nose and it came away quite bloody. He was still woozy, so he finally looked up at Noah and nodded, doing what he could to help as Noah got him on his feet. He felt the Glock's muzzle against his side and looked at Noah, but didn't say anything.

"Now, we're going out and down the stairs, then over to my truck. If anyone sees us, I'm going to say I'm taking you to a doctor because you hurt yourself in an accident. If you try to tell them anything different, I will have to kill them, so their deaths will be on you, got that?"

Iverson only nodded. A moment later, Moose came out of the bathroom carrying a large bundle wrapped in blankets. He glanced at Noah and said, "This ain't light," and went out the flat's door. Noah nudged Iverson, and they followed him.

One woman happened to open her own door as they went by, but she only looked at Iverson with disgust and said nothing. Noah shrugged and went on, and they got to the truck without incident. Neil opened the back door and Noah shoved Iverson in, where he found himself facing Neil's machine pistol. Moose dumped his burden into the back of the truck and slid in beside their prisoner, while Noah got into the front seat again. He nodded to Sarah, and she put the truck in gear and headed for the house.

Noah turned back to look at Iverson. "So what were you cooking the explosives for?" he asked. "What's about to go down?"

Iverson looked at him, but said nothing. Noah smiled. "Okay, look, you're going to tell me, let's get that straight. You can do it before I rip off your balls, or after, but you're going to tell me."

Iverson sneered, but then Moose reached down and grabbed his crotch and began to squeeze. Iverson's eyes went wide as he squealed loudly, grabbing at Moose's arm and trying futilely to push it away.

Noah waved a hand to get his attention. "If I tell him to stop, he will," he said, and Iverson stared at him for a few seconds before nodding vigorously.

"'Twas for them black glundies," he said. "Them what moved in down floor. They wanted guns and some bombs, and someone told 'em I knew the makin'. That was worth two thou to me, if ya hadn't bunged me up!"

Noah looked at him. "What were they going to do with it?" he asked.

"How do I know? All they do is pay me, I don't hold they hands!"

Noah turned back to face the road, and Moose moved his hand to the back of Iverson's neck.

When they got back to the house, Noah got out and opened the garage door and Sarah drove the truck inside. Once the door was closed again, Moose dragged Iverson out and walked him into the house. He took him into one of the extra bedrooms and tied his hands and feet so that the man couldn't get loose, then gagged him and closed the door. He stood outside it for a moment, and when the thumping began, he opened it again quickly. "Nobody said we had to keep you alive," he said. "Piss me off and I won't bother." He closed the door again and listened for a few minutes, but there was only silence from the room.

He found the rest of the team in the kitchen, where Sarah was looking into the "fully stocked pantry." "Well, with what's here, we can have peanut butter and jelly sandwiches, or we can have canned soup that has an inch of dust on top. For what they charge for this place, they could at least stock in some pizza."

"Did you look in the freezer?" Neil asked.

"Yep. There's ice in there, but no food."

"What time is it? There was a row of fast food places about a mile down the road."

"It's only seven-thirty," Noah said. "Take Moose with you and go get some burgers or whatever. I'll watch Iverson while you go."

Sarah picked up her purse from the counter and started for the garage while Moose followed, and the truck backed out a few moments later.

Noah walked down the hallway and opened the door to the room where Iverson lay on a bed, hands and feet still firmly bound. The man looked up at him, and Noah could see the fear in his eyes. He reached down and checked the knots, then closed the door again and went back out to where Neil was sitting at the table in the kitchen.

"It'll be dark by the time they get back. We'll eat, then go on out to look the garage over with the drone. How likely is it that he'll spot it?"

Neil shrugged. "If he's wearing night vision gear, he probably will. Other than that, my idea is to try to stay high and look for any obvious places he might be able to hide, and then work my way down through the levels. I've checked it out online, it's a four-story parking garage. The walls are only partial, so there's a way in on every level. If I stay near the ceilings and close to the edges, I should be able to look through it pretty thoroughly."

Noah nodded. "We'll leave as soon as we eat."

Moose and Sarah pulled back in a few minutes later with a bag full of small hamburgers and fries, and they sat at the table while they ate. Sarah managed to get half a burger down before she shoved the rest away. She sat quietly while the rest of them ate, but Noah could tell she was worried.

"Relax," he said after a few minutes. "This is just going to be a recon mission. Neil's drone is the only one who'll be in any danger right now. If Adrian spots it, he'll probably blow it out of the air."

"It isn't right now I'm concerned about," she said. "You're going back there in a few hours, and he's gonna be trying to kill you. What happens if he manages to do that, Noah, have you thought about that? What happens to me, to us?"

Noah looked at each of them in turn, and then turned back to Sarah. "You'll all be reassigned, of course. Allison isn't going to waste the best support team in the organization."

Sarah leaned toward him, then, and he could see the tears threatening to brim over. "But we won't have you," she said, and even he could hear the potential grief in her words.

He said nothing, and after a moment she leaned back in her chair once again. When all three of the men had finished eating, Moose and Noah went to check on Iverson once more, and then they went out through the garage.

It took them almost an hour to get to the garage, but Sarah drove past it as if it was of no importance. A half-mile further along, she pulled over and parked beside an abandoned building, and all four of them got out. Neil set his computer on the hood and powered up the drone in the bed of the truck.

Like a ghostly apparition, it rose almost silently and went straight up for almost four hundred feet, then veered off in the direction of the garage. The four of them watched the monitor as the images captured by the onboard camera were transmitted back through Neil's phone. The phone was connected by cable to the computer, so all of the video was relayed to the bigger screen. A moment later, the top of the garage came into view, and Neil used the camera's magnification to zoom in for a close look.

There were a half-dozen cars on the top level, scattered around in no discernible pattern. Neil tapped a key and the view suddenly split into two separate screens. One of them was the normal view, but the other was infrared, allowing them to see that there was no one hiding in any of the cars.

"That's neat," Moose said. "If he's in that building you ought to be able to find him with that."

"That's the plan," Neil said, grinning. He continued maneuvering the drone around from well above, looking for other possible hiding places on the roof. He scanned a large box that seemed to hold a fan for drawing exhaust fumes out of the structure, but the only heat source in it was the fan's motor itself, so he sucked in breath and began bringing the drone down slowly.

He backed off the zoom so the image was stable, and after a couple of minutes, he was able to hover the drone just three feet over the top-level floor. From there he moved toward the ramp that started down, and followed it, staying just below the ceiling and constantly swinging the camera from side to side.

This level also held a few cars, and one of them showed a heat signature that was consistent with a human body. Neil moved toward it slowly, watching for any sign that the figure inside had seen or heard the drone, but it appeared the figure was lying prone in the back seat. There was no visible movement, so Neil went in for a closer look and saw the silhouette of a man who was apparently sleeping in his car.

He pulled back slowly and rose to just under the ceiling again, then continued searching the level. When he came to the next down ramp, he followed it.

"This is spooky," Sarah said. "Doesn't it seem strange that he'd say he wanted you to meet on the top floor, but he isn't up there waiting?"

Noah shook his head. "Not really," he said. "If I'm heading for the top floor, I have to drive through the lower three to get there, right? He'll most likely be hiding somewhere on one of them."

The drone continued its search pattern, but the second level was completely empty of cars and heat signatures. Neil shook his head and started down the final ramp.

There were several cars on the lowest level, and four of them had heat signatures. Neil hissed as he tried to slide the drone quietly over each of them, watching for movement that might indicate someone awake and watching with a gun.

"Over in the corner," Noah said suddenly. "There's a heat signature there, not in a car. Can you tell what it is?"

Neil turned the drone in the direction Noah indicated

and moved toward it slowly. "It's pretty bright," he said. "Could be a man, I guess. I don't see any movement yet. Let me try to get closer."

The image on the screen continued to get closer to the heat source, but a moment later Neil shook his head. "That's not a man," he said. "I don't know for sure what it is, but it isn't a person. Some kind of machinery, I'd guess."

"Then he isn't here?" Sarah asked.

"We can't say that for certain," Noah said, "but it doesn't look like it. Moose, take one of the assault rifles and go do a careful recon of your own. If you don't find him, then try to find a good hiding spot of your own and be ready when the action starts. I'll be back here at midnight on schedule."

Moose reached into the back of the truck and picked up one of the rifles, then took three extra magazines and shoved them into his jacket pockets. The street was fairly well lit, but there was little traffic; he jogged across it and began moving through shadows and alleys on his way back to the parking garage.

"What if he doesn't find him?" Sarah asked. "Or worse, what if Adrian finds Moose?"

Neil kept the drone on station until Moose got there, and then he brought it back to the truck and landed it in the bed. The three of them got in and headed to the house as Noah's phone rang.

It was Moose, reporting that he had found no one in the building except a few homeless people sleeping in battered old cars. "It looks really clean, Boss," he said. "I came in by hopping the wall in the back, so I don't think anyone saw me. I've got a spot where I can watch the main entrance, and I should be able to spot any movement here on the ground floor. I'll keep you posted."

"Thanks," Noah said. "I'll be back in a couple of hours."

TWENTY-TWO

I t was a moonless night, so the only light striking the top of the car park was the glow of the city that reflected off the clouds above. From his position, two stories higher on the roof of the neighboring building, Adrian watched for any sign of movement, both on the car park and on all of the taller buildings around it. Surely the imposter would make some attempt to reconnoiter these premises before the scheduled meeting at midnight, wouldn't he?

He glanced down at the street that ran in front of the building, but there was very little traffic about. This was an area given mostly to office buildings, and all of their staff and occupants were gone hours ago. Only a few of them had any sort of security, and none of those were close by. It wasn't likely anyone would be roaming the streets, so the next vehicle he saw would likely be his intended prey.

He checked his watch and confirmed that it was almost eleven. Another hour to wait, he mused, but he had wanted to be in position long before the other arrived. Sitting on top of a building for six hours would be a small price to pay if he was able to eliminate this complication.

* * *

Noah checked on Iverson one more time and then came back to the kitchen and looked at Neil. "He's asleep, I think," he said. "Check on him now and then, but don't get close to him. If he manages to get loose, just shoot him. I'd prefer to keep him alive to turn over to Catherine and her people, but it isn't an absolute necessity."

"Yes, sir," Neil said. "Boss, you're gonna be really careful, right? You're coming back?"

"I intend to," Noah replied. "If I can get Adrian, this whole operation might still have a chance of success, but as long as he's out there, I don't see any way to get to IAR's top man, and that's the actual mission."

"What about just taking out the ones you already know?" Sarah asked. "Wouldn't that send enough of a message to the guy at the top? He'd have to start all over, wouldn't he? That would give us time to find out who he is."

"He's probably got people ready to step in and take over from each of them within days of anything happening to them. No, I don't think it would slow IAR down for more than a week. I've got to find out who he is, and then take him down. That's the mission, and it's the only way."

Sarah started to say something more, but then closed her mouth. She knew she couldn't convince him to do things her way, so there was no point in trying.

"It's almost eleven," Noah said. "Let's go. Since the meeting is on top of the parking garage, he's going to expect me to drive up there. That means I need to snag a car along the way."

Sarah stood up from the chair and reached for her purse. "Come on, then," she said. "If there's one thing I know how to do, it's steal a car." Noah stood, and she followed him out to the truck and slid behind the wheel. He got in beside her and nodded, and she started it up and began driving in the general direction of the garage once again.

The ride was quiet, interrupted only once when she made a comment about the lack of traffic. Noah knew she was worried, but there was nothing he could say that would allay her fears, so he said nothing.

She pulled into a parking lot about a mile from the building and then turned to face him. "I know you've got to do this," she said, "but I'm scared, Noah. I know there's this big gap between us, between the way I feel and the way you feel, but I don't know what I'll do if anything happens to you tonight. I love you, and I need you to know that before...." She stopped talking suddenly, and leaned over to grab his collar and pull him to her for a kiss.

He held her for a few extra seconds, and then slowly let her go. "I'm going to come back," he said. "Have some faith. My grandfather would have told you to say a prayer, and I believe it couldn't hurt if you want to."

She gave him a weak grin. "I already have been," she said.

"Then what's there to worry about? Like I said, just have some faith."

She leaned her forehead against his own for a moment, then pulled away and got out of the truck. Noah stepped out and followed her as she walked over to where a few cars were clustered together. She glanced into each of them, then turned to him with a grin.

"This is too easy," she said. "Somebody left the keys for you."

Noah stepped up to the Volkswagen she indicated and glanced inside. Sure enough, the keys were hanging from the ignition. "This will be fine," he said. "Stay back out of sight, and I'll call when this is over."

He tugged on the door handle and cocked his head to one side when it didn't open. He leaned down and looked again, then turned back to Sarah. "I think the reason they left the keys in it is because they locked them inside," he said.

Sarah burst out laughing. "Oh, my gosh, I can't believe I missed that! Give me a minute and I'll…"

"I've got this," Noah said. He reached behind his back and withdrew his pistol, using its butt to break the window. He reached in and unlocked the door, then pulled it open and began brushing broken glass off the seat. "It's still the most convenient solution." He climbed inside and started the car, then reached out and caught her hand. He looked into her eyes for a moment, before letting her go and putting the car in gear.

* * *

Neil was nervous. While it was likely Noah was correct and the team would be reassigned if anything happened to him, Neil didn't like the idea of losing the little family he had finally discovered. As an orphan, he had often felt alone in the world; Noah, Sarah and Moose had become the family he had always longed for. As a result, he was frustrated at not being able to do anything to help in this particular situation.

He peeked in on Iverson, but the fellow had not moved since the last time. The snoring sounded real, so

Neil was convinced he was genuinely asleep. He went out to the garage, intending to play with the drone for a little bit in order to take his mind off the situation.

"If only you had a longer range," he said irritably to the machine. "I could sit right here and keep an eye on the whole thing." He tapped the power button on the remote app he had installed on his phone and it came to life. He guided it through the screen to hover a few feet off the floor, and was about to send it out the garage door when a thought occurred to him.

He landed the drone again, then hurried inside and dug out the toolkit from one of his bags. He carried it back to the garage and was delighted to find a workbench along one wall. Once the tools were all set up, he took the cheap phone they had picked up from the Holy Smoke restaurant and laid it on the bench beside them.

"A signal is a signal as a signal," he said. "The receiver doesn't care where it comes from, as long as it can receive and interpret it!" He hurried over to the drone and picked it up, then set it on the workbench and began taking its covers off.

Fifteen minutes later, the speaker and microphone wires from the cheap phone were soldered into the drone's processor, replacing the input and output wires from its original radio transceiver. Neil turned his attention to his own phone, carrying it into the house and plugging it into his computer. It took him only minutes to find the drone's control app, and a few more allowed him to get into its code and begin making modifications. After a couple of false starts, he found the correct section of code to alter that would allow the app to transmit commands directly through the cell signal, rather than bouncing them through the remote control unit via Bluetooth connection.

He ran back to the garage and powered on the phone that was now connected to the drone, then told his own phone to connect with it. He had set the receiver unit to answer automatically, so the connection was almost instantaneous.

Now to test it. He tapped the icon to launch the drone, and shouted, "Yes!" when the little aerial vehicle lifted off the floor. He hurried back into the kitchen and connected his phone to the computer, so that the video image appeared on the larger screen, then programmed the drone to fly directly to the GPS coordinates of the parking garage. Its built-in proximity detectors kept it from hitting anything as it flew out of the garage and high up into the air.

With the range now virtually unlimited, Neil watched the display as the drone flew at almost 60 miles per hour toward its destination. Going as the crow flies, it arrived in less than twenty minutes and came to a hovering stop directly over the structure.

Neal piloted it down to just a few dozen feet above the upper floor and looked around, but there was no one visible yet. It was still almost 15 minutes before midnight, so he hadn't expected Noah to be there yet. He quickly flew down the ramps, scanning each floor for only a couple of minutes, but there were no new heat signatures on either the third or second levels.

The ground level was different. There was one new heat signature that he hadn't seen before, hiding behind a car in the far back corner. Neil zoomed over in that direction, keeping the drone just under the ceiling, and then aimed the camera.

Then he laughed, as Moose looked up at him and

waved frantically for him to get the drone away. Neil bobbled it a couple of times and then took off again. This time, he went out through one of the gaps in the side wall and made a low reconnaissance around the building, moving through the alleys and along the street.

He found no one hiding outside, and began to wonder if perhaps Adrian had only set up this meeting as some kind of diversion. That wouldn't make sense, though, since he certainly knew that Noah would be forced to show up. There had to be something he was missing.

He took the drone up again, going up high enough to once again get a bird's eye view of the entire building. The darkness still covered it completely, and the infrared showed no sign of anyone hiding there, but Neil was sure that Adrian must be around somewhere. He held the altitude and began rotating the drone, raising the angle of the camera to scan the surrounding area.

* * *

Noah pointed the car toward the garage and took out his phone to call Moose. The call was answered on the second ring. "I'm on the way," Noah said. "Where are you?"

"Ground floor. I've been watching for anyone coming in and haven't seen a single thing. Maybe he's standing you up?"

"I doubt it. He's around there somewhere, you can be sure of it. We just haven't found where he's hiding."

"What do you want to do, then?" Moose asked.

"I'm coming in, driving a Volkswagen Golf diesel. Watch for me, I'll be turning in in about fifteen seconds. Hop in and ride up with me, maybe we'll draw him out and can get this over with."

"Roger that," Moose said. A moment later, Noah pulled in and saw Moose waiting for him in the main aisle, so he stopped and let him get inside.

"Keep your eyes peeled," he said as he eased the clutch out again and started up the ramps.

* * *

A small car came toward the building on the street, and slowed as it approached. Neil swung the drone over the side of the building to watch as it turned to enter, realizing that it must be Noah making his appearance. He moved back to watch the ramp exit on the top, and sure enough the car came slowly out into view.

It stopped just outside the exit and sat there for a moment. Neil expected Noah to step out, but he only sat in the car, as if watching to see if anyone else was there. After a moment, Neil went back to looking around the area.

A flash of red at the edge of the screen caught his eye, and then a second, much brighter flash left a glow near the same spot. Neil spun the drone toward it and saw movement, but the residual glow was too great to see through at that moment.

That was a gunshot, Neil thought. *Adrian is on the roof of that building! Noah is a sitting duck!*

He spun the drone around again and zipped toward the little car on the roof, but it was already moving. Noah had thrown it into reverse and backed into the exit again. Neil flew the drone down until it was just in front of the car and followed as it moved down to the third level.

Noah braked the car to a halt once it was out of the

line of fire, and suddenly saw the drone in his headlights. There was no reaction from the car, but then Neil waggled the drone and saw Noah and Moose step out of the car, staring at the machine. He moved slowly, easing toward them and then backing away, until he saw they had caught on and were following the drone. Moving slowly, he led them to just inside the exit to the top.

He stopped there and turned the drone to face Noah and Moose, moving toward them for just a moment and then hovering. Noah said something that Neil couldn't hear, then pointed down at the floor to indicate he understood he was to wait there. Neil turned the drone again and zipped out quickly, rapidly taking it high into the air. He aimed it at the spot where he was sure Adrian was hiding, and sure enough the infrared picked up the glow of his body.

"Okay, guys," Neil whispered to himself, "I hope you're paying attention!"

Neil hit an icon on his phone and every light on the drone suddenly came to life. He dived at Adrian, trying to hit him with the small spotlights that were mounted under the drone, and was rewarded with a clear glimpse of the man.

And then the screen went dark, as Adrian realized what was happening and put a bullet through the camera and the main body of the drone.

TWENTY-THREE

Noah pulled the car out onto the roof, but there was no visible sign of anyone there, so he paused. He was sure that would be the natural response to finding yourself alone if you were expecting a meeting, but he also knew it put him right into the open. When a shot rang out and a bullet struck the roof of the car, he was only half surprised, but his instincts took over and he slammed the little car into reverse and floored the accelerator as he dumped the clutch. It flew back into the ramp leading downward, and he braked to a halt when he was sure they were out of the line of fire.

"You okay?" he asked Moose, and the big guy nodded.

"I'm fine," he said. "The bullet came through just behind me. If you'd waited another second or two, he'd have gotten shots into the windshield and we'd both probably be dead."

Something crossed between the car and the slight glow of the light reflecting on the ever-present clouds. Noah stared hard to try to see what was coming at them. "What the hell?" he asked when he saw the drone hovering just in front of the car.

"It's Neil," Moose said. "He's using the drone to scout for us. You didn't know?"

Noah shook his head. "Neil is back at the house," he said, "he can't run the drone from that far away, can he?"

Moose shrugged. "He seems to have found a way. You know how he is with electronics, making them do things they weren't meant to? I don't put anything past him." The drone was wiggling around. "What's he doing?"

"I'd say he wants us to follow the drone. Maybe he's seen something we haven't." Noah opened his door and got out, and Moose did likewise. Sure enough, the drone started slowly back toward the exit onto the roof, and the two of them followed.

When they got to the opening, the drone stopped and seemed to push back at them for a moment. Noah looked at Moose. "I think we're supposed to wait here. Get over where you can keep an eye on the drone, and I'll do the same from this side." He looked at the camera lens of the drone and pointed down at the floor, then nodded. The drone waggled once more, then turned and moved quickly out of the exit and up into the air.

With its lights off it was almost impossible to see as it flew around in the dark, and Noah lost track of it only a moment later. He tried to keep his eyes focused on where it had seemed to be going, and it paid off.

The drone's marker and landing lights came on suddenly, and it dived to the far left. Noah leaned around the concrete wall he was hiding beside and caught a glimpse of a man on the roof of a building next door. The drone seemed to be attacking him like a bumblebee, and as Noah watched, the man raised a rifle and fired three shots in quick succession. The drone's lights went out, and it crashed down onto the roof of the garage.

"There he is," Noah said, but he didn't need to say anything. Moose had already moved over beside him and dropped to one knee, aiming the rifle and squeezing the trigger. He fired several bursts of automatic fire, and after one of them he was rewarded with the sound of a man screaming in pain.

"You hit him," Noah said. "He'll be coming down through the building. Let's get down there and try to head him off if we can!"

They ran down through the ramps and out onto the street, but saw no sign of Adrian. A back door on the building was broken, and a spot of blood smeared on it showed that he had brushed against it as he made his escape.

"He's gone," Noah said. "Let's get out of here before the police show up." He took out his phone and called Sarah for a pickup as they walked quickly through the alley to the next street over.

* * *

"*No!*" Neil yelled as the screen died. He knew what had happened, of course, but it left him with no way to know what was going on. "*Damn it!*"

He shut off his phone and tossed it onto the table, then decided to go and check on Iverson again. He reached across the table for his machine pistol, but a sudden sound behind him made him turn just in time to see a blur that struck him hard on the side of his head, and then everything went dark.

* * *

Sarah pulled up alongside them only a moment later and both of them quickly got into the truck. Moose laid the rifle on the floorboard under his feet as she sped away.

"What happened?" Sarah demanded.

"He was there," Noah said, "hiding on the roof next door. It never occurred to me to think of him as a sniper, I should've seen that coming. Neil somehow got the drone working and managed to spot him up there, so when Adrian got a shot off at us he was able to use the drone to show us where to find him. We're pretty sure Moose managed to hit him, but it may not be serious. He got away before we could get to him."

"Damn," Sarah said. "Are you guys okay?"

"We're fine," Noah said. "He only got one shot at us, and he missed."

"He got the drone, though," Moose said. "It's definitely dead. Maybe we should have grabbed it, to keep it from leading back to us."

"We'll deal with that if it happens," Noah said. "Right now, I think I want to get my hands on Broussard. With any luck, Adrian is going to be dealing with his wounds for the rest of the night. If we move fast, we might be able to convince Broussard to help us turn the tables on him."

Sarah shook her head, but she pointed the truck out toward Broussard's home. Sensing the urgency, she pushed the truck as fast as she dared, ripping the speed limits to shreds all the way.

Still, it took them almost 40 minutes to get there. She parked on the same dark side street, and Noah told her to wait right there until they got back.

He and Moose each took an assault rifle and began moving through the brush that would lead into Broussard's estate.

"Funny", Moose said, "seems like just yesterday I was making jokes about having to invade this place. Oh, wait, that was yesterday, wasn't it?"

"The day before," Noah said with a straight face. "Pisses me off I never bothered to find out if he has security at this place. I was hoping we'd never have to do this."

"Well, look at it this way," Moose said. "We could just go back to the house and take it easy, or we can invade this place and try to make this mission work. Personally, I think this way is going to be more fun."

They came to the fence that surrounded the estate and watched it carefully for a few moments. There was no sign of any guards inside the perimeter, and they saw no indication that the fence was wired for alarms. Noah was about to climb over it when Moose nudged his arm.

"Look over here," he said. "The last good storm must've knocked that tree down, it's leaning right over the fence. We can go right up it and hop over without ever touching the wires."

Noah nodded. "Let's do it," he said. Both of them ran up the leaning tree and hopped onto the ground on the other side of the eight-foot fence. They crouched there for a moment, but there was no sign that they'd been detected so they began moving toward the house once again.

A few minutes later, they made it to the east end of the house. There were only a few lights on inside, and none of the lighted rooms seemed to have anyone in them. Noah scanned a window looking for an indication of the security system and found it after only a few seconds.

"It's a simple breakaway," Moose said. "If we slide the

window, the contacts come apart and that's what sets off the alarm."

"The contacts are pretty simple. The one on the wall is connected to a pair of wires, and the other is just a strip of metal that completes the circuit. If we could slide another piece of metal in between and keep it there as we raise the window…"

"Say no more," Moose said. A moment later he had pulled a thin-bladed knife out of his pocket and forced it between the contacts so that the blade completed the circuit. Noah took another knife from his own pockets and used it to unlatch the window at the top, then began slowly lifting. He managed to raise it up a foot and a half without causing Moose to lose his connection. With the knife in place, the window was jammed tight, so Noah reached in and laid his rifle on the floor before crawling through the opening himself. Moose followed a moment later.

They picked up their weapons and moved quietly through the house, surprised to find no kind of security inside. The ground floor was empty, so they moved carefully up the stairs to the second floor. Broussard was asleep in the third bedroom they checked.

Noah moved stealthily to the bed and quickly shoved his hand over Broussard's mouth. The man woke instantly, and his eyes went wide. Noah put a finger to his own lips to warn Broussard to be quiet and the man nodded his understanding.

"Do not lie to me," Noah said, reverting to his Adrian impersonation. "Is there anyone else in the house?"

Broussard shook his head. "No," he said softly. "I live alone." The look on his face suggested that he might be considering that the gravest error of his life at that moment.

"You set me up to be killed, Monsieur Broussard," he said. "This is not the way business associates should treat one another, is it?"

Broussard opened his mouth to speak, but then closed it. A tear leaked out of one eye as he stared up at Noah. After a moment, he opened his mouth again. "We are confused," he said at last. "There is another who has contacted us, claiming that he is Adrian. He says you are an imposter, an agent sent to learn who we are so that we may be arrested."

"And so you tried to have me killed? Did you not realize that I would come for you after such an attempt?"

Broussard licked his lips as he looked into Noah's eyes. "As I say, we are confused. It was my sincere hope that the survivor of the encounter would be the one we truly wish to deal with. It seems that you may be the real Adrian, after all."

Noah stared at him for a moment. When he spoke, it was without Adrian's accent and affectations. "When we met the other day, Broussard, you told me how you had been forced into this position. Was that true?"

Broussard nodded his head. "It is true," he said, "every word of it."

Noah nodded. "I had thought it was," he said. "Mr. Broussard, I was not sent to arrest you, not any of you. My orders are to identify the leadership of IAR and kill them. If things had gone as I expected the other night, you and the Council would already be dead, but there was a monkey wrench thrown into my plans when Deanna had to call your Executive Director. In order to complete my mission, I have to find him, as well." He looked down at Broussard, who now had tears flowing freely from both eyes. "Mr. Broussard, I can offer you one chance to save your life. Understand that it will mean I own you, and that you will from now on do whatever I tell you to do. The only thing different about your life will be that I am not the same as your current master. I, or someone who speaks for me, will come to you when we need information that you can provide, or when we need your help to accomplish a mission of our own. We will never, however, ask you to participate in terrorism. That's what we are out to stop. Are you interested in this offer?"

Broussard hesitated for a moment, then nodded his head, not trusting himself to speak.

"Very good. When we were in the meeting the other night, one of the other members looked at Deanna and asked her if she would like to make the call to the director. From that, I gather she is not the only one who knows how to reach him?"

"That is correct," Broussard said. "Each of us has a number by which we can reach him, but we can use each number only once. After that, we are to be given a new one. I have never used mine, but I was given one in case I need it."

"Give it to me." Noah picked up a pad and pen that lay on Broussard's nightstand and passed it to him. The old man scribbled the number down and handed it back.

Noah looked closely at him. "Do you know who he is?"

The old man shook his head. "No. I was never told, and I have never asked. Knowledge like that is too dangerous for a man in my position."

"I can understand that," Noah said. He stared at Broussard for a long moment, and then asked, "Do we have an arrangement, Mr. Broussard?"

"We do," Broussard said.

"Adrian may not be dead," Noah said. "We wounded him tonight but I don't know how badly. If he contacts you again, do not tell him about my visit or what we discussed. If you can find out where he's at or how I can track him down, let me know. Use the number I called you from earlier today, I'll keep it on for you." He rose from the bed and looked down at Broussard once more. "And don't double cross me. You won't believe how cruel I can be if I'm double crossed."

He turned and motioned for Moose to follow as he left the room. They went out the same way they'd come in, through the window, and Moose retrieved his knife after they closed it behind them.

"Do you trust him?" Moose asked.

"Strangely enough, I do," Noah said. "He didn't want to be in bed with these people, and we've just offered him a way out. If I can kill them all, then he's in the clear, and we've just gained a new intelligence asset."

TWENTY-FOUR

Sarah was relieved when they came back so quickly, but she was worried when Noah told her about the deal he'd made.

"We've got what is probably a number Neil can locate," Noah said, "and that old man never wanted to be any part of IAR in the first place. He can be an asset to both us and the UK, but not if he's dead. I think I made the right call."

"You didn't see the old guy, Sarah," Moose said. "He was definitely relieved at the chance to get out and stay alive. I'm with Noah on this one."

She clamped her mouth shut and didn't say anything more.

Getting back to the house took almost an hour and a half, since they had to go so much farther across the city. It was close to three by the time they got there, and Sarah parked the truck just outside the garage, but they went through it to get to the kitchen entrance.

Moose was in the lead and pushed the door open, but it hit something. He tried to see what was blocking it but couldn't, so he called out, "Neil? Hey, Neil?"

There was no answer. Noah tapped Moose on the shoulder and motioned for him to wait there, then jogged out and around to the front door. They hadn't locked it after moving in, and it was still unlocked, so Noah took out his Glock and made his way quietly inside.

The lights were out in the front of the house, but there was one burning in the kitchen that he could see. He moved as stealthily as possible until he could look into the kitchen and then saw Neil lying on the floor with his head blocking the other door.

Noah looked down the hall toward the room where Iverson had been kept and made his way toward it. The door was ajar, so he used his toe to push it open and then leveled his gun at the bed. Iverson was gone, of course, and Noah made a quick search of the rest of the rooms before going back to the kitchen.

Neil's head seemed to be bleeding profusely, so Noah gently lifted him away from the door. The bleeding had actually stopped at some point, but the boy was breathing.

"Come on in," Noah called. "Neil's been hurt."

Moose and Sarah rushed in, and Sarah demanded Moose put him up on the table while she got clean washcloths. She wiped away the blood, and let out a squeal of relief when Neil began to groan.

A few moments later, Neil was sitting up in a chair at the table, drinking a cup of instant coffee Sarah had found and made for him while she looked at the gash on the side of his head. She dug into her purse and came out with a tube of antiseptic cream and began smearing it into the wound.

"*Ooowww*," Neil yelled. "Damn, that stuff burns!"

"Shut up," Sarah said. "You really need some stitches in this, but at least I can get it cleaned out so you won't die of an infection. You're gonna have a dickens of a scar, but at least it'll be mostly under your hair."

"Not if you keep pulling it all out—*Ooowww!*" He yanked away from her and then looked up at Noah while holding the spot with one hand.

"I'm sorry, Boss, I blew it," he said. "I got so into working the drone that I forgot to keep checking on him. He got loose, somehow, and by the time I realized it, he had already split my skull open."

"Be glad," Moose said. "If he'd gotten hold of your gun, I think there's a good chance he might have shot you."

"But I messed up. I let him get away, and now he's got my machine gun, all because I had some wild idea about using cell phones to control the drone...."

"Stop it," Noah said. "Your wild idea probably saved both of our lives tonight, mine and Moose's. As for Iverson, we'll let the British deal with him. He's not our priority, the mission is." He took out his phone and dialed Catherine Potts.

She answered sleepily. "Hello?"

"Catherine, it's Alex Colson. I'm sorry to bother you at this time of night, but I've got a bit of information your friends at MI6 need to know about." He quickly explained about Iverson and his illicit guns and explosives business. She agreed to contact the appropriate department and claim she got it from an anonymous source. He thanked her and ended the call.

He pulled the slip of paper he'd gotten from Broussard out of his pocket and passed it to Neil. "I'm pretty sure that's the number to a satellite phone held by the Executive Director. Can you get a location on it?"

"Noah!" Sarah said. "Give him a break, he just got his head knocked half off."

"No, no, it's okay," Neil said. "Yeah, I can track it down. Let me get to my..." He had started to rise, but suddenly sank back into his chair. "Hey, Moose? Would you drag my computer over here, please?"

Moose got up and got the laptop, and set it in front of Neil. The boy picked up the slip of paper and looked at it, then pulled up the program he had used before. He entered the number and set the machines to scanning for the satellite phone.

Only a moment passed before it beeped, and then a map appeared. A marker showed the location of the phone, somewhere in the middle of Damascus. "That's where the phone is at this moment," Neil said. "I can set this to keep track of it when it moves, if you want."

Noah nodded. "Yes, do that. Now tell me if Deanna and James are still at her building."

Neil turned back to the computer and began working again. After a minute, he grinned, but the grin faded fast when it pulled on the skin to one side. "Yeah, they're still there. At least those two phones are."

Noah took out his phone and dialed a number, then held it to his ear. "Switchboard," said a feminine voice.

"This is Camelot," Noah said. "I need operations."

"One moment." There was silence for a few seconds, and then a male voice came on the line. "Camelot? What can I do for you, boy?"

Noah's eyebrows raised a quarter-inch. "Doctor Parker? I didn't expect you to be on duty, sir."

"We're still a bit shorthanded, so I get drafted now and then. Tonight I get the privilege of sitting up so you youngsters can talk to me when you have a problem. What's on your mind?"

"Sir, I wonder if we have any assets in Syria at the moment. I have a location in Damascus I need to check out. I need to get the identity of someone there."

"Damascus? Hang on," Parker said, and then there was silence again. It lasted almost three minutes. "Okay, give me the address. I've got hold of someone who can find out who we're dealing with."

Noah read it off to him. Parker put him on hold again, but was back in less than five minutes.

"That's a house, it belongs to Saleh Hussein Abdul. According to CIA, Abdul was occasionally rumored to have been an associate of bin Laden. No concrete evidence ever came to light, but the rumors have persisted for some time. What's the significance?"

"The IAR is run by an Executive Council that answers to one man, someone they call their Executive Director. Each member of the Council has a special phone number they can use to contact the director, and I've gotten hold of one of them. The number goes to a sat phone that is located at that address. That makes Mr. Abdul the number one candidate for director of IAR."

"I agree, and it would make sense considering the rumors we just discussed. IAR is primarily a funding organization, arranging and financing terrorism throughout most of Europe. If he and bin Laden were working together at any time in the past, he probably had enough contacts to continue once bin Laden was dead. Hold another moment."

This time the hold lasted almost 10 minutes. When he came back, Parker sounded as close to excited as Noah had ever heard him. "Camelot, it turns out that team Hercules is currently in Syria, not more than an hour from Damascus. I'm going to wake Allison and ask her to sign off on sending Hercules in to terminate him immediately. What's the situation on your end?"

"The other members of the Council are still here in London, where I can get to them. If Hercules can handle Abdul, I'm going to go ahead and take them out immediately."

"Go ahead. There's no doubt in my mind Allison will agree to letting Hercules handle Abdul. Between the two strikes, we should be able to put this mission to bed."

The line went dead and Noah turned to Moose. "Let's get going," he said. "We're taking the Council out tonight, before they have a chance to let anyone know what's happening. Neil, I need you to go back into the building's security system and kill the cameras for a couple of hours. Can you do that?"

Neil started to nod, but winced. "Yeah, no problem," he said. "I'll have it done before you get there."

Sarah reached over and picked up her purse, but Noah stopped her. "You're staying here with Neil. I can drive myself for this one, but he's still hurt. I don't want him here alone if Iverson decides to come back. Keep your gun where you can reach it, okay?"

Sarah's eyes took on the look of a pair of glowing coals. "If he shows up here, he's dead," she said.

Noah nodded once. "I'm counting on it." He held out a hand and Sarah dropped the keys into it, and then he and Moose headed out through the kitchen door. They went through the garage and got into the truck, and Noah pointed it toward the Florentine Global building.

The same attendant was on duty in the parking garage when they arrived, but he was engrossed in something on his phone. Noah drove past the booth and turned the next corner, then parked on the side of the street. He and Moose walked nonchalantly back toward the garage and were able to slip in without being noticed, just as Moose had done before.

"If this is what they call security in England," Moose said as they rode the elevator up to the sixth floor, "then I want to come back and go into competition with them. Guy like me could make a fortune here."

"Yeah," Noah said, "but you'd get bored."

As the elevator rose, each of them withdrew his pistol from its hidden holster and twisted on a silencer. As soon as the doors opened they moved out, Noah going high while Moose went low, guns ready. There was no one in the hallway, so they went to the far end first.

"As far as we know," Noah said softly, "they only have two bodyguards. When I was watching the video with Neil from their security cameras, both of them went into this room." He indicated a door that was just in front of them.

Moose shrugged. "Easy enough," he said. He reached up and knocked on the door, and a moment later they could hear someone moving around inside. The peephole in the door lit up as the lights inside were turned on, but then it went dark a second later as someone looked through it.

Moose was standing there grinning, and after a couple of seconds they heard the safety chain being removed and then the door opened. A large, dark-haired man with a mustache looked out at them. "Help you with somethin'?" he asked.

"Yeah," Moose said, and then he slammed his weight into the door. The man was thrown back and landed on his butt, but he was trying to bring a pistol of his own up as he fell. Moose shot him between the eyes, while

Noah took aim at his partner, who was trying to grab a pistol out of the holster that was hanging on the back of the chair. Noah squeezed his trigger once, and the man fell to the floor with a third eye.

"We probably could've done that a little quieter," Noah said.

Moose shrugged. "We gotta get their attention somehow, right?"

They moved to the next door down and Moose simply kicked it in. Noah stepped inside to find François struggling up from his bed, jerked awake by the crashing of the door. A single shot through his temple put an end to his struggles. Noah spun and stepped back out into the hall, where Moose was already kicking in the next door.

Roberto was in this one, and was already out of bed and trying to get his pants on. Moose raised his pistol and fired twice, both rounds taking Roberto through the heart. He dropped like a slab of meat to the floor and Moose stepped back out into the hallway.

The next door opened before they got to it, and James burst out of it with a gun in his hand. He tried to aim it at Moose, but Noah fired once and struck him through the Adam's apple. James went down holding his throat, the gun falling from his grip as he tried to stem the flow of blood.

They stepped over James as he gurgled his last, and Noah pointed at Deanna's door. Moose kicked it in and Noah stepped inside. Deanna DiPrizio was sitting up in her bed, and tears were streaming down her face. She opened her mouth to speak, but no words came out at first. Noah raised his gun and aimed it at her, and suddenly she began to beg.

"Please, please don't kill me," she said. "I know who

you are, I know you're with the police, I can give you information..."

"Can you tell me the name of the Director?" Noah said coldly.

Deanna's eyes looked confused for a moment, but then she shook her head. "None of us know his name," she said. "But I can..."

"Then you have nothing I want," Noah said. He squeezed the trigger and blew her brains across the wall behind her bed. Her face went slack as she fell backward.

He turned and walked out of the room and stepped directly back into the elevator. Moose followed, and Noah pushed the button for the garage level. They stepped out and moved along the walls, staying in darkness until they got close to the exit. The attendant was still staring at his phone with his back to them, so they quickly turned the corner and were out of sight within seconds. Neither of them spoke until they got into the truck and pulled away from the curb.

"That was easy," Moose said then, but Noah could tell that he was pumped with adrenaline.

Noah shrugged. "Sometimes it is," he said. "The operation, I mean. I've been watching you, you're trying to act like killing these people doesn't bother you at all, but it does. You don't have to be like me, Moose. You don't even want to be like me, trust me on that."

Moose was silent for a few seconds, then he looked over at Noah. "When we're in a firefight, it doesn't bother me a bit when I put someone down. When we have to go in and just put them down, though, like tonight, I can't help wondering if it's any different than regular, cold-blooded murder. I'll be honest, it eats at me, but I get over it. I know it's our job, but right now I'm just feeling like it's going to come back to haunt me someday." He turned his eyes back to face the road. "Sometimes, when I'm not even thinking about any of the people we've killed, I'll suddenly think I see one of them staring at me. It happens in the street, sometimes, sometimes in restaurants—it's just a fleeting glimpse, like a ghost looking at me and asking why I killed them."

"I've heard that from others," Noah said, "guys I served with. Some of them said they could see the faces of the soldiers they killed everywhere they looked."

"But you don't." Moose was quiet for a moment, and then turned to look at Noah once again. "Yeah, Boss, sometimes I wish I was just like you."

TWENTY-FIVE

They got back to the house and Noah walked straight past Neil and Sarah to his bedroom. Sarah followed him and found him stripping off his clothes to get into the shower. She stood in the door without saying anything, but at last he turned to look at her.

"That part's done," he said. "Now we wait for word on the man in Damascus. As soon as we have confirmation, that's where we're headed."

"What about Adrian?" she asked. "Do we do anything about him?"

"Hopefully the bullet Moose put into him will take care of that problem," Noah said. "If he turns up while we're still here, then we'll see what we can do. Otherwise, I'm ready to put him behind me."

He turned and walked into the bathroom, and a moment later she heard the shower running. By the time he came out, she was already in bed waiting for him. He slid in beside her and snuggled up close, wrapping his arms around her from behind.

"Noah," she said softly, "you're acting like something's bothering you. Want to talk?"

"It won't make any sense to you," he said. "What's

bothering me is that nothing is bothering me. Everyone else feels some kind of remorse or guilt or something when they have to kill somebody. I just looked into the eyes of a woman as I blew her brains out, and felt nothing."

Sarah rolled toward him and put a hand on the side of his face. "That's not your fault, you know," she said. "It's just who you are. After what happened when you were a kid, it's what your mind had to do to survive."

Noah looked into her eyes quietly for several seconds, then stroked her cheek with his fingers. "I look at you, and I see all the emotion, all the feelings you have for me, they glow in your eyes. I want to know what that feels like. I want to know what everything feels like. I want to feel love, I want to feel guilt, I want to feel every emotion—but the closest I can come is those brief moments when desire takes over." He kept his hand around the back of her head and pulled her toward him, kissing her lips gently. "Right then, I wanted to kiss you. It just seems like there should be more that I feel at a moment like that."

Sarah extended her pinky and rubbed it over his lips. "Sometimes, I think—I think that it's not that you don't have the emotions, it's just that you don't let yourself feel them. They're not gone, they're just blocked, and to be honest I'm a little afraid of what will happen if they ever come back."

Noah pulled her close and kissed her again, and then they stopped talking.

* * *

The car came out of the rooftop ramp and stopped, and Adrian aimed the scope down at it. He couldn't see through the windshield, but there was almost no doubt in his mind that the imposter was sitting behind the wheel. He released the safety on the rifle and took careful aim, centering the crosshairs on the spot where a driver would be sitting, and squeezed down on the trigger.

The first shot was high, puncturing the roof of the car but missing the driver's head. He worked the bolt to chamber another round just as the car lurched in reverse and shot back into the enclosed ramp. His second shot struck the concrete and ricocheted off into the night.

So, it would come down to a fight between the two of them. It never occurred to Adrian that the imposter would simply turn and run; they were both professional killers, and neither could simply walk away at this point. He stayed where he was, waiting for his opponent to make the next move.

He sat perfectly still, his sights trained on the entrance to the ramp. As soon as anything appeared in that opening he planned to put a bullet through it. He knew the scope was just a little off, a little high at this range, so he lowered it a bit to compensate. If the imposter stepped out, he was dead.

Suddenly there was a burst of light, high and to his left. He instinctively raised his eyes to see what it was, and bright white light ruined his night vision for the moment. He turned the rifle and fired, jacking the bolt to get off three shots as quickly as he could, and he was rewarded when the lights went out and whatever that thing was went crashing onto the garage below.

The sound of shots from the garage roof made him spin, but he was on his feet rather than sitting. He raised the rifle and aimed back at the entrance, determined to bring this to a conclusion, but then something tore through his left forearm. A bullet, he knew, he'd been hit! He squeezed off one shot that went wild, and then another bullet grazed his hip. He fell to the surface of the roof and knew that he had lost all advantage.

The flesh wound on his hip wouldn't slow him down, but the throbbing in his arm meant that it would be useless for a time. He dropped the rifle where he stood and bolted for the access door that led into the stairwell. He'd left it slightly ajar, so he smashed it open with his good right arm and rushed down the stairs. These were service stairs that went all the way down, six flights that took him to the main floor. He had come in through a back entrance and had secured from the inside with a simple hook. He threw it open and hurried down the alley, grimacing in pain as his injured left arm brushed against the door.

The imposter would be on the way, he knew, hoping to catch him before he could get away. He had a pistol, but didn't dare try to make a stand at this point. His arm was bleeding profusely and needed to be taken care of. Survival was more important than victory at that moment, so when he rounded a corner in the alley and saw a trash container, he leapt inside and buried himself in the garbage.

He heard footsteps circling the building he had just left, but they didn't come close to the container. Two men were talking, and he realized that the imposter had not come alone. He should have expected it, but it was too late to worry about it now. Luckily, they decided to leave before the police could be called in. Adrian waited a couple of minutes, then climbed out of the trash container and walked as quickly and calmly as he could to where he had left his own car.

His arm was throbbing as he got into the vehicle. He had chosen an automatic transmission, so he was fortunately able to drive with only one hand. He made it several blocks away before he heard the first police siren.

He came to a traffic light and stopped, then quickly took out his phone and punched in a number with his thumb. He put the phone on speaker and tucked it back into his pocket so that he could drive while he talked.

"Hello?" came a sleepy, female voice.

"Oi, Judy," Adrian said, reverting to a cockney sound. "It's Arthur, you remember me?"

"Arthur? God, yeah, it's been a while." She seemed a bit more awake.

"Yeah, well, been a bit busy, luv. Listen, I've got a bit of a problem, the kind that needs your help. Can I come round?"

"My help? You're hurt, then?" Judy sounded exasperated. "Why's it men only call me when they've got hurt?"

"It's because we know you're the best, luv. Come on, then, I've got a bloody hole in my arm, and I think it smashed the bones a bit. Just need you to patch me up so I can get back on what I got to do."

She snorted into the phone. "Fine, come on round. Back door, off the alley. I'll come down and let you in."

"Right, see you then." She hung up her phone without another word, but Adrian didn't care. He was beginning to feel weak and worried that he was losing too much blood. A couple more turns brought him into the alley behind her building, and he found a spot to park.

Getting out of the car and standing left him feeling a little dizzy, so he leaned against the car for a moment to get his balance. Despite the fact that he left a fair puddle of blood on the ground, it wasn't so much blood loss as shock that was affecting him, he knew. He pushed off the car and staggered toward the door. She opened it as he got there and pulled his right arm around her shoulders as she helped him up the stairs to her apartment. Neither of them spoke until they were inside with the door shut. She helped him take off his jacket and laid it on the table as he settled into a chair.

"Let's see what you've done," Judy said. She cut his sleeve away with a pair of scissors. "Ach, this is a mess!" She took hold of his arm and tugged on it gently, but Adrian hissed with the pain. "The radius is okay, but the ulna is broken. The bullet passed through, that's good, and the artery isn't severed. You really need surgery."

"Yeah, well, not today. Can you patch me up?"

"Yeah, but it's gonna hurt. I got to clean this thoroughly, then try to set the bone the best I can. I can manage a splint, but not a cast."

Adrian nodded. "That'll do," he said. "I still got things to do, can't be laid up right now."

Judy looked at his face, which was sweating. "You're in a bit of shock," she said. She went and got a blanket and wrapped it around him, then brought him a cup of tea. "Drink that," she said. "It'll make you sleep, but at least you won't feel everything I got to do."

He nodded again and picked up the cup with his good hand, then drank it down all at once. "That's good," he said. "Just don't let me sleep too long."

The drug hit him quickly, and he was out cold less than ten minutes later. Judy set to work, and finally got everything cleaned and stitched and wrapped and splinted by the time the sun came up. Her patient was sleeping peacefully, so she put the arm in a sling and sat down to watch over him.

Arthur was a strange one. She'd known him for about five years, by then, and every time she saw him it was because of another injury of some sort. The last one had been a year back, when he'd supposedly gotten stabbed in a row at the pub. She patched him up, but something about the wound had bothered her.

No, face the facts, she thought to herself, it was Arthur that bothered her. She'd always been one of those girls who went for the bad boys, and something about him told her he was about as bad as they could get. She'd tried flirting with him, even tried outright seduction, but he'd only smiled and driven away each time. The simple mystery of him had been driving her crazy, and she'd been thinking about him almost daily ever since that last time.

Who are you, really? she asked mentally, but of course he didn't respond. She stared at him for a few moments more, and then her gaze fell on the jacket. Watching carefully in case he might wake and catch her at it, she reached over and picked it up, then went through the pockets.

There was a wallet, and she pulled it out carefully. She glanced at his face once more to be sure he was still asleep, then opened it. The driving license had his picture, but the name on it said William Hensley, not Arthur. With her eyes narrowed in curiosity, she began looking through the rest of the wallet.

There wasn't much in it, not the sort of things you'd normally find in a man's wallet. Old pictures, scribbled notes, business cards—none of that was present, but tucked in the hidden pocket was a photo of himself with a blonde lady. Judy felt her face go red as she looked at it, realizing that this was the reason her attempts to win his favor went unrewarded. She put the picture back and slid the wallet back into the pocket she'd taken it from, then carefully laid the jacket back exactly where it had been. After a few minutes, she decided to get a little sleep and went to her bed. A few dozen tears later, she finally drifted off.

She was up again at eight, shortly before Adrian woke. She gave him another cup of tea, this one without any drugs, and sat down at the table with him to drink one of her own.

"Care to tell me how this happened?"

Adrian shrugged his right shoulder. "Wrong place, wrong time," he said. "One of my mates decided to rob an express shop, and the bloody clerk started shooting." He reached into a pocket and pulled out a wad of money, peeled off a thousand pounds and handed it to her. "I appreciate the help," he said. "I'll be getting out of your way, then." He struggled to his feet.

"You'll be careful, then? You'll need to change the dressing at least once a day, and you should get yourself some antibiotics. I'm afraid I don't have any to hand."

"I can do that. My thanks once again," he said as he walked toward the door. "Like always, best you forget I was here. Don't wanna be associated with the likes of me."

Judy said nothing, so he went on out to the car and drove away back to the flat he used whenever he was in London. He had made his way to it immediately after his escape, fairly sure it hadn't been discovered. There were things he kept hidden there that he surely would have been questioned about if it had been.

He let himself in when he arrived, then opened a kitchen cabinet and removed the pots and pans inside it. That done, he reached to the back and pulled out the false panel that hid one of his many secret compartments. He was always prepared for just about anything, and the prescription pad inside bore the signature and drug control number of a well-known physician. He scribbled out an order for some heavy antibiotics that he would pick up from the druggist later, then sat down to begin planning.

It was Monday, and there were only three days until Prince Charles would make his appearance at Albemarle, but Adrian had not yet heard from Eddie. He didn't feel a need to worry just yet; he'd give it another day and hopefully everything would be arranged.

Meanwhile, there was the problem of the imposter. Broussard needed to know the man was still running loose, so he took out his phone and dialed the old man's number.

"Hello?" Broussard said.

"You know who this is," Adrian said.

"Yes, of course," Broussard said.

"My encounter last night ran into difficulties. The imposter is still at large. Should he contact you, I want to know about it immediately."

There was a slight hesitation in Broussard's voice, but Adrian had become accustomed to it. It came from the man's innate terror at dealing directly with the assassin. "Of course," Broussard said. "I shall notify you immediately if I hear from him."

"Now, as for the assignment I accepted," Adrian went

on. "It will be completed on Thursday. The method is one that will be immediately connected to certain known enemies of the UK. Let your people know that I shall expect the balance of my payment within twenty-four hours after it is done."

"Of course," Broussard said. "That will be no problem at all."

* * *

Noah had slept until almost 11, and was wakened by the sound of his phone. He reached across to pick it up from the nightstand and saw that it was a call from the E & E headquarters.

"Camelot."

"Camelot, this is Allison. I'm reporting to you that Hercules was able to handle the situation in Damascus, and the CIA has confirmed your assessment on Abdul; he was definitely running the IAR. From the news reports coming out of London this morning, I gather the Council has also been terminated?"

"Yes. Parker said to go ahead, so we did. It all came off without a hitch as far as I know right now."

"Good work, then. You can wrap this one up and come on home whenever you're ready."

"Ma'am, with your permission I'd like to stay a little longer. We still got one loose end to tie up. The real Adrian is on the loose, and I've got a hunch that he and I are not done with each other. We had one little confrontation last night, but he got away with a bullet wound, not sure how serious. I've turned Pierre Broussard into an intelligence asset. He was blackmailed into his cooperation with IAR, and with them gone, he's a free man again. I've got him in a position to work with me on Adrian, because Adrian is trying to complete the assassination of Prince Charles."

"Yes, I'd been advised of his escape. Perhaps we should notify the Brits to get Charles out of sight for a while?"

"I'd thought about that, but if we do, Adrian is going to vanish. He seems to have a serious grudge against me, though, so I'm hoping he'll want to try to take me out again. Broussard is his only contact with IAR, so he probably doesn't realize they're gone. My guess is that he will contact Broussard again to try to set me up for another shot."

"I'll leave this up to you," Allison said after a moment. "Just remember that it would be a serious blow to US and British diplomatic relations if anything happens to the Prince, and they find out we could've warned them."

"Well, as it happens," Noah said, "our local station chief is currently assigned to the MI6 team that is hunting Adrian. I've made her aware of the threat and told her that I may need to get his appearances canceled on short notice. She assured me she could arrange that if necessary."

"Good thinking. Incidentally, when you get done with Mr. Broussard, you might want to turn him over to her as a handler. That way we both have access to him. Never know when he might come in handy, right?"

"That was my thought exactly," Noah said. "I'll let you know of any further developments."

"Sounds good. I'll talk to you later."

TWENTY-SIX

T he phone went dead, and Noah put it back on the nightstand. Sarah was looking up at him, so he leaned down and gave her a kiss.

"Mmmm. What'd I do to deserve that?"

"That's for just being you," Noah said. "Unfortunately, I think we slept long enough. Allison says the news of last night's activity has already gone global, and the Executive Director of IAR has joined the rest of his council. As soon as we settle the Adrian issue, we're headed home."

He rolled out of bed with Sarah following, and they took another shower before leaving the bedroom. Moose was sitting at the kitchen table, but Neil was still sleeping. Noah filled him in on the call from Allison, and he grinned.

"So what do we do about Adrian?" he asked.

"There isn't really anything to do at the moment. All we can do is wait and see if he contacts Broussard again. We need to wake Neil up, let him know what's going on."

"I'll get him," Sarah said as she walked off down the hall.

"You know," said Moose, "it's always possible Adrian isn't an issue anymore. I mean, yeah, it looks like he got out of the building but we don't know how badly he was hit. He could be laying dead in an alley somewhere."

"Possible, but somehow I doubt it. Still, we'll have Neil run a search through news reports, see if any John Does have turned up dead."

There was coffee in the pot, and Noah got up to get himself a cup. By the time he got back to the table, Neil and Sarah were coming into the kitchen. "I need a cup of that," Neil mumbled. Sarah went to the pot and poured a cup for him and another for herself.

Noah brought Neil up to speed while he sipped his coffee, then told him what he wanted. The computer was still on the table, so Neil pulled it over close and started tapping on the keys. "Okay, scanning the news reports. It seems somebody murdered six people in an office building during the night. Security guards saw nothing, and for some strange reason the building's security video was on the fritz. One of the victims was the CEO of Florentine Global Export, and three of the others were on its Board of Directors. The other two men were reported to be bodyguards who worked for the CEO." He tapped a key. "A stolen car was recovered in the Limehouse Central Car Park early this morning, with a bullet hole through its roof. A remote control drone was found shot to pieces on top of the same garage, and police suspect there's a connection between the two. The drone had a cell phone attached to it, but the bullet that destroyed it had gone through the phone, so police are guessing that it might've been some sort of training exercise for a terrorist or paramilitary group. They did notice that a neighboring building had been broken into during the night, and found a rifle on its roof. They're speculating that the rifle may have fired the shots that destroyed the drone. They also found bloodstains on the roof, and in the stairs leading down from it, as well as on the back door." A few more taps. "Three apparently unrelated bodies were discovered in different places during the night, but none of them died of a bullet. Two overdoses and a suicide. Nothing that matches up to Adrian at all. Checking hospital reports— nope, only one gunshot wound reported overnight and it was a woman who was accidentally shot in the butt by her husband, while he was cleaning a gun. Oh, and here's a tidbit I personally like. It seems a Mr. Patrick Iverson was arrested this morning at his apartment, charged with terrorist activities for making explosives." He looked up at Noah. "Unfortunately, I don't see anything that could connect to Adrian. Any other ideas?"

Noah shook his head. "No, we'll just need to wait…" He was cut off by the ringing of his phone. He left it on the nightstand, so Sarah hurried down the hall to get it. She got it back to him on the fourth ring, and he answered it immediately.

"Yes?" he said.

"You told me to call if I heard from—from him. He called only a few minutes ago."

"That's good," Noah said. "What did he have to say?"

"Well, at first he simply demanded that I let him know if I hear from you, as you said he would. Then he began talking about the assignment, the same one the Council spoke to you about. He said it will be completed on Thursday, and wanted me to make sure he received the balance of his payment within twenty-four hours after. I assured him I would see to it, and that was all."

"Thursday, is it? All right, I don't want you to do anything at the moment. I'm sure by now you've heard the news?"

Broussard hesitated for just a moment. "Yes," he said. "And the director?"

"Also eliminated at his home in Damascus. I suspect the IAR is finished, but I will shortly provide you with a contact in case anyone ever tries to drag you back into it. For now, I don't want you to do anything. If he contacts you again, say you have not heard from me yet but that you'll notify him immediately if and when you do."

"Yes, sir," Broussard said. "I will do exactly as you tell me."

Noah ended the call and turned to Neil. "Thursday is the day Prince Charles goes to the elementary schools, right?"

Neil tapped the keyboard for a few seconds, then nodded. "Yep," he said. "Three different ones. Royal Academy, Albemarle and Hempstead Preparatory."

"Adrian told Broussard the assassination will take place on Thursday. That means he's going to strike at one of those three schools. The only question is, which one?"

* * *

Sam Little stomped into the conference room and dropped heavily into his chair. He looked around at the faces of his team, glaring at each of them in turn.

"We're going on thirty-six hours since the bloody bastard escaped," he said icily, "and already we've got some pretty strange shit happening around the city. You've all seen the reports on the shot-up camera drone, right? The rifle they found that took it down is one of Adrian's favorites, an LM308 sniper rifle. There were no fingerprints on it, but I've no doubt he was using it. What I want to know is what the hell the drone has to do with anything. Anybody got any ideas?"

Stamper shrugged. "Perhaps he was getting in some target practice?" The others did their best not to chuckle, but a few sniggers escaped.

"That would suggest he's practicing for an aerial target. Anybody got a reasonable suggestion why he might be doing that?"

No one spoke up, so Sam went on. "Fine, I'll suggest one. We know that he was planning something big when we took him, so it's reasonable to assume he intends to complete that hit now that he's out. It's entirely possible that his target is going to be moving around by helicopter. That would explain trying to get a practice on an aerial moving target, wouldn't it?"

The team all looked at one another, and Catherine spoke first. "That actually would make some sense," she said. "Do we have any information on major figures who might be airborne in the near future?"

"Unfortunately, no," Sam said. "None of the Ministers are scheduled for any type of low-level flight anytime soon. Since the practice was obviously with the rifle, it would have to be either helicopter or light plane; that weapon couldn't do much to anything bigger."

The meeting went on for more than an hour, with several different ideas bandied about without appealing to anyone. The whole team felt that they came out of it knowing even less than they did going in.

Sam caught Catherine as they were leaving the conference room. "Kate," he said, "could I have a minute?"

She turned to him with a smile. "Certainly, Sam," she said. She waited as the others filed out, and then Sam closed the door and turned to her.

"Look," he began, "I was called in this morning for a chat with Mr. Younger. He raised my clearance two points in order to fill me in on a little detail regarding a member of my team who happens to be privy to some information he thinks I ought to ask about. Care to enlighten me?"

Catherine gave him an innocent look. "Enlighten you? About what?"

"Come on, don't be coy," Sam said. "Alex says you work with the Yanks, and that you know something about Adrian that I don't. He didn't want to overstep, so he said I should ask you point-blank. What's going on, Kate?"

Catherine sighed. "It's true I'm a liaison officer with an American organization," she said, "but I seriously can't tell you anything about them. As for the current situation, there's an American agent in the city who was impersonating Adrian as a cover, trying to get information on IAR. When our lot let him get away, it caused some complications in that operation. In fact, it's highly likely Adrian is trying to track him down even now." She leaned toward him conspiratorially. "In my unofficial opinion, that likely has more to do with the drone situation than any sort of target practice."

Sam stared at her. "So what, this Yank is trying to get to Adrian before we do?"

"No, Sam, I think it's the other way round. Adrian found out that someone was impersonating him, and apparently he's trying to find out who it is and put a stop to it. The American agent is hoping for the chance to turn the tables."

Sam's jaw worked furiously for a couple of seconds. "All right, Alex says I can't order you to tell me anything you don't want to, and that's fine. But I want you to get your Yank on the horn and find out exactly what's going on. If Adrian is really trying to pull off an assassination, I can't see how he'd be wasting time on something as unimportant as bloody identity theft. There must be more to this, somewhere, and I want to know what the hell it is." He turned and yanked the door open, stalking away from her.

Catherine chewed her bottom lip for a moment, then went to her own little office. She closed the door and sat down at her desk, then reached into her upper desk drawer and pushed a button on a small device. After that, she took out her phone and dialed the number that would connect her to Alex Colson.

It rang twice before he answered. "Mr. Colson, it's Catherine Potts. I'm afraid I need to ask you to let me know what's going on."

"Yeah, I sort of thought I'd be getting this call," Noah said. "I had a bit of a close encounter with Adrian last night, out in Limehouse. Unfortunately, as far as I know he's still alive and still in the game. He made contact with our old friend Broussard today, hoping to get another crack at me."

"I see. And what about all the dead bodies over at Florentine? Any connection there?"

"A small connection, yes. Four of those people were on the Executive Council of IAR. They were my original mission."

"Right, I understand. Back to Adrian, is there anything you can give me that I can hand off to my superiors? It seems my boss has been made privy to my dual association, after all, and he's rather furious."

Noah hesitated for a moment. "Catherine, I'm going

to tell you something, but I need you to keep it under your hat until the last possible moment. Adrian accepted the same assignment that IAR wanted to give me, when they thought I was him. It's possible he's actually going to try. At the moment, I'm doing everything I can to set up a trap that can shut him down for good, but if I can't, I'll be needing you to make the cancellation we discussed earlier."

It was Catherine's turn to hesitate. "Very well," she said. "I'll cooperate, but contact me immediately if you need me to do anything. As much as he's irritated a lot of the populace, we really cannot let anything happen to the crown prince."

"I don't intend to," Noah said. "But the best way to prevent it is to eliminate the threat, don't you agree?"

"Oh, I absolutely do," she said. "I'll be waiting for a call."

She closed the phone and sat back for a moment to gather her thoughts, then got up and walked out of her own office and straight to Sam's. He was at his desk, and looked up at her with ice in his eyes as she entered.

"You're right," she said. "Adrian is planning an assassination, and the American is working to stop him. I've been assured that as soon as he learns who the target is, I'll be notified."

Sam stared at her without speaking, but the anger in his eyes gradually faded. "How long, Kate? How long have you been playing both sides?"

"The Americans asked for someone in our ranks to be liaison and station chief," she said, "about two years ago. I was handed the job and told to keep it to myself. It's a symbiotic relationship, you might say; occasionally, we need the very special services the American outfit offers. In return, I'm given access to information that can assist whenever they have a mission in our jurisdiction."

"Special services? Dear God, are we talking about the Icemen?"

Catherine couldn't suppress the grin all the way. "Well, I'll admit I've heard them called that, though they never speak of themselves that way. But, yes, we're talking about those people."

Sam stared at her in silence for a full minute, then shook his head. "Forget I ever asked about it, can you do that?"

"Certainly, Sam," Catherine said.

"I've only one more question, then," Sam said. "When this bloody mess is all over, would you be free for dinner some evening?"

Catherine smiled. "When this bloody mess is all over," she said, "I'll make certain to be free any evening you like."

TWENTY-SEVEN

One of the things fiction writers tend to get wrong about espionage work is the illusion that it's all action and glamor. In reality, most of it involves tedium and boredom. Noah wasn't much affected by such things, but his team was going stir crazy by the following evening.

Nothing more had happened after Catherine's call. Noah had checked in with Broussard later that night, only to learn that he'd heard nothing from Adrian. The following day, Tuesday, was just as quiet so that by the time evening rolled around, Moose, Neil and Sarah were all suffering from anxiety. They knew something was going to happen, but the waiting was worse than they had expected it to be.

At a little after seven, Noah called Broussard once more. "Do you have a way to reach Adrian?" he asked when the old man answered.

"I have a number, of course," he said. "Should I give it to you?"

"Yes," Noah said. "I should've thought of this earlier. Let me have it, but be sure to let me know if you hear from him."

Broussard gave him the number, and Noah scribbled

it down and passed it to Neil. He said goodbye to Brous-sard and ended the call, then looked at the skinny kid on the computer.

"Well," Neil said, "I've got good news and I've got bad news."

"Let's get the bad news out of the way," Noah said.

"Okay. That number isn't really tied to a cell phone. It's a VoIP number, Voice over Internet Protocol. A for-warding number, basically. If you dial that number, the call is forwarded to an actual phone somewhere else."

"So you can't track down the location of the phone that receives the call, is that what you're saying?"

"Yes, but there is still the good news. The good news is that I may be able to hack the server that reroutes the call, and find out where it's actually going. That should get me the real number, and a shot at locating the phone it's connected to. And before you ask, I'm already work-ing on it."

Noah sighed and nodded. "Okay, let me know if you get anything."

Unfortunately, hacking the server proved to be diffi-cult. Its encryption was equal to that of most financial websites, Neil told Noah, so getting into it without an actual username and password was nearly impossible. Still, he set up a program to keep trying even after they finally went to bed at close to midnight.

* * *

Adrian wasn't as bored. Eddie finally called that morning, and he drove out to meet him at yet another restaurant. This one had tables outside, and he saw Eddie and Georgie sitting at one off by itself.

"Are we set, then?" Adrian asked as he took a seat.

"Wasn't any problem at all," he said. "My new bird was happy to let me pick her up after work at the school, took her out for a few drinks then shagged her 'til she squealed. Georgie here nicked her keys and took them out to get a copy made, had 'em back in her bag by the time we were done. She's a bit sweet, I might hang onto her for a bit."

"And she never saw Georgie?"

"Not even once. There's nothing to tie us to the job. Georgie got in and out of the auditorium in the wee small, everything's set."

Georgie giggled. "Shaped charges," he said, "just like we said. They'll blow straight up, anybody on that stage is gonna be part of the ceiling."

"And the detonator?" Adrian asked.

Eddie pulled a small, cheap cell phone out of his pocket and slid it across the table. "This won't make any calls," he said, "it's just a simple remote made to look like a mobile. Just push the little red button," he said, "and it all goes boom. Just make sure you're not standing too close when it does; it'll blow straight up, right enough, but some of the roof might come falling back down. You've only got to be within 500 meters, that'll do the trick."

Adrian smiled and pulled another envelope out of his pocket. He slid across the table and Eddie made it disappear.

"I added a bit of a bonus," Adrian said. "You boys do good work, and I'm sure we'll be talking again."

Eddie and Georgie both smiled from ear to ear. "Our pleasure," Eddie said.

* * *

Wednesday turned out to be bright and clear, but Noah was no closer to any ideas about how to track down Adrian than he had been before. By nine o'clock, even he was beginning to feel the strain of inactivity. Twice he picked up the phone to call Broussard, but both times he put it down. He was quite certain the old man would call him if he had anything to report.

* * *

Halfway across the city, a young boy decided to take a shortcut through an alley. He had cut through it many times, but this time he noticed something he had never seen before: there was a big splotch of nearly dried blood, and the sight of it bothered him for some reason he couldn't comprehend. He stepped carefully around it and went on home.

"Ma," he said to his mother, who was putting soup into a bowl for his lunch, "why d'ye reckon there'd be a puddle of blood over in the next alley?"

"Blood? And where did you see blood?" she asked him.

"Next alley back," he said. "Right behind the flats, where Miss Judy lives."

Judy Woodbridge was well known in the neighborhood. She had been a nurse at hospital until a few years back, when she had been caught stealing drugs from the hospital pharmacy and selling them on the street. She'd been arrested and gone to jail for a year, and she lost her nursing license and found herself tending bar just to make rent.

Still, she had the knowledge and the skills. It was no secret that she offered black-market medical care, and many of the neighbors had taken advantage of her abilities. Unfortunately, so did much of the riffraff around the area, and a lot of the neighbors were sick of the unsavory characters that came in and out of her back door. They had told her so on more than one occasion, and she had promised to stop the traffic, but obviously she was starting up again.

The boy's mother said nothing as her son ate his lunch, but when he finished and rushed off to see his mates again, she went to her phone. No one would know it was her, she reasoned, so there was no cause to worry about any sort of retaliation. She told the inspector she was transferred to that she was sure there was something illegal going on in flat D over at number 321 Dibble St. After all, what possible lawful reason could there be for big puddles of blood in the alley behind where the outlaw nurse lived?

The inspector filed a report on the call, but he didn't have time to go and take a look for himself. It probably wasn't anything important, anyway.

The report of blood in a suspicious location, however, triggered a program in the computers. Sam Little received a notice only a few minutes later, and decided it was worth checking out. The rest of the team was working its own leads, but Catherine was in her office. He poked his head in and asked her to join him for a ride, and she agreed instantly.

"Coppers got a report of a lot of blood in an alley," he said. "There was blood all around where the rifle was found, too, and this alley happens to be right behind a flat where lives a former nurse who tends to the misfortunes and injuries of those who prefer not to go to hospital. I thought it's worth taking a look."

"Certainly," Catherine said. "Might be nothing, but you never know."

They pulled up in the alley a short time later and found the blood with no problem. There wasn't quite as much as the caller had indicated, but still enough to make Sam think somebody had suffered quite an injury. He started toward the back door of the building and spotted several more drops of blood along the way. "Look there," he said. "That's good and dry, could easily be old enough to match with the blood we found on the roof, by the rifle." Catherine only nodded, so Sam knocked on the back door of the building. When one of the tenants came to open it, he flashed his ID and sent the man scurrying back to his own flat. Sam and Catherine went up the stairs and found flat D. Sam knocked, and a female voice from inside demanded to know who was there.

"MI6," Sam said. "Got a few questions for you."

The door opened ten seconds later and a tired-looking woman stared out at them. "MI6?"

Sam and Catherine both showed their IDs, and the woman opened the door and allowed them inside. "I've got some tea on," she said, "if you'd like a cup?"

"That won't be necessary," Sam said. "We wanted to ask you about all the blood in the alley, leading right up to the back door. I noticed a couple of little drops on the stairs coming up, as well."

The woman looked at him for a moment, and then shrugged. "Why should I know?"

Sam started to speak, but Catherine cut him off. "Judy —your name is Judy, right? Judy, we know who you are and we know what you do. We are not here to cause you any problems, we just want to know about the man who came to you with a bullet wound night before last." She stared pointedly into Judy's eyes, and after a moment the woman looked down at the floor.

"He's a real bad one, ain't he?" Judy asked. "Only I thought he was just like the others, but I was wrong, wasn't I?"

Catherine felt adrenaline building up, and nodded. Sam kept his mouth shut and watched.

"Yes, he's a bad one. He's a very dangerous man, and sooner or later he's going to decide you know too much. We need to find him, and we need to find him soon, or he's going to do something terrible. When he does, he may start to worry that we might find you. Do you understand what I'm saying?"

Judy raised her eyes to Catherine's face and nodded slowly. "You're saying he might decide to kill me. Right?"

"That's exactly what I'm saying. Judy, if you know anything that can help us find him, please tell us now. If we can get to him, we can put him away so that he can't ever start to worry about how much you know."

Judy stared at her for a moment, but then the little bit of defiance she was trying to display seemed to wash away. She sank into a chair at the table, and Catherine sat in the one opposite. Sam continued to stand where he was, trying to be invisible so as not to interfere in what Catherine was accomplishing.

"I fancied him for a while," Judy said. "Tried over and over to make him notice, but he never would. Always said he had to go, wouldn't ever stay any longer than he had to. I always thought it was just me, you know, like maybe I wasn't pretty enough or something. I mean, he never said he had a wife, so how was I to know, right?"

"Of course," Catherine said. "Did he tell you this time?"

Judy shook her head. "No, he didn't say nothin'. Only I got nosy, you know? He'd been shot, and the bullet broke the bone in his left forearm. I had to set it and stitch it, so I gave him a cup of tea with codeine, to put him to sleep, you know? Worked right good it did, too. He was out like a light in two shakes. I patched up his arm and set the bone, wrapped it up real good and put it in a sling, then I got curious. He had his jacket laying on the table, here, and I took a peek through his wallet, you know?"

Catherine was nodding. "And what did you find?"

Judy's face clouded over. "He'd always said his name was Arthur," she said. "His driving license, though, I saw it, his name is William, William Hensley. And then I found the picture, picture of him and his wife." The anger suddenly faded, and a tear started to leak out of her right eye. "Pretty thing, she is. Lot prettier than me. Guess that's why he never wanted to stay the night, right?"

Catherine reached out and put a hand on Judy's arm. "You're pretty enough," she said. "Maybe for all he's bad, there's a tiny spot of good in him that wants to be faithful to his wife. But Judy, that doesn't change the facts. He does some bad things, Judy, very bad things. We need to put a stop to him. You said you saw his driving license. Did you see an address?"

Judy nodded. "Over in Harrow," she said. "891 Westridge, flat 12." She looked up at Catherine. "Do you know, I toyed with the idea of going there? Just wanted to meet her, see what she's like. Probably would've been a bad idea, right?"

"I think it would have been a very bad idea," Catherine said.

* * *

Sam called the rest of the team and told them to meet him and Catherine at the address Judy had given them, then headed for it as quickly as he could. It took almost an hour to get across the city, so the others had arrived and were waiting by the time they showed up.

"Okay, there's a good possibility this is our boy," Sam said. "If it is, this could get pretty dangerous pretty quickly. Terry, you and Nick and I are going to the front door. Harry, I want you and Lloyd to go up the fire escape. The flat's on the third floor, east side of the building to the back. Keep out of sight, just in case he's in and decides to bolt out the window. We want him alive if we can, but don't take any chances. Everybody set?"

"Now, wait a minute," Catherine said. "And what about me, Sam Little?"

"You're the watch," Sam said. "You stay out of sight by the car, in case we need you to call in backup."

She stared at him for a moment. "You're a bloody chauvinist, you know that, Sam?"

"No doubt, but I'm also the case officer. Do as you're told, right?"

"Fine," she said. Sam and the others split up and started toward the building from two different directions.

Sam and the two with him made it up the stairs with no problem, and Sam knocked on the door. There was no answer, so he knocked again, more loudly this time. When there was still no response a moment later, he looked at Nick and nodded. "Do it," he said.

Nick reached into a pocket and pulled out a little leather case, and a moment later he had picked the lock on the door. He, Sam and Terry slipped inside, and after quickly checking to be sure no one was present, Sam went to the window and opened it so the others could come in.

"All right, let's search quickly, but be careful. We're dealing with an assassin, you never know what sort of booby-traps he might've hidden around." The others nodded, and began looking through the apartment.

Nothing jumped out at them at first, but then Lloyd discovered a loose floorboard and pried it out. Underneath, he found a number of wallets and passports. "Sam," he called, "you'll be wanting to see this."

The photos in the passports and IDs showed Adrian in various disguises. Sam was ecstatic, for there was now no doubt they had found his London base of operations.

"Keep looking," he said. "God only knows what else he might have stashed around here."

Down at the car, parked a half block away, Catherine was still fuming about being left out of the action. She had come up with a number of rude and witty things that she would say to Sam when she got him alone. He'd bloody well think twice before he ever pulled this sort of thing on her again, he would.

A car pulled up across the street from the building, and a lone man got out of it. Catherine glanced at him, but he seemed shorter than the description she'd been given of Adrian. She leaned her head back and began thinking of more things she might say to Sam, but then something about the man suddenly made her look again.

He wasn't short; he was simply bent over, slightly stooped as he walked. He looked like an older gentleman, but there was something in the way he was holding his left arm that threw it off. That arm was stiff, she could tell, and she instantly realized she was looking at Adrian in disguise.

He was already at the door by the time she realized it, and there was no way she could get to him in time. She grabbed her phone and dialed Sam's number, praying that he would answer before Adrian got to the door of the flat.

Sam felt the phone vibrate in his pocket and pulled it out. It was Catherine calling, so he answered immediately. "Sam," he said.

"He's here," Catherine said. "He's coming up the stairs now. He's made up like a little old man, but I'm telling you it's him."

"Thanks, luv," Sam said and he instantly ended the call. He hissed to get the attention of the others and whispered that they were about to be joined by their prey.

Lloyd and Terry were closest to the front door, so they hurried to get behind it. In doing so, they bumped into each other, and Terry lost his balance for just a second. His arm bumped into a lamp and it crashed to the floor.

They all froze. There was a very small chance Adrian had not heard the lamp breaking, so they held position.

In the hallway outside, Adrian had frozen. A noise from inside the flat could mean only one thing: his hideaway had been discovered. He breathed a sigh of regret, then stepped up to the door. He reached up over the woodwork around it and felt until his fingers found the button he had hidden there years earlier. He pressed it, and then turned and started back toward the stairs and down.

Every one of his operational bases had a similar button. It started a timer hidden in the wall that was wired to explosives under the floors. There were other buttons hidden inside, so that he could always set the timer and escape out the window or through the hidden hatch in the closet ceiling. The timer would count down two minutes, by which time he would need to be out of the building.

He stepped out the front door and walked with his stooped gait back toward his car, but Catherine spotted him instantly. She leaped out of her own car, drawing her pistol and aiming at him.

"Adrian!" she screamed, and he turned his head instinctively. "Freeze where you are!"

Without being able to see who was shouting at him, Adrian froze. He slowly raised his hand and turned to face the voice. A lone woman stood in the street, a small automatic in her hand.

"Do not move," she commanded. "Keep your hands up where I can see them, or I will fire."

"What is this about?" Adrian asked, trying to look confused. "I'm only going out for a drive, luv."

Catherine kept her pistol trained on him with her right hand, while taking her phone out again with her left. She tried twice to hit the redial key, but her left hand wasn't as agile as her right, and she missed. Without lowering her gun, she glanced down at the device for a split second to press it with her thumb, but that was all Adrian needed.

* * *

Sam and the others were crouched in the flat, guns trained on the door, but Adrian hadn't appeared. He glanced at Terry and started to rise to his feet, but then, faintly, he heard Catherine's voice from down in the street.

"He's got out," Sam yelled, and they all started toward the door...

* * *

As soon as her eyes left him, he dropped to the ground, rolling and snatching his own pistol out of its holster. He came up onto one knee and aimed the pistol in a single fluid motion, then squeezed the trigger once. His bullet struck her just over her left breast, and she fell.

Adrian rose and started toward her, his gun extended for a second shot, but just then the explosives went off. Debris came flying down at him, so he turned and ran for his car. He got in and started it quickly, then jammed it into gear and floored the accelerator. By the time people came running out of the surrounding buildings, he was out of sight. The apartment building he had used as a safe haven for so long was collapsing from the top down, and no one inside escaped.

Catherine lay in the street, staring at the destruction. She'd been shot, but all that mattered to her at that moment was that Sam and the rest had been inside when the bombs went off.

People were running and screaming, and several came to see if she was all right. She could hear them talking to her, but couldn't make out what they were saying because she couldn't get past her own thoughts.

She shoved away those who tried to help her and grabbed for her phone in her jacket pocket. Her left hand wouldn't work, so she used her right thumb to scroll through the call history and punched redial on the number she wanted.

It was answered almost immediately. "He killed them," she said, "Adrian, he killed them all, Sam and everyone. I don't care what it takes, Colson, find him. Find him and kill him!"

Her head swam suddenly, and she let her eyes glance down at her chest. Blood was pulsing out of where the bullet had struck her, and she knew that an artery had been hit. Weakness started to set in, and the phone fell out of her hand as everything went dark.

TWENTY-EIGHT

"Catherine? Catherine, are you there?" Noah called into the phone, but there was no answer. He could hear people talking, as if milling about, but Catherine seemed to be gone.

"Hello?" A male voice came onto the line.

"Hello, can you hear me?" Noah asked. "What happened to the woman I was talking to?"

"She's laying here bleeding, mate," the man said. "Whole bloody building blew up, don't know what hit her, but she's got a bloody hole in her chest. Blood squirtin' out all over the place."

"Hang up and call 999," Noah said. "Do you hear me? Call for help, right now."

He ended the call and looked at the others, gathered around him at the table. "That was Catherine Potts," he said. "I'm not sure what just happened, but she said Adrian killed her entire team, and a passerby said she's laying in the street, bleeding badly. She wants me to find Adrian and kill him."

"Oh, God, Noah," Sarah said. "Is she…"

"The man I spoke to said blood was squirting out. That's not good, but it means she's alive at the moment. I don't know if she's going to make it, but I told him to call for an ambulance immediately. Hopefully he'll do it."

"So what do we do now?" Moose asked.

"We figure out how to find Adrian, and do exactly what she asked. Everybody think, there's got to be something we've missed. Something that will tell us when he's planning to strike."

"I don't know what it would be," Neil said. "I've gone over everything possible about Charles. I know his movements for the next week, everywhere he's going to be, everything. We know Adrian's supposed to strike tomorrow, so it's bound to be one of the schools, but which one? Could we possibly cover them all?"

"Tell me about them again," Noah said. "Maybe there's something that will give us a clue as to which one he's planning to strike at."

Neil rolled his eyes, but turned to the computer again. He called up the itinerary he'd looked at before and began reading it off. "Thursday, he goes to Royal Academy at eight AM to hear their choir sing. Ten-thirty, he'll be at Albemarle Primary to speak to the students about the British Constitutional Monarchy form of government—the Prime Minister is also going to be there, by the way—and then at three, he's supposed to be at Hempstead…"

"Wait," Noah said. "You said the Prime Minister is going to be at Albemarle with him?"

"Yeah, that's what it says right here. I hadn't seen that before."

"That's because they were keeping it under wraps," Noah said. "Catherine told me that Adrian had been planning some kind of a big assassination when he was captured, but they never found out who the target was.

There was speculation, though, that it was the PM. If she's right, that's got to be it. He can take both of them out at the same time."

"That would make sense," Moose said. "Two birds, one stone."

"Neil, can you get me the specs on that building? And I want to know exactly where this program is taking place."

"Give me a few minutes," Neil said. His fingers began flying over the keys.

"Noah," Sarah said, "should we notify somebody? Get the whole thing canceled?"

Noah shook his head. "Not just yet," he said. "If it gets canceled, we may never get another chance to nail Adrian. What we got to do is figure out just what it is he plans to do, so that we can stop it."

Sarah stared at him. "Are you getting a little personal about this?"

"No," Noah said. "If we can't figure it out in time, you'll make the call yourself just before they arrive. I just can't take the chance that Adrian might find out it's been canceled and failed to show up. It's the only time we know of where we know exactly where he'll be."

"Okay, I've got it," Neil said. "The program takes place in their main auditorium. Both Prince Charles and the Prime Minister will be on the stage, taking turns explaining the British system of government to the kids. I've also managed to get the blueprints for the building, take a look."

Noah leaned in and stared at the screen. The auditorium was one large room, set up theater-style with gradually rising seats. The stage was large, but open; there were no wings on it for anyone to hide in.

"There's nowhere he can take a shot from," Noah said. "There's no balcony, no booth anywhere. There's no place I can see where a rifle could be concealed, and there should be enough security to make sure he can't get close enough to make a pistol shot. How in the world is he planning to pull this off?"

Neil was also studying the diagram on the screen, his finger tracing different possible paths toward the stage. He shook his head, dragging his finger back to try again, but he still couldn't figure out how anyone could make a shot that would be certain, let alone two of them. "It's a clear span building," he said. "There's not even any place in the ceiling or on the roof he could possibly hide. He'd have a better chance of making the shot from underneath the damned stage!"

Noah shook his head. "No, there's no trapdoors. Nowhere he can peek out of, he couldn't be sure of..." He suddenly leaned forward and looked at the diagram again. "Neil, you're a genius!"

"I am? I mean, I know I am but..."

"You said it, the only way he could possibly make the shot is from under the stage. What's the only way to make a shot count when you can't possibly see the target?"

"Explosives!" Moose blurted. "He's going to blow up the entire stage!"

"Exactly," Noah said. "That's the only thing that could make any possible sense. He can take out both Prince Charles and the Prime Minister at the same time."

"God, he'd be killing God-only-knows how many kids!" Sarah said.

"Yes, but he won't care. Remember when they asked me to do this job? They wanted it to look like the work of some known enemy of the British state. I'll guarantee you the explosives will be a type used by the Irish Republican Army or some other such group. They'll get the blame, but whoever's behind the assassination of the PM will reap all the benefits."

Neil was pounding on the keyboard. "Okay, there's like ungodly security on that school for the next couple of days," he said. "How can we put a stop to this without canceling the appearance and evacuating the school? We've got to find some way to get into that building tonight."

Noah nodded. "You're right, but how?"

"I'm looking, I'm looking," Neil said. "Give me a minute, will you?"

Noah sat back in his chair and waited, while Moose chuckled. A moment later, Neil pointed his finger at a spot on the screen.

"There's only one possibility," he said. "See this, on the roof of the auditorium? That's where an air conditioner used to be, but they upgraded the system sometime recently and took that one out. There's a cover over it, probably screwed down. If you could get up there and take it off, you could rappel down a rope and end up right in front of the stage. From there, you can get to the access panel to get onto the stage right over here on the left, see it?"

Noah nodded. "Okay, I see it," he said. "Got any brilliant ideas on how to get me on that roof?"

"Actually, I do. Can either of you guys fly a plane?"

"Yes," Noah said, "My grandfather taught me. What have you got in mind?"

"There's a small private airfield about 10 miles out of the city. It's the kind of place that doesn't have its own tower, no security for anything, but there is a school there for people to learn how to jump with a parachute. I'm thinking we could go there, snag a parachute, steal a small plane and fly over the school. Moose can use a parachute, right?"

"Right," Moose said.

"Okay, so Noah flies the plane over the school, and Moose jumps out—with me strapped onto him."

"Oh, no," Sarah said, "no way!"

"I really don't see any choice," Neil said. "Does anybody else here have the necessary electronic or chemical knowledge that might be necessary to defuse a bomb? I'm telling you, this will work. Like I said, there's a parachute school there. They'll have one of those rigs they use, where they strap the student to the instructor and let them jump out together."

"And you think nobody will spot a parachute landing on top of that auditorium?"

"Not if there's a big enough diversion," Neil said. "That's where you come in, Sis. You're always claiming you can outdrive anybody, right? Well, we steal you one of those fast and furious type cars, and you go racing around the parking lot of the school just before we get ready to jump. You make enough of a fuss, and all the security is going to be watching you. All you got to do is outrun the police cars that decide to go after you. Compared to making my first-ever jump out of an airplane, sliding down a rope and disarming God knows how big a bomb, you've got it easy."

Noah, Moose and Sarah sat there for a moment just staring at him. It was Moose who spoke up first.

"As crazy as it sounds," he said, "it actually might work."

"I was thinking the same thing," Noah said. "This is why we are a team, right? Because each of us is the best at what we do. Neil's right, it has to be him that goes in to disarm the bomb, nobody else here has his skills. I'm the only one here that can fly a plane, Moose is the perfect candidate for the parachute jump." He turned his eyes to Sarah. "And you're the best driver on the planet."

"Oh, my God," Sarah said. "Geez, we're really going to do this, aren't we? Can I point out that there's just one big flaw in this plan?"

"What's that?" Neil asked.

"How we get you guys back out of there after you deactivate the bomb. Anybody figured that one out yet?"

"Oh, that's the easiest part of all," Neil said. "We walk right out through the front door."

"The front door? What, you want me to come back and make another diversion?"

"Not necessary," Neil said. "Moose and I will just stay under the stage and get some sleep. When all the festivities end tomorrow, we can slip out and leave with everybody else."

Sarah just stared at him.

"Okay, that's the plan, then," Noah said. "Let's get busy putting it into action."

It was only a little past one, so they worked on refining the plan throughout the afternoon. Neil spent a good part of the time studying up on IEDs, and Sarah used her phone to plan her own escape route after her automotive diversion. Noah sent her out to grab some necessary supplies and dinner at five, and she came back with everything, plus a bucket of KFC. They sat down and ate, waiting for it to start getting dark.

Finally, it was time to go. Neil gathered up the tools he would need and shoved them into his pockets, and then they locked up the house and headed out in the pickup truck. Sarah drove as they went out to the little airport, but there were a couple of cars at the airport when they arrived, and a number of people looking over an older twin-engine Beechcraft. They spent an extra forty-five minutes driving around the sparsely populated countryside, and were glad to find that the place was deserted when they came back.

"Okay," Noah said as he, Moose and Neil climbed out of the truck. "Go find yourself a car to steal, but then stay out of sight with it as much as you can until you hear from us. We're only going to get one shot at this, so it's got to work the first time. You'll need to keep their attention on you for several minutes, at least, long enough for Moose and Neil to make their jump and gather up the parachute on the roof. As soon as they're down, you make a run for it and find somewhere to ditch that car. Get somewhere safe, then you can take a taxi back to the truck and come to pick me up."

Sarah rolled her eyes. "I've got it, Noah," she said. "It's not like we haven't been over this five hundred times, right?"

Noah was standing beside her door, with the window rolled down. He looked at her for a moment, then leaned in and kissed her. She stopped complaining and wrapped her hand around the back of his head to prolong the kiss. When she finally let go, it was with a smile on her face.

"Stay safe," Noah said.

"You, too," she said. She put the truck in gear and drove away.

It took Moose only a few seconds to break into the parachute school's little building. Finding the instructor rig that would allow him to take Neil along with him on the jump took nearly 10 minutes. Unlike the rental parachutes, the instructor rig was kept in a cabinet in the manager's office.

Meanwhile, Noah had been looking over the few airplanes that were tied down on the apron. The jump school owned a single-engine Cessna that had been modified for its purpose. Only the pilot's seat remained inside, and the right-side door was rigged with a mechanism that would swing it upward, rather than outward. That got it completely out of the way so that it didn't interfere with the jumpers.

Moose found the key to the plane in the office and brought it out. "I thought this might make life a little easier for you," he said. "Something about riding in a hot-wired airplane doesn't appeal to me."

Noah took the key and nodded. "I can imagine," he said.

They climbed into the plane and Noah fired it up. He let the engine warm up for a minute, then gave it a little throttle so that it could taxi to the end of the runway. A moment later, they were airborne.

Sarah had hurried back into the city, looking for a car that she felt would be suitable for her own part in this crazy operation. She was heading into heavy traffic when she spotted the one she thought would be ideal. It was a 2015 Subaru WRX sTI, and from the look and sound of it, it was one that had felt the touch of a high-performance shop. It was cruising along with a number of other such cars, and she followed it until the driver pulled into the parking lot of a small restaurant.

She drove past as the driver got out of the car and went inside, then parked the truck behind the store a block away. She locked her purse inside and jogged back to the little restaurant, glad to see the Subaru still sitting in its parking space.

She'd gotten a good look at the young man who was driving, and found him sitting with a couple of other boys in a booth inside. She ordered a Pepsi, then took it to a table right beside where they were sitting.

It took only a moment for the boys to notice her, and she flashed them a slightly flirtatious grin.

"Care to join us, luv?" one of the other boys asked.

"Thanks, but I'm okay," she said. "Hey, do you happen to know who owns that beautiful Subaru outside? The one with the flames painted on it?"

Two of the boys started hooting, and pointed at their companion. "Oi, that's Mikey's car," one of them said. "Fastest thing on the road, it is!"

"Really?" Sarah said, her eyes going wide. "I've heard a lot about those cars, are they really as fast as they say?"

Mikey grinned from ear to ear. "Mine is," he said. "She's been pumped up a bit. Over 500 hp coming out of her engine, she'll break three hundred KpH. Ever ridden in one?"

Sarah got up and slid into the seat beside him. "No," she said as if awestruck. "I'm Linda. Would you take me for a ride?"

Mikey smiled, and she could see the lecherous thoughts dancing across his mind. "Sure, baby," he said. "Let's go."

Sarah jumped up and let Mikey lead her out to the car, and tittered when he held the door open for her. She could see the other two boys gawking at them through the window as Mikey walked around and got behind the wheel. He fired the car up and backed it out of its space, then eased it onto the street.

He made a couple of turns and got onto a fairly deserted street, then downshifted to second gear and floored the accelerator. The all-wheel drive grabbed the road and the car shot forward. The road had a couple of curves in it, and he took them fast, fast enough that Sarah could hear the tires squealing.

When he finally slowed down, Sarah gushed over how fast the car seemed to be. "You know, I've never told anyone," she said, "but going fast in a car really turns me on." She made her eyes and smile as seductive as she possibly could. "I don't suppose you know anyplace private we could go, do you?"

"Oh, yeah," Mikey said. "Just hang on, luv." He sped up again, and headed out of the populated parts of the city. Within minutes they were cruising down a lane that seemed to be completely devoid of either traffic or houses.

Sarah reached over and ran a hand down his chest. "Find somewhere to park," she said, her voice thick and sultry.

Mikey laid a hand on her thigh for just a moment, but then had to downshift as he made a turn into what looked like an old cemetery. "This okay for you?" he asked with a grin.

Sarah nodded. "It's perfect," she said. "Let's get out so we can do it on the ground."

Mikey's grin got even wider as he opened his door and stepped out of the car. Sarah jumped out of the passenger side and ran around to where he was standing. She threw her arms around his neck and put her face just in front of his, then said, "Mikey, do you like surprises?"

Mikey kept smiling, but his eyes suddenly held a question. "Surprises?"

The question was answered quickly, as Sarah's little Beretta suddenly materialized in front of his face. "Surprise," she said. "I'm so sorry, but you're not getting lucky tonight. In fact, what you're going to do is take off all your clothes and toss them into the car."

The grin vanished, to be replaced by a look of shock and anger. "Are you crazy? I'm not gonna..."

Sarah pointed the pistol slightly to the right of his head and squeezed the trigger once. The bullet whizzed by, but the sound of the gunshot nearly burst his eardrum.

"Geez, you crazy bint," he yelled.

She pointed the gun back at his face, but then lowered it until it was aimed at his crotch. "Strip, I said. Everything off, right now. Toss it all inside the car and then start walking."

Mikey's gaze followed the aim of the gun, and then his clothes started coming off. He threw them into the open window, finally ending with his underwear.

"Now, start walking." Sarah pointed toward the far back of the cemetery. "Keep going in that direction, and don't stop until you find some clothes. Got it?"

Mikey started walking, screaming obscenities at her as he went. Sarah watched until he was a good 500 yards away, then opened the driver's door. She had to throw his clothes into the backseat before she could get in, and then it took her a moment to adjust the seat for her shorter legs. She honked the horn twice, and then roared out of the cemetery and back toward the city.

It would take Mikey at least a couple of hours to make his way back to civilization, she figured, especially since his nudity would make him want to avoid being seen. Hopefully, this crazy plan would be over and done with by then.

TWENTY-NINE

S arah took out her phone and called Noah. He answered, but she could barely hear him over the noise of the airplane's engine. "Can you hear me?" she shouted.

"Yes, just barely," Noah said loudly. "Are you ready?"

"Yeah, I'm just about half a mile from the school. Tell me when you're ready and I'll go into my act."

"All right," Noah yelled, "I've been circling the school. Give me two minutes to get lined up, and then go for it."

"Two minutes, got it," she yelled back. She started driving toward the school, going slowly to give Noah the two minutes he asked for.

Just as she got close enough to think about turning into the parking lot, Noah yelled, "Now!"

Sarah made the turn and immediately noticed several policemen standing around the doors that led into the auditorium. She smiled and waved, then suddenly floored the accelerator and started driving in circles in the parking lot. The tires were screaming as they tried to hold onto the tarmac, but the power of the engine was too much for them. The car was doing doughnuts, with all four wheels.

The officers shouted at her, and then they all started

running in her direction. She gave them another wave, and then cut the wheel hard to the right and zipped right around them. She spun the car around so that she was behind them, and then floored it again.

They scattered like bowling pins, and a couple of them even fell down. She flew through the gap they created and whipped the wheel around to circle them once again. All of them were yelling at her, and she suddenly saw more officers coming out of the building. One of them jumped into a Ford patrol car and started it up, but Sarah wasn't through having fun. As the car launched itself in her direction, she cranked the steering wheel the opposite way and threw herself into a skid that took her completely around the police car. As she came out from behind it on its opposite side, she punched the accelerator again and then started running circles around it.

The officer behind the wheel slammed on his brakes, completely shocked at her behavior. The rest of them were standing around the perimeter of the action, jumping up and down and screaming at her to stop, and Sarah suddenly found it all absolutely hilarious.

She could hear a droning sound, and realize that it had to be the airplane. That meant she needed to keep their attention on her for at least another few moments, so she whipped the wheel the other way and broke out of the circle of policemen, now doing laps all the way around the parking lot. The officers were turning in place so rapidly, trying to keep track of where she was at, but at least a couple of them were starting to show signs of dizziness.

Another patrol car started up and started her way, the officer's intent obviously being to try to ram her and bring her to a stop. She waited until he was close enough that she could see his face, then shoved the accelerator to the floor and shot past him. He was so surprised that he kept his eyes trained on her, and ended up crashing into the first patrol car.

Sarah ran a couple more rings around them, squealing her tires as she did so, but then a glance showed her the blinking lights of the airplane flying away. She made two more complete circuits, deliberately aiming herself at clusters of policemen and then dodging around them at the last second, then shot out the parking lot exit and onto the road. The speedometer was reading 160 when she straightened out, which put her at nearly 100 miles an hour.

Three more patrol cars came out of the parking lot in pursuit, and she could see flashing lights off in the distance as reinforcements were headed her way. Her hours of map study would pay off, as she began whipping the little car around corners faster than the patrol cars could ever hope to take them.

She was still laughing, and it suddenly dawned on her that she hadn't had so much fun since the last time she had run blocker for her dad. Some things, she figured, must be in your blood.

It took her about fifteen minutes to lose her pursuit, and then she managed to drive sedately and quietly into another part of the city. She parked the car in a recessed loading dock, where it couldn't be seen from any street, then locked it up with the keys inside. She walked about a mile through back streets and alleys before she started looking for a taxi.

* * *

Noah, Moose and Neil caught a brief glimpse of Sarah's shenanigans, but they were too busy to pay much attention. Moose had carefully judged the winds and chosen the direction he wanted Noah to approach the school from, and he and Neil were already strapped together and kneeling just inside the open jumper's door. Noah kept the plane steady, and Moose watched through the windscreen.

Suddenly Moose tapped Noah on the leg, and Noah cut the throttle. The engine dropped to an idle as Moose grabbed hold of Neil and flung them sideways out of the plane. As soon as they were out, Noah pulled the throttle out again and gave the little airplane all the power it had.

Noah flew off into the countryside, and ten minutes later he landed the plane in a field. He got out quickly and started jogging toward the road he had seen on his approach, then kept jogging back toward the city.

* * *

Neil managed not to scream, but it took all his self-control to do it. Moose had warned him that this was a low-altitude jump, so he was prepared when the parachute snapped open right after they left the plane. Still, the whole thing was quite a shock and Neil kept his eyes closed until Moose warned him that they were about to land.

They hit the roof of the auditorium almost dead center, and Moose began frantically pulling the parachute down and gathering it up. "We've got to bunch it up now," he said, "or it could catch the wind and drag us right off." Neil grabbed some of the lines and began helping immediately.

A minute and a half later, Moose had the parachute gathered into a wad and tied it all together with its own cords. He released Neil from the harness, and then shrugged the rest of it off himself. They carried the harness and parachute to one of the remaining air conditioner units, and Moose secured it there with another piece of cord.

"Okay," Moose said. "Let's get inside."

They crouched low and waddled over to the hatch, where the older air handler had been removed. Neil had been right, and it was secured with screws. They took out a pair of screwdrivers and had all but one of them out within a couple of minutes. They slowly twisted the hatch and peeked through the gap, but after a moment Moose said he was certain there was no one inside the auditorium to see them. He swung the hatch further open, then moved over to another air handler and looped a rope around it, then let both ends fall down through the opening.

"Okay," he said to Neil. "Climb onto my back and hold on as tight as you can without choking me to death, okay? You hang on, and I'll climb down the rope."

"O–okay," Neil said. "You know, I can't believe this was my stupid idea."

"I can," Moose said with a straight face. "Climb on, and like I said, hold on tight."

Moose was kneeling beside the opening, and Neil climbed onto his back, wrapping both arms and both legs around him. Moose scooted the rest of the way to the opening and slid into it, causing Neil to panic for just a moment before he caught their descent on the rope. "Ow," Moose hissed. "I said hold on, not break my neck."

Moose hung on to the rope just below the opening, and reached up with one hand to push the hatch back over the hole. He had left a couple of screws partly in the lower edge, and they caught in the holes in the roof. As soon as that was done, he scrambled down the ropes, hand over hand, keeping a grip on both strands so that they wouldn't fall. As soon as they touched down onto the floor, Neil slid off his back and Moose pulled on one of the ropes. By tugging on it steadily, he pulled down on one side while the other side went up and around the air handler. When he pulled it back through the open hatch, the hatch itself dropped perfectly back into place. No one looking up from inside would ever know it had been removed.

Five minutes later, both they and the rope were up under the stage. Neil produced a flashlight and began looking around, trying to find any sign of bombs strapped to the supports, but he started to think they were on the wrong track when he didn't find any.

"Moose," he said. "Remember what I said about being a genius? Maybe I'm not all that smart, after all. Do you see any bombs?"

Moose had his own flashlight out and was looking just as thoroughly. "Can't say I do," he said. "Got any other bright ideas?"

Neil was sitting on the subfloor under the stage, shaking his head. "It's got to be here," he said. "We looked at it from every possible angle, and this is the only answer. There has to be a bomb under here, somewhere."

"I understand that," Moose said, "but there isn't one. You see it for yourself, there's..." He suddenly stopped talking and began crawling forward, his light shining ahead of him. He paused, looking at one of the structural supports under the stage, and then turned to look back at me. "Come take a look at this," he said.

Neil crawled over to where he was crouched and looked at the support. It looked like a solid block of wood, roughly eight inches square and three feet tall, holding up a section of the stage floor. When Neil looked where Moose was pointing, though, his eyes suddenly went wide. There was a quarter-inch hole drilled into the side of the post, and a thin wire was sticking out of it. The wire was uninsulated, and simply stuck out about two inches to the side.

"What do you make of that?" Moose asked.

"Holy crap," Neil said. "That's an antenna. The bomb is inside this solid block of wood, and it's designed to be detonated by a radio signal. The antenna is sticking out so that it can pick up the signal without interference from the wood around it."

Neil suddenly began scrambling all around, and found three more identical posts with wires sticking out. "Four bombs," he said. "There are just four of them, but the way they're placed, there won't be anything left of the stage or anyone on it once they go off."

"Okay, I get that," Moose said. "The question is, how are you going to defuse them when they're inside solid blocks of wood?"

"Oh, that's the easy part," Neil said. He pointed at the framework of the stage, just beside the post they were looking at. "Put your back against that for a moment and push."

Moose looked up at the framework and shrugged, then put his shoulders against it and gathered his legs underneath him. He pushed upward, straining a bit, and then watched as Neil simply pulled the post over and laid it on its side.

"Okay, you can relax for a minute," Neil said. He was shining a light at the top of the post, where they could now see a six-inch diameter hole. He reached inside and carefully withdrew a metal canister with a nine-volt battery and a small circuit board on top. The antenna wire that was protruding through the hole was attached to that circuit board.

Neil pointed at the battery. "This is a pretty simple design," he said. "All I have to do is disconnect the battery, and this thing is harmless." He reached out and took hold of the battery, then looked at Moose. "Or it may go off when I pull it. I guess there's only one way to find out, though."

Moose's eyes went wide as Neil yanked the battery free, but then Neil started snickering. "Gotcha," he said. "Lift the floor again so I can put the post back in place, okay?"

Moose shook his head and glared at the kid, but then he pushed up with his shoulders again while Neil replaced the support. Fifteen minutes later, they had all of the bombs out and disarmed.

Now all they had to do was wait.

THIRTY

Adrian had been busy, and a great deal of it had involved thinking. Someone had managed to find out where his base was and tipped off MI6, that was obvious. That told him that at least one of his contacts in London had betrayed him, but which one? As far as he knew, none of them was aware of the flat he used as a base of operations. The only thing he could imagine was that someone had followed him, but he'd never seen any sign that he was being tailed.

It didn't really matter, anymore. In the past ten years, his activities had earned him nearly half a billion dollars, while his investments had almost doubled it. When he collected the final payment on these two contracts, it would put him over that mark. It was time for Adrian the assassin to retire, and he had already been making plans in that direction.

He wondered if Eddie and Georgie had enjoyed the bonus? Yes, there was an extra five thousand pounds in the envelope, but the real bonus was the chemical poison that he had soaked the money in. It would be absorbed through their fingertips as they counted out the money, something he knew they would both do. It would act fast, shutting down their nervous systems so that they would be paralyzed, unable to breathe. They would be dead within less than twenty minutes, hopefully fast enough that they wouldn't even get a chance to spend any of the money. If they did, they'd be taking a few others with them.

What other loose ends did he have? He thought of Judy, and while he didn't think she could possibly have been the one to give up his address, he still needed to put an end to her. Once this explosion went off, there would be an investigation like none other. He needed to have no one who could possibly mention him still be breathing at that point.

Of course, there was Broussard. Adrian had seen the news reports of the murders at Florentine Global, and suspected it might have been the work of the imposter. If they were the Council, then why was Broussard still alive? That was another loose end he would take care of before he left the city that afternoon.

There was the imposter, as well. Unfortunately, Adrian had missed his chance to eliminate that one, but at least there was nothing connecting the two of them. Perhaps later, after things died down, he might be able to track the imposter on his own and finalize that situation. He could be patient; patience was something you learned in his business.

He looked at the clock on his car radio and saw that it was already past nine. He had been forced to rush the day before to get new identification, but he was certain it would pass inspection. The forger who made it for him was one of the best, or at least she had been. He wondered if she realized what was happening before he put the bullet through her brain.

No loose ends.

DAVID ARCHER

His identification named him as Walter Smyth. The real Walter Smyth was now resting permanently in a landfill, thanks to the automated trash compactors on the new city trucks. They simply dumped the containers into the back, where everything was shredded and smashed into a block, to be shoved out the back and into a hole waiting to be filled. With his identification, however, naming him as a visiting professor from Cambridge, he had no trouble getting admitted to the day's program.

He had no intention of remaining in the auditorium for the explosion, of course. He simply wanted to be certain that both of his targets were on the stage, and then he would push the button in his pocket as he exited the building. The detonator, disguised as a cheap old cell phone that didn't even have a camera on it, would draw no suspicion even if it were discovered.

Yes, it was almost time.

* * *

Sarah had called Noah as soon as she got back to the truck and her purse, and he'd told her where to pick him up. It'd taken her a little while to get to him, but then they went back to the house and got some sleep.

They were up at seven, showered and got ready to face the day, then went out for breakfast. Noah called Allison while they were on the way and explained what was going on, and she put him on hold for a couple of moments. When she came back, she told him that she had pulled in a couple of favors owed to her by MI6, and gotten his and Sarah's cover names added to the guest list at the Albemarle event. They were listed as diplomatic guests, which meant they would not be searched or subjected to any particular scrutiny. He thanked her and ended the call as they pulled into the parking lot of a restaurant.

By the time they finished eating, it was getting close to nine. Albemarle was some distance across the city from where they were, so they drove on out and got there early enough to find a parking place. A police officer stopped them as they were preparing to enter and asked for their identification.

"Oh, yes, Mr. Jamison," he said after a moment. "Yes, you and Ms. Porter were added to the list just a bit ago. I understand you are in diplomatic work?"

"Yes," Noah said. "We work for an arm of the American State Department that handles land negotiations. We were sent over to help with some new property acquisition, and the ambassador suggested we might want to come and sit in on this presentation."

"I've never actually gotten to see anyone who was royalty before," Sarah gushed. "This is such an honor."

The officer smiled at her and handed back their identifications, then gave them each a card on a lanyard that would identify them as diplomatic guests. "Just put these on," he said, "and go on in and find a seat. There's a section already reserved for diplomatic visitors. Someone inside will be happy to show you to it."

The two of them walked inside and were escorted to the diplomatic seating area. They were very near the front of the auditorium, but at least they could see the entry doors. Noah kept an eye on them, certain that Adrian would be walking in wearing some sort of disguise. He intended to make sure the man didn't get away this time.

"You think they're still under there?" Sarah asked, indicating the stage with her eyes.

"I guarantee it," Noah said. "If they'd been caught, we'd know about it, and if they found a way to slip out during the night, they would've called us. They're still there. Let's just hope they accomplished what they came for."

"Yeah," Sarah said. "No kidding."

They sat in their seats as other guests entered and found their own sections, and Noah saw three or four men who could possibly have been Adrian. None of them acted particularly suspicious, so he tried to keep track of where each of them sat. Every once in a while he would look around, just keeping track of them. If he looked and saw one of them out of place, he would be almost certain that one was Adrian.

At a little before ten-thirty, the kids who made up the student body of the school were escorted in. There were about three hundred of them, and more than half the seats in the auditorium had been reserved for them. They filed in calmly and orderly, reminding Noah of little soldiers marching in step.

Suddenly, a man walked onto the stage and approached the lectern.

"Students, welcome guests," he said, "we are most delighted to bring you a pair of distinguished visitors, today. Everyone please stand for a moment and show a warm welcome to the Prince of Wales and our own Prime Minister."

The formerly quiet students all leapt to their feet and began shouting and applauding, and it took only a few seconds for the rest of the guests to join in. Noah and Sarah stood as well, clapping and cheering with the rest, even as Noah pretended to stretch his back in order to look around at his suspects. All of them were in place, and everyone sat down a moment later.

This would be the moment, Noah thought. If Adrian was going to strike, if you were going to detonate the bombs he'd arranged, it would probably be shortly after the two world leaders appeared on it. Noah craned his neck to watch his suspects as first Prince Charles and then the Prime Minister walked onto the stage.

"I'd like to take this opportunity," Charles said, "to thank all of you for coming today. There is little more important, in my opinion, than to instill in our youth a thorough and complete understanding of how our government functions. Only with that understanding can they truly attain to be productive and valuable citizens of our great nation, and so it is with great pride that I stand here before you today in my humble attempt to impart a small bit of wisdom to our future generation."

The crowd broke into applause again, and the Prince stood there, smiling and waving and waiting for the noise to die down. It took a long moment, and Noah glanced around at his suspects again.

One of them was moving. A man of the proper build, with black hair and a neatly trimmed beard, had risen from his seat and was headed toward the exit. As Noah watched, he glanced at the stage and the expression on his face was one of excitement, almost as if seeing his victims was giving him some sort of thrill.

Noah tapped Sarah on the shoulder and pointed surreptitiously. "That's him," he said. "I'm going after him." He stood and began making his way to the aisle, but suddenly he realized Sarah was right behind him.

"Not without me, you're not," she said. He kept his eyes on his man and let her follow without saying a word.

Adrian—Noah was certain of it, now—would get to the exit at least thirty seconds before he and Sarah would reach it, simply because he had been sitting closer to an aisle and didn't have to fight his way past other seated guests. He considered shouting to try to get his attention, but decided against it. If anything happened to incite the crowd into a panic, Adrian would certainly be able to escape.

Noah finally reached the aisle and began walking as fast as he could, hearing Sarah's footsteps moving just as quickly behind him. Adrian slipped through the exit, and Noah broke into a light jog. He managed to cut Adrian's lead by several seconds, but by the time Noah got through the door, he was nowhere in sight.

A policeman was standing by the door and Noah turned to him. "Pardon me, guv," he said, "my mate was feeling ill and came out just a moment ago. Red shirt, got a fluffy beard, did you see which way he went?"

The officer smiled. "Yes, sir," he said. "He went that way, toward the car park." He pointed in the general direction of the parking lot.

Noah didn't even bother to thank him, but started jogging in that direction. Sarah made it out of the auditorium just then, and began running after him.

Noah passed a delivery truck and suddenly saw Adrian again. He was standing 50 yards away, and seemed to be trying to make a phone call. He was looking down at a phone in his hand, pressing a button, but then he looked back toward the auditorium and Noah realized that the phone was actually the detonator.

Adrian saw him coming, then, and even from that distance, he saw the large nose and build, and realized that he was suddenly facing the very imposter who had tried to take his place. He had pushed the red button on the phone a half-dozen times, but there had been no explosion. Seeing that bloody imposter told him why. The bastard had somehow learned what he was doing and managed to stop it.

Adrian, who had never been very well hinged to begin with, suddenly snapped. He dropped the phone and took off running, surprising Noah with his speed. Noah leaned into his run and began kicking for all he was worth. There was still a good 50 yards between him and Adrian, and he was doing everything he could to make it up.

One of the many police officers saw them running and stepped out in front of Adrian, ordering him to halt. Instead, Adrian ran head-on into him, knocking him to the ground and stumbling over him, but managing to grab the short assault rifle he was carrying and snatch it away. He ran a few more steps, then turned and pointed the weapon at Noah.

Noah had snatched his pistol out as he ran, and quickly snapped off three shots toward Adrian. He missed, but Adrian flinched and then turned and ran to the side. Another officer ordered him to halt, but Adrian fired a quick burst and put him down. He kept running, and Noah rounded the corner just in time to see him step over the fallen officer and snatch open one of the emergency exits of the auditorium. It would put him just inside, at the very back behind the audience seating. Noah ran harder, but then thought to pick up the fallen policeman's own rifle as he ran past, shoving his pistol back into its holster.

He caught the door just before it closed and snapped

it open again, expecting to see Adrian standing just inside and firing toward the stage. Instead, he saw absolute pandemonium. Someone had seen Adrian with the rifle and screamed, and now the entire crowd was trying to find its way to the exits.

Noah cast a glance at the stage and saw that security personnel had grabbed the Prince and the PM and were covering them with their own bodies as they hustled them off the stage and through the side door that would get them out of Adrian's line of fire. Noah whipped his head from right to left, and finally saw Adrian running down the far outer aisle. The people in the seats on that side were stampeding away from him, but there were too many of them clambering about for Noah to get a clear shot. He turned and ran for that side of the room, intending to follow Adrian.

Adrian suddenly turned into the seats and dropped down behind them. He popped up quickly and snapped off a short burst in Noah's direction, but there were too many people behind him for Noah to be able to return fire. Adrian shouted something, but there was no way Noah could make it out over all of the screaming, so he crouched low and continued moving toward where the man was hiding.

Adrian wasn't holding still, however. He had moved down the row of seats and suddenly popped up again. Another three-round burst struck the wall just above Noah's head, but he still didn't have a clear shot.

"Noah!" he heard, and suddenly saw Moose up near the stage, his Glock in hand. Noah pointed to where he had last seen Adrian, and Moose nodded as he turned and ran along the front row of seats. Adrian was staying low, and neither of them could see him at the moment.

Suddenly, Adrian popped up and fired again, this time shooting into the fleeing crowd. Several people fell, and Noah decided it was time to risk returning fire. He slid to a stop and raised the rifle to his shoulder, aiming at the seat that Adrian had dropped down behind and squeezing off a three-round burst of his own.

"He's moving, he's moving," Moose shouted, but Noah kept the weapon to his shoulder. He was scanning the seats, waiting for Adrian to show himself again, but to no avail. Moose had his pistol in hand, and suddenly began climbing over the seats to try to get to the man.

"I see him," he shouted, and leveled his pistol to squeeze off a shot. He shook his head, indicating that it missed, and suddenly a new voice rang out. "Right there," Neil shouted, pointing, "he's right there."

Adrian suddenly popped up again, but this time he wasn't looking toward Noah. The rifle was aimed at Neil, and Noah swung his own weapon and squeezed the trigger, but Adrian leaned at the last second and his shots plowed into empty seats behind. Noah could see Adrian focusing on Neil, but Moose was raising his pistol again. He fired once but the shot went wild, and then Adrian spun and fired, and Noah saw Moose go down.

Everything went into slow motion. Noah heard a scream from Sarah, behind him, but kept his eyes focused on Adrian as he tried to turn and drop at the same time. Noah lowered the barrel of his rifle and squeezed the trigger three times in rapid succession, sending nine rounds directly at his target.

Three of them struck Adrian, knocking him back. Noah took off running again, threading his way through the seats a row or two behind where Adrian had been. He knew he'd hit his target, but was startled

DAVID ARCHER

when Adrian managed to rise once more.

Body armor, he thought, just as Sam Little had done in his own confrontation with the assassin. *The bastard's wearing body armor!*

Noah tried to aim for a headshot, but Adrian's weapon was already pointed directly at him. Noah braced himself for the impact he knew was coming, but then two other shots rang out, as first Neil and then Sarah aimed and fired, and Adrian was rocked. His aim wavered, his shot went wild, and Noah took the opportunity to center his sights on the man's face and squeeze his trigger.

Adrian's face exploded, as three bullets passed through his nose and each of his eyes. The body fell, and Noah hurriedly clambered over the seats to be certain Adrian was dead.

There was no doubt. The world's most feared assassin had come up against his own agent of death, and his brains were now splattered across the seats where children had sat only minutes before.

Time sped up again, and Noah heard his name being called. He looked up to see Neil screaming at him, and he made his way to the aisle and ran down to the front as quickly as he could. Sarah reached Neil at the same time Noah did.

"I tried," Sarah said, sobbing as she spoke. "I shot him, but he didn't go down..."

"He was wearing armor," Noah said. He leaned over the seat to get to Neil and Moose.

Neil was sitting on the back of one of the seats, holding Moose and screaming for help. Noah looked down and saw the jagged red hole that was just slightly off center in Moose's chest, then looked at his face.

Moose was blinking and trickles of blood were running from his nose and mouth, but he managed to focus his eyes on Noah. He tried to speak, and Noah bent down close to hear what he had to say, but it was very faint. All he caught was five words: "... honor to serve with you..."

Moose's eyes glazed over, and Noah quickly put a hand to his throat. There was no pulse, and Noah knew that Moose was gone.

Suddenly there was noise, and Noah looked up to see a dozen policemen surrounding them, weapons aimed directly at them. Noah lowered the rifle he was holding carefully to the floor, then reached out and took the pistol from Neil and laid it down, as Sarah lowered her own. As soon as he was finished, the officers swarmed over them all.

EPILOGUE

All three of them were arrested, handcuffed, then dragged out and shoved into separate police cars, where they sat for more than an hour while investigators tried to piece together what had happened.

Finally, they were driven to a police station and locked into separate cells. Noah and Neil were directly across from one another, but Sarah was taken to an entirely different part of the building.

Neal looked up at Noah, and his face was streaked with the tracks of his tears. "I can't—I can't believe he's gone," the boy said. "He can't be gone, Noah, he just can't be."

"Yes," Noah said, "I'm afraid he's gone. He drew Adrian's fire away from you."

"But why would he do that?" Neil wailed, his anguish almost palpable. "I could have ducked, I could have run away, why would he do that?"

Noah looked at the skinny young man for a moment, and then he spoke the truth. "He did it because he loved you," he said. "You were the one he called his little brother, remember? What else could he have done when he saw Adrian ready to shoot you down?"

"But it's not fair!"

They sat in their cells for almost four hours before anyone came to get them. They were handcuffed again and marched through hallways into separate interview rooms, and the only good part was when Noah saw Sarah through the door of one of them.

He was handcuffed to a table and told to wait. He sat there for another fifteen minutes before a man walked in holding a single sheet of paper and sat down across the table from him.

"Are you Michael Jamison?"

Noah simply nodded. Being arrested on foreign soil meant being disavowed, he knew. Trying to tell these people the truth would not help anything.

"Mr. Jamison," the man said, "my name is Simmons. I'm with MI6. I've been going over the witness statements from the events at Albemarle today, and they all seem to indicate that you fired the shots that killed a man who had apparently gone crazy, bringing a gun into the auditorium and shooting the place up. Would you care to tell me why you did that?"

Noah looked him in the eye. "It seemed like a good idea at the time," he said.

"Mr. Jamison, I wonder if you are aware that the man you killed was in fact an extremely dangerous assassin. He had in fact been the subject of a massive manhunt over the last few days, ever since he escaped from custody. Any comment on that?"

Noah cocked his head and looked closely at Simmons. "How would I know that?"

Simmons looked down at the paper in his hand for a moment, and then looked back up into Noah's face.

"I have an agent who works for me," he said carefully. "Yesterday, she was badly wounded when she tried to apprehend that same man. She's currently in hospital, and still in quite critical condition, actually, but she's conscious. She caught the news on the telly about Albemarle, and shortly thereafter began demanding a telephone. She called me, and asked me—no, she bloody ordered me—to go to one of my superiors and ask to be informed about something special about her. Do you know what my superior told me?"

Noah shook his head.

"He bloody well told me that I had better listen to anything she had to say, because she was one hell of a lot more important to him than I will ever be. He then told me to get my arse out to that hospital and find out what it was she wanted me to know. I did, I did exactly as he told me to do. Because of that, I now know that you are not in fact, Michael Jamison. I also now know that you are some sort of bloody American agent who was apparently sent here to prevent that assassin from carrying out his dastardly deeds. I know that the young man and young lady with you are part of—of whatever it is you do, as was the other young man who unfortunately lost his life today." Simmons took a deep breath. "Now, does any of that sound familiar to you?"

Noah looked at him for a moment before speaking, thinking about what he wanted to say. Finally, he said, "Catherine is still alive?"

Simmons blew out his breath all at once. "Damned right she's alive," he said. "According to her, even that is thanks to you. She said it was you who convinced some drugged-out passerby to call an ambulance for her, is that true?"

Noah only shrugged.

"Well, let me tell you how this is going to go. Michael Jamison, as it turns out, is a bloody hero, as are your two young friends. You'll be paraded in front of the Queen tomorrow morning so that she can personally thank you for saving the lives of her son and the Prime Minister, immediately after which you and your friends will be escorted onto an airplane and flown out to an American aircraft carrier somewhere in the bloody Atlantic. Your late friend, incidentally, will be accompanying you on that journey. Now, what happens to you after that, I have no idea. I'm sure I don't even want to know, but I can tell you this: if you ever come back to the UK, it's a bloody tossup whether you'll be greeted with hugs and kisses or stood in front of a firing squad. Do I make myself clear, *Mister* Jamison?"

"Perfectly," Noah said.

* * *

A few minutes after Simmons left, a policeman came in and unshackled Noah from the table. He was led out of the room and down the hall to another room with comfortable chairs and asked politely to wait there for a few minutes. Less than a minute later, Sarah was brought into the room and immediately threw her arms around Noah's neck and began to cry. Neil joined them only a couple of minutes after that.

They made it through the Royal Review the next day, with Moose represented by a tall, wooden cross that was carried by one of the Buckingham Palace Guards. The three of them walked alongside it as they were led before Queen Elizabeth II.

"I have been briefed about the events of yesterday,"

the elegant old woman said to them when they stood before her. "I am aware that you are American agents, and that your mission here was to stop the assassin who was trying to destroy our country by his acts. My first words to you, therefore, are from the Crown. My nation thanks you for the courage and devotion you showed in performing your duties, and were it possible, I would see each of you created a Baron or Baroness, at the very least."

She sighed and looked up at her son Charles, who stood just behind and to one side, then turned her eyes back to them.

"My next words are from a mother," she said. "I must express to you my personal gratitude for the life of my son. I am told that each one of you put your own lives on the line, firing your own weapons at the man who was trying to take him from me. While your own laws prevent me from giving you any kind of official reward, I cannot allow your heroism to go completely unrecognized, and so I have hastily arranged a gift for each of you."

She waved a hand, and a young woman stepped up beside her, bearing a silver tray. The Queen reached over and picked up a small box, then turned to Neil. "Young man," she said, "I saw the video recording of the events, and have been told that the man who died deliberately drew the assassin's fire away from you. This tells me that he was your friend, and while nothing can truly ease the loss you must be feeling, I would like you to have this." She opened the box, and Neil saw, through his tears, a large silver ring. "This ring was once worn by Arthur Wellesly, the First Duke of Wellington, who commanded the armies that defeated Napoleon. It is a treasure of our country, for it speaks of courage in the face of overwhelming odds, and I thought it a fitting tribute to the man who gave his life defending not only you, but our Prince and Prime Minister. Please take it as my personal gift."

Neil sobbed as he accepted the box from her hand, and stepped back. Queen Elizabeth looked at Sarah.

"I saw that you also fired your weapon at the assassin, doing all you could to draw his fire yourself. This tells me that you are equally as brave as the fallen man, and so..." She took another box from the tray, opening it to reveal a diamond brooch. "I have this for you. It was given to me by Diana, the Princess of Wales, shortly after she gave birth to my grandson, William. Let it always remind you that you are a jewel among women, and remember that Diana, no matter how we may have quarreled, never displayed anything but the greatest courage in her life."

Sarah accepted the gift with a smile, but her own tears were still in evidence. The Queen turned to Noah.

"What can I give the man who led the mission to save us all? I thought about this for a long time last evening, and I decided it must be something that reflects the courage of a man who undertakes missions that seem impossible. For that reason," she said, reaching to the tray for a larger box, "I chose the one item in my possession that reflects that courage."

She opened the box to reveal a pistol, a Walther PPK. "This is the pistol that was carried by Ian Fleming during a number of missions that remain classified as unrevealable even to this day. Less than twenty people in the government knew that he was active in those missions, but I can tell you that our nation might well not have survived without him. His personal weapon strikes me as the best reward I might give to you."

Noah accepted the box from her hands, and then looked the Queen of England in the eye. "Your Majesty, we are all honored to have been of service, both to your gracious self and to the United Kingdom. If my fallen comrade were alive, he would express the same sentiments."

The review ended then, and the three of them followed the cross and its bearer out of the room. They were taken to a garage where a limousine awaited them, with their luggage already inside, and driven to Heathrow, followed by a hearse. They stood by and watched as Moose's body was loaded onto the plane, and were then escorted up the ramp and seated in the plane, which took off only a few minutes later. The flight lasted slightly more than two hours, and then the plane touched down on the aircraft carrier.

The coffin was removed and transferred into yet another airplane, and the three of them were ordered to board it as well. This time they were told the flight would last far longer, so they all ended up sleeping for the majority of the ride home.

They were met at Denver by Allison, Don Jefferson and Dr. Parker, and driven home in one of the biggest limousines they had ever seen. Moose rode back to Kirtland in the back of another hearse.

Noah, Sarah and Neil were met by Lacey and Elaine when they were dropped off at home. The five of them went into Noah's house, where they spent a long night getting completely drunk and remembering the man they had loved and called a friend.

"Why?" Elaine asked. "Why did he have to die?"

Neil was sitting beside her, with Lacey on his other side, but neither of them spoke. Sarah was opposite them, one hand resting on Elaine's shoulder, but even though she tried to say something, nothing would come out.

Finally Noah leaned toward her. "Elaine, Moose was a soldier, and he died doing his job. I know that isn't any consolation, but it's likely that both Neil and I would be dead if it hadn't been for him. None of us are ever going to forget him, and we'll never stop missing him, but he did what had to be done. He was a hero, and sometimes a hero is called on to make the ultimate sacrifice."

Elaine looked at him and nodded, but it was obvious she was only trying to avoid saying anything herself. Noah realized it, and said nothing more. They all sat in silence for another hour until Elaine had drunk enough that she passed out on the couch.

Moose was buried two days later, in a special cere-mony. It was attended by Allison, Don Jefferson and his wife and daughter, the Jacksons, both of the other ac-tive teams and dozens of E&E staff and trainees. Moose had not been the first to fall in the line of duty with the organization, but he had been popular throughout the outfit.

Because he had no other family, Elaine was given his posthumous Medal of Valor and the flag that had draped his coffin.

Noah, Sarah and Neil all thought that was a good idea.

Read on for a sneak peak of The Wolf's Bite (Noah Wolf book 5), or buy your copy now:
davidarcherbooks.com/the-wolfs-bite

Be the first to receive Noah Wolf updates. Sign up here:
davidarcherbooks.com/noah-updates

DAVID ARCHER

THE WOLF'S BITE

A
NOAH WOLF
THRILLER

RIGHT HOUSE

ONE

Noah's phone vibrated in his pocket, and he took it out to read the text message that had just come in.

My office 13:00.

He looked up at Sarah and Neil, who were sitting across his kitchen table from him. They had been eating lunch, but their phones had gone off at the same time as his, and he knew they were reading the same message.

"I guess the Dragon Lady thinks it's time to get us back in the saddle," Neil said.

Sarah nodded. "I've kinda been expecting it," she said. "It's been a month. I'm surprised they gave us that long."

Neil looked up at Noah. "Don't suppose they gave you any heads up on what's happening, did they?"

"No," Noah said. "I'm sure this has to do with filling the gap in our team. With Moose gone, we need a new backup man. I would imagine we're going to meet him today."

Neil and Sarah looked at one another but didn't say anything. They had both felt the incredible impact of Moose's loss, but they had finally stopped breaking into tears each time they thought of him. Moose Conway had been more than just a part of their team; he had been like a brother to each of them, and had given his life in an effort to save theirs. Their last mission, to ferret out the people behind a little-known but powerful terrorist organization, had gone sour and they had been forced to go after one of the most deadly assassins the world had ever known. When it came down to a firefight, that assassin had drawn a bead on Neil, but Moose had drawn his fire and taken the bullet. His heroism had cost him his life.

Noah Wolf, their team leader, had fired the shots that ended that assassin's career, along with his life. Noah was an assassin, himself, the shining star of the American organization known simply as E & E. He had been recruited after a short but illustrious military career, specifically because he suffered from something known as atypical blunted affect disorder, a rare condition that leaves its victims without emotions—or conscience—of any kind. Noah had not been afflicted with the ravaging grief that Sarah and Neil had known, but he still felt the vacancy that Moose's death had left in his life. There was something wrong, with Moose gone, something that simply would never be right again in Noah's world.

Unfortunately, the work that they did was dangerous. As an assassin, it was often up to Noah to eliminate dangerous or evil persons from the world, just the way any soldier might have to eliminate an enemy. There were always risks in any kind of war, and Moose was not the first to die in the service of E & E, nor would he be the last. Noah had come to the conclusion that the Grim Reaper knew each of their names, and probably had them written on some future to-do list.

"Man," Neil said, "I hope whoever we get isn't an asshole. Moose is gonna be a tough act to follow."

"It's almost a quarter after twelve," Sarah said. "We should probably get on the way, if we're going to get there on time."

She put away the bread and cold cuts they had used for making sandwiches while Noah cleared their plates and put them in the dishwasher. Neil walked out ahead of them and managed to twist his long, lanky frame into the back seat of Sarah's Camaro when they joined him. Noah slid into the front passenger seat as Sarah got behind the wheel, and they headed into Kirtland.

Sarah had to push the car a bit to make it on time, but they stepped out of the elevator at two minutes before one. Getting to Allison's office took only a minute, so they were actually slightly early when her secretary waved them in.

Don Jefferson, Allison's right-hand man, was already sitting on one of the big leather sofas in her office. Allison was in the wingback chair she used when she was holding an informal meeting, so Noah and the others settled onto the sofa across from the one Jefferson occupied.

Allison Peterson was the director of E & E. She answered only to the President of the United States, and her approval was required before any assassination could be ordered by American operatives. In most cases, any assassination she sanctioned would be carried out by one of the teams that worked for her.

"I'm assuming you've all had time to cope with the loss of Mr. Conway," Allison said without preamble. "We understand how devastating such a loss can be to a team, but it's also necessary to get you past it and back into action as soon as possible. We have to replace him today, and your new teammate will be here in just a few minutes."

"Because you're our very best team," Jefferson said, "we're giving you the best man we have available. His name is Marco Turin, and I'm fairly sure you've all met him before."

Noah nodded. "I have," he said. "He showed me around my first day here, but you know that. He struck me then as a pretty good guy."

"He's an asshole," Neil said with a disappointed sigh. "When I was in PT, he was always picking on me about how tall I am."

Sarah grinned at him. "That's because most people aren't tall enough to bang their heads on a doorway." She turned to Jefferson. "I've met him a couple of times, just around town. He seems okay."

Allison rolled her eyes. "Good, that's two out of three of you he won't have to win over. Listen, kids, it's very rough on anyone who has to step in when a team member is lost. Don't be too hard on him, okay?"

There was a tap on the door, and it opened to reveal Marco. He grinned when he saw Noah and stepped into the room, taking a seat beside Jefferson.

Marco was a dark-haired, stocky and muscular man of about five foot ten. His hair was a little long and parted in the middle, and he wore a short and obviously untrimmed beard. He sat quietly for a few seconds, simply allowing the team to look him over. When he finally spoke, it was softly, and with an accent that sounded like the Deep South.

"When they told me I was gonna be joining your team," he said, "I remembered Noah and I talked about that possibility when we first met. I know you had a good run with Moose, and I can tell you that I had nothing but the greatest respect for him. I know I can never replace him, but I promise you I'll do my best at whatever you need me to do."

Noah leaned forward and extended a hand to him. "I'm sure you will," he said. "None of us expect you to become Moose, so just be yourself. That's all we ask."

Neil shook hands with Marco, and then Sarah followed suit. "Just don't start with the tall jokes, okay?" Neil asked. "Let's leave that behind us."

Marco grinned. "No problem," he said. "I never make jokes about a man I always look up to."

Neil groaned, but Sarah chuckled. "We're all just here to do our jobs," she said. "You'll be fine, I'm sure."

Allison smiled at them all. "Marco has been our utility man, filling in wherever he was needed up until now. This will be his first permanent assignment to a team, but there was literally no one better that we could give you." She leaned forward and put her elbows on her knees, her hands clasped together. "Noah, I want you guys to spend the next few days getting used to each other, because there's a mission waiting for you. I won't go into the specifics right now, but I need your team ready to start mission-specific training next Monday morning."

Jefferson cleared his throat. "I'd suggest you spend your time recreationally until then," he said. "Try to spot any personality differences that could interfere and overcome them, because there won't be time for it once your training begins. The new mission will be critical, but it's also going to be different from what you've done up till now. We need to know you guys can work together properly."

"That's it for the moment," Allison said. "You kids get out of here and go have some fun. We'll all meet again oh eight hundred Monday morning, in the briefing room."

Noah stood and the others all rose immediately after. "Okay," he said. "Let's go have a beer."

"Sounds good," Marco said. He and the others followed Noah out the door, and they rode down the elevator together. "Hey, Stretch, why don't you ride with me?" He pointed at the Mustang that was parked two spaces over from Sarah's Camaro.

Neil glared at him. "Do not call me that," he said menacingly. "Remember that I can spit onto your head without you even noticing, okay?"

Marco laughed. "Okay, okay, I just had to get one more out of my system. I promise I won't do it again, good enough?"

Neil's narrowed eyes bore into him for a moment, but then he nodded. "Okay, fine," he said. He followed Marco to the Mustang and slid the passenger seat all the way back before he got in.

Noah and Sarah got into the Camaro and backed out, and she led the way out of the garage. "Where to?" she asked Noah.

"Let's go on out to the Sagebrush," Noah said, naming their favorite restaurant and bar. "A beer actually does sound pretty good about now."

Sarah nodded and pointed the car in that direction. From town, it took them almost 30 minutes to get to the saloon, and she was just mischievous enough to force Marco to break the speed limits to keep up with her. When they pulled into the parking lot, Noah noticed that both Marco and Neil were grinning when they got out of the car.

They walked into the restaurant and were greeted by Don Jefferson's daughter, Elaine. Elaine had been Moose's girlfriend, and the smile she gave them had a hint of sadness in it. "Hey, Guys," she said. She looked Marco over. "This the new guy?"

"Yep," Sarah said. "Elaine, this is Marco. Marco, this is Elaine Jefferson."

Marco and Elaine nodded at one another. "We've met before," Elaine said. "You've got a rough job ahead of you, Marco. Filling Moose's shoes isn't going to be easy."

"I'm not even gonna try," Marco said. "We all know he was the best at what he did, so I'm just going to try to do my job the best I can."

Elaine looked into his eyes for a moment, then nodded once. "That's good," she said. "Moose and I were pretty close, but I love the rest of these guys, too. You better take care of them for me, whenever you're out on the job."

Marco grinned and winked. "That's my plan," he said.

"Good," she said. "Come on, guys, I've got a table right over here."

Elaine led them to a table that was situated some distance away from the few other customers in the restaurant, then brought them each the beer they had ordered. Neil, who was actually still a few months shy of being old enough to drink legally, knew that she wouldn't bother to card him.

The table had five chairs. Noah took one, with his back to the wall, with Sarah sitting beside him on his left and Neil on the opposite side of her. Marco had taken the chair on Noah's right, and now he nodded at the fifth chair.

"Are we expecting someone else?"

"No," Noah said. "That's Moose's chair. It's sort of a tradition we developed after we lost him."

"Yeah," Neil said. "He's always with us, so we always keep a chair open for him."

Marco nodded. "I get it," he said. "Look, y'all, it's like I told Elaine. I'm not out to replace him, I've been around the outfit enough to know that that's impossible. You guys all had something going, something that let you work together in one of the worst possible jobs you could ever have. Believe me when I say I'm fully aware that I may never find that same closeness. I've been a utility man for the last two years, filling in wherever they needed me. Don't worry about making me feel like the odd man out, I'm used to it. Just know that I'll do my absolute best at whatever y'all need me to do."

Noah cocked his head and looked at Marco quizzically. "No problem there," he said. "I'm just wondering, though, where did you get that Southern drawl? I don't remember you sounding like that back when we met."

Marco laughed. "Back then I was doing all I could not to let it show," he said. "Lately, I just got to the point I don't worry about it. It comes from my upbringing. I grew up down in Florida, in a small town near the Georgia line."

"Good," Neil said. "Next time you make wise cracks about how tall I am, I'll remind you that you're just a cracker."

The four of them made small talk through a couple of beers apiece, then Noah suggested they all head back to his place. They settled their tabs with Elaine, leaving the generous tip they always did, and Noah noticed that Neil automatically went to the passenger door of

Marco's car.

It looked like Marco might just fit in.

TWO

"This is likely to be one of the toughest missions we'll ever give you," Allison said during their briefing on the following Monday. "It is not, and I repeat not, an assassination. This time you get to experience the other E, eradication. The goal this time is to make the target disappear and seem to be dead, while we move them into an entirely new life."

"That's only one of the differences," Jefferson said, sitting beside her at the conference table. "Another one is that it won't be Noah on point position, this time. The target is a young woman who is currently held in a women's prison in Thailand. Sarah, you'll be going into the prison yourself to make contact. Noah and the others will be planning and arranging your escape, so your job is to get this girl to come with you."

Sarah's eyes had gone suddenly wide. "I have to go to prison?"

"Yes," Allison said. "You'll be arrested for possession of methamphetamine, the most common charge in Thailand. As a result, you'll be quickly sentenced to a term of years in the prison known as the 'Bangkok Hilton.' A part of it is designated as a women's prison, and that's where you'll find your target." He pushed a button on a remote he held in his hand, and the image of a pretty young woman with long brown hair appeared on the screen behind him. "That's her. Her name is Sharon Ingersoll, and she's been sentenced to five years for possession and sale of *yaba*, or meth."

"Wait," Neil said, "we're going into a prison to rescue a drug dealer?"

"Actually, no," Allison said. "Miss Ingersoll was innocent. She was simply visiting Thailand on vacation, and was sharing a room with another American girl that she met after she arrived. That girl had purchased the drugs for her own use, but because it was more than what the government there recognizes as a recreational amount and they were both in the room at the time, both of them were charged. Thailand doesn't provide any kind of quality in defense attorneys and she wasn't given a chance to secure her own, so they were railroaded through a rapid trial, convicted and sentenced in less than a week."

"Okay, but still," Neil went on. "If she was innocent, isn't there something our embassy could do? Why does it have to involve us?"

"As it happens," Jefferson took over, "Miss Ingersoll is considered a rising star in the field of particle beam technology. She's been working with DARPA for the last two years, and the research team she's part of insists they can't continue without her. The work she does concerns mostly weapons and energy transmission and is classified Most Secret, so normal diplomatic channels that require tons of background information could run the risk of exposing her. If any of our enemies were to learn about her current situation, she'd be at risk of abduction or termination, so the Joint Chiefs want us to move on this as soon as possible. Since she has no family, and very few friends outside of those she works with, a complete change of identity seems to be the ideal solution."

Sarah swallowed hard. "Okay," she said. "And how do we get her out?"

"That's going to be the tricky part," Jefferson said. "We considered trying to bribe the guards, but that runs the risk of discovery that could make the mission even more difficult. The most likely chance of success is going to come down to a stealth incursion. Noah, Neil and Marco are going to have to break into the prison, locate you and the target, and then get you both out."

"Earth to Jefferson," Neil said. "You're including me in this insanity? You do remember that I'm the clumsy one, right?"

Jefferson grinned at him. "Of course," he said. "But don't worry, Neil, we've got you covered. Ms. Ingersoll was arrested almost two months ago, so we've had some time to work on the problem. We've had a detailed mockup of the prison constructed out in the training areas, and filled it with more than a hundred actors who have been briefed on how the staff and prisoners would act. It's accurate even down to the colors of the walls, so you'll be able to practice every move dozens of times before you actually get on the plane to Thailand. You've got a week; I'm sure you can get it down to a science in that time, can't you?"

Neil rolled his eyes and sank into his seat. Noah leaned forward slightly.

"You said a stealth incursion," he said. "What about weapons?"

"Special and silent," Jefferson replied. "While there aren't many escapes from the Bangkok Hilton, it has happened in the past. Usually, it involves help from someone on the inside, but this one is going to be different. You'll have some special weapons for this mission, because you've got to make every effort not to leave any corpses behind you, this time. Live guards who were stunned or don't know what happened will probably be punished for dereliction of duty, but dead guards would be grounds for a massive investigation. The last thing we need is for anyone to associate the escape of a pair of American girls with potential agencies of the US government."

"And that's exactly what they would think," Allison added. "The diplomatic nightmare that would ensue would make the fallout over Benghazi look like a picnic. I'm not telling you not to take whatever steps are necessary to accomplish the mission, Noah, I'm just asking you to be very, very careful. I told R&D to work up some nonlethal weapons for you. Hopefully, that will avoid leaving any bodies in your wake."

"Okay," Noah said. "Mr. Jefferson, you said there is a mockup of the prison for us to practice in?"

"Yep, a duplicate of the women's section. The entire prison is pretty large, but the women are housed in one small part of it. That section is up against what amounts to the eastern walls of the prison, so we made a mockup of about a fifth of the whole structure. It's laid out exactly like the real thing, so you'll be able to get familiar with every twist and turn you might have to make when you go in."

"Now," Allison interrupted, "the trickiest part will be after you get them out. You have to stage the escape in such a way that it leaves a trail, and some of our operatives in Bangkok will provide you with a corpse that has been modified to look a lot like Ms. Ingersoll, even down to the fingerprints. The body is of a young woman who has been declared brain-dead after a drug overdose but is currently being kept alive on the physical level. A portable life support unit will keep it breathing until it's time for Ms. Ingersoll to become officially dead, and then, Noah, you will fire the shot that will become her official cause of death. Once they have the body, the Thai authorities will be more than happy to close the case on her. Sarah, of course, will simply disappear with you. She'll become one of the legends of people who escaped the Bangkok Hilton."

"That's a relief," Sarah said. "For a minute there, I was afraid I was going to have to get caught with the corpse in order to make it all convincing."

"Oh, no," Allison said with a grin. "You're not getting away that easily, young lady. We still need you."

"I'm glad to hear it," Sarah said, smiling.

Allison turned to Noah. "Noah, despite your lack of normal emotions, I know that you've gone to extreme lengths to rescue Sarah in the past. I have to ask this question, even though I don't want to. Is this situation we are putting her in going to create a problem?"

"No, Ma'am," Noah said without hesitation. "I understand the necessity, and rescuing her seems to be part of my regular job description, anyway. The mission comes first."

"Hey!" Sarah said, but she was grinning.

"Don't get your panties in a bunch," Neil said. "We all know good and well that Noah won't let anything bad happen to you."

Marco chuckled. "Heck, yeah, even I can tell that."

Allison smiled, but her eyes were boring into Noah. "It is necessary, and there isn't another team I could trust with this mission. I'm counting on you, Camelot."

"Yes, Ma'am," Noah said. "How soon can we begin training?"

"Today. I want you to make a stop out to see Wally, then report to the training center. The gate will know where to send you, and someone will be there to give you a tour. Start working up your mission plans as soon as possible, Noah, because DARPA wants this girl back within the next three weeks. That gives you one week training, one week to get into position and one to pull it all off. If anyone can do it, I know that Team Camelot can."

The team rose, and Neil grabbed a couple of extra doughnuts on his way out of the briefing room. They had ridden to the briefing in his Hummer, so they climbed back into it in the parking garage and headed out to see Wally at the R&D section.

THREE

Wally Lawson missed out on becoming a mad scientist only because he just didn't have enough evil in his heart. Had that not been the case, he might well have been the type of genius who could invent orbital death rays and use them to blackmail every nation on the earth to submit to his domination.

Still, Wally's need to devise creative methods of dealing death and destruction seemed to be inherent in him, and so he had submitted patent applications for several items that would have made James Bond sit up and take notice, all before the age of seventeen. Someone in the patent office had enough intelligence to realize just what the devices were capable of, and referred them to the FBI, who then passed them on to the CIA. A week later, Wally was paid a visit by three people claiming to represent a major defense contractor. Since he had already graduated high school two years earlier and dropped out of college simply because it was boring, he happily accepted the lucrative income that came with the job they offered him in their research department.

Wally Lawson was a genius. Despite a massive charade, it took him less than three days to figure out who he was really working for. That didn't bother him, so he was running the entire department by the time he was twenty-two. He'd held that position for more than twelve years.

Allison had learned about Wally while she herself worked for the CIA, so when the president tasked her with creating E & E, she had demanded the right to take him along. He'd been with the agency for three years and seemed to be happier than ever. He had also brought along some of the talent he had been developing for the company, and Allison's recruiting had brought him several more. The R&D center covered almost 30 acres and employed more than sixty people with degrees ranging from engineering to physics and even quantum mechanics. Many of their creations could do things that would've still been thought impossible with publicly known technology, but they remained highly classified.

The security guards, who all knew Noah and the others by sight—even Marco had been there numerous times—nevertheless spent more than a minute carefully examining their identification and confirming their identities with retinal scans. Once they were satisfied they were not dealing with impostors, they opened the inner door and allowed the team to enter.

"Camelot!" Wally shouted as he walked quickly up the hall toward them. He stopped in front of Noah and extended a hand, and the two men shook. "They called ahead and told me you were coming. I got a quick briefing on your mission last month, so I've had my people working round-the-clock to come up with ways to help you out. Ready to see what they've got for you?"

"Yes," Noah said. "I hope they're giving us something good. Sarah's going to be dangerously exposed on this mission, and I don't want anything to happen to her. She's been through enough already."

"Well, yeah," Wally said. "Don't you worry, we'll keep her as safe as we possibly can." He stopped and looked at Marco, then turned his eyes back to Noah. His normally jovial face turned solemn. "I was really sad to hear about Moose," he said. "He was one of the best."

"Yes, but he was also a soldier. We all know the risks of our job, and Moose gave his life to protect Sarah and Neil, and even me. I suspect his only regret would be missing out on the next mission."

"Amen," Neil said. "That was Moose."

Wally nodded, and then the smile spread over his face again. "I see they gave you Marco," he said. "He's pretty good, think he can keep up with you guys?"

Noah glanced at Marco. "He's going to have to. We're being tossed right into the fray, but I think he knows what he's doing. We'll all do the jobs we have to do, and do them the best we can."

"Okay, then, let's go see what we've got. I put Nancy and Mickey in charge of this project, they're right down this hall." He turned and started walking even before he finished. Noah and his team followed along.

They came to a green door and Wally opened it and stepped inside, then held it for them all to enter. A young man who looked younger than Neil glanced up from the computer in front of him.

"Mickey, this is Team Camelot," Wally said. "Where's Nancy at?"

"Ladies' room," the boy said. "She should be back any

minute." He stood and extended a hand to Noah. "Camelot, right? Heard a lot about you, it's a pleasure to finally meet you."

Noah shook hands with him, and then the others did likewise. "Pleasure is mine," he said. "I understand you've been working on some things to help us with our new mission?"

"Yeah," the boy said, nodding. "Nancy is the actual brains, here. I just do what she tells me, putting all the pieces together."

"Don't let him fool you," said a feminine voice. A blonde woman in her thirties stepped into the room behind them. "I come up with some ideas, but Mickey refines them. We're a pretty good team, but I doubt either of us could accomplish much on our own. Every project we do is a collaboration."

"Which is why I trust them with the important stuff," Wally said. "All I have to do is tell them what the situation is, and then they start bouncing the ideas back and forth. Before you know it, they've invented something so new and exciting that we have to keep them completely under wraps. If any of our enemies ever found out just how bright these two are, they'd do whatever it takes to steal them away."

Nancy burst out laughing. "I hope you're all aware that Wally tends to exaggerate."

"Just show them what you've got," Wally said. "I haven't seen this stuff yet, either, so we can all make up our minds together."

Nancy nodded at Mickey, and he reached over to pick up a small plastic box off his desk. It was about the size of a ring box, but when he opened it up, they saw what looked like a small plastic rod.

"This is the latest thing in subdermal trackers," he said. "It works like a contraceptive implant, just under the skin. 433 megahertz, ultrahigh frequency RFID chip inside." He pointed at three small, round devices that were still on his desk. "These units can read the chip from up to half a mile away, or up to 1500 feet through brick and concrete. If you set them around the area where the women's prison is located within the compound, they'll triangulate its position within only a few inches. Each one has a battery that's good for about two weeks of continuous use. We'll give you these to practice with during your training, but when it comes down to the real mission you will have fresh units with new batteries."

He picked up something else from the desk. This time it was a device that looked like a common tablet computer. "This is the monitor that receives the encrypted data from the scanners and translates it into an image it can display on a tactical blueprint of the prison, with every room and section marked. That way, you'll know exactly where Sarah is at all times."

Noah nodded his head. "Okay," he said. "That'll definitely help when it's time to get her out."

"Exactly," Nancy said. "But that isn't all we've got for you." She nodded to Mickey again.

"The rest isn't quite as high-tech as that," the young man said, "but it should come in handy." He held out another small box, this one containing three devices that looked like small plastic cones. "These little gadgets, when you place them against a wall, can detect movement on the other side. They're fairly simple, because all they do is pick up vibrations transmitted through the wall. That could be vibrations from someone speaking, or somebody walking along, just about anything. Even the sound of someone breathing will create tiny vibrations in the walls that can be detected. They are ultrasensitive, but only in the direction they're focused. You can be talking while you're holding it, and it won't even notice."

"You can use these to make sure a room is empty before you enter it," Nancy added. "You just hold the big end against a wall or door, and watch the needle on the smaller end. If it moves at all, there is something on the other side that's causing vibrations. You can get an idea of the type of vibration, as well, by watching the needle. People walking will be rhythmic, people talking will be erratic and fluctuate. Breathing will be rhythmic, but soft."

Mickey nodded. "You'll get the hang of it pretty quickly," he said, then stepped around his desk to a workbench and picked up what looked like a toy submachine gun. "Now, this little baby will come in handy when you go in, and especially if you encounter resistance. It fires a gel capsule filled with a gas at surprisingly high pressure. The gas is derived from scopolamine, and a single whiff of it is enough to render someone essentially motionless for several minutes. It doesn't knock them out, but it inhibits thought and intention. Basically, anybody who gets a sniff of it suddenly can't remember what they were doing or think of anything else to do, so they just stop wherever they're at and do nothing until it wears off. A side effect is that they usually won't remember anything from the last few minutes before it hit them until the point where they realize they've been out of it, so they won't even be aware they've been affected. We'll also give you some little sticks of chewing gum that act as an antidote, so it won't affect you even if you walk through a cloud of it."

"Chewing gum?" Neil asked.

"Yes," Mickey said. "The antidote is embedded in it, and it is absorbed rapidly into the bloodstream through the tissues under your tongue. We're talking like within one or two seconds, that fast."

"Okay," Noah said. "And how long does the effect last, once we shoot somebody with these?"

"The immobility will last seven to nine minutes, so you'll have to move pretty quickly once you use it. We've got three of these ready for you, and they each hold about 120 shots."

Neil grinned. "So, we just shoot somebody in the face with it?"

Mickey chuckled at him. "You don't even have to hit them. The gas will spread out quite a ways, so if you hit the wall anywhere near them, they're going to get a sniff. The guns are set for three round bursts, and even one burst can stop a small group of people."

"How accurate are they?" Noah asked. "Do you have any dummy rounds we can practice with?"

"Actually, yes," Mickey said. "I figured you'd want to get the hang of them, so we made up a thousand rounds with just air inside. The gel capsules burst on impact with anything, because the pressure inside is just barely low enough to keep them from bursting on their own."

Noah nodded. "Okay, so we can keep track of where Sarah is at inside the prison all the time, we can scan a room for occupants before we enter it and we can incapacitate anyone who gets in the way. What about a way for her to let us know when she's made contact with her target?"

Nancy smiled and took a step closer to Noah. "Well, that presented a bit of a problem, because there's no way she can take any sort of communication device in with her. We thought about adding a transmitter to the implant, but anything that emits an active radio signal is likely to be detected and might even expose her. I was forced to resort to desperate measures, so I just told Mickey there was no possible way we could accomplish it."

Wally let out a loud guffaw. "Telling Mickey something can't be done is a surefire way to get it accomplished. Right, Nancy?"

She nodded, still smiling. "Exactly," she said. "Mickey came up with the idea of yet another little implant, one that will emit a signal just once. The same receivers that triangulate the tracker will receive that signal, letting you know that she's ready for extraction."

Sarah spoke for the first time. "You guys sure get off on shoving stuff into my body," she said. "Are you certain none of this will hurt me?"

"Not a bit," Nancy said. "We've got some anesthetic gel that will keep you from even feeling it when we implant them. The tracker is going into your right thigh, and the extraction signal…"

"I call it the panic button," Mickey put in.

"Okay, the panic button will be inserted just under the skin outside your left rib cage. You'll be able to feel it with your fingers, and all you have to do to set it off is press it until it snaps. You'll be able to tell when you got it done, and your team will get the signal to come snatch you out."

Sarah gave her a sour grin. "Okay, so when do you stick me with this stuff?"

"Oh, not until you're ready to go. We've got some made up that won't be actually implanted for you to use during your training." She nodded at Mickey, who picked up a larger plastic box and passed it to Sarah. "There are three panic buttons and one tracker in there. They have tape on them, just stick them to yourself. Other than that, they work just like the real one. Camelot, you'll use the scanners and monitor during training, so that you get the hang of them."

Noah nodded. "Set us up, then," he said. "We need to get started on the practice runs today."

Wally grinned at them. "Hold on," he said, "not so fast. We got a couple other little surprises for you. Follow me."

He led them through a series of hallways and into yet another room. An older, balding man rose from his seat as they entered.

"Jeremiah, this is Team Camelot. Noah, this is Jeremiah. Whenever we run into a need for a special tool, he's the guy we come to."

Noah shook hands with Jeremiah, who smiled softly.

"Pleased to meet you," the older man said. "Wally briefed me on your mission and told me to think about what tools you might need. I managed to get a copy of the blueprints of the prison, and started thinking about what might be required if you had to create your own way in." He turned to a large table where the blueprints were laid out. "Looking at what we got on their security, it appears to me there are numerous places where it would be possible to literally cut through a wall or roof to gain entry. The trick to that, of course, is how to do so without attracting a lot of attention. Now, I looked at every angle I could think of, including the possibility of going in from under the building. It has a basement level, but that would require digging. Any kind of excavation would be pretty difficult to keep hidden unless you started some distance away and constructed a tunnel. For that reason, I decided to look at simply going through the building itself."

He pointed at various places on the designated walls near the women's section. "These are spots where I think it would be possible to cut through the wall and make an entry point, but the problem is that such an entry would be difficult to conceal. On the other hand, if you take a look at the top of the building," he added, as he flipped the blueprint away to show what appeared to be a large print of a satellite photo, "there are some pretty big sections that aren't easily observable by security. According to our intelligence, these areas that I've marked aren't even subject to video surveillance."

He turned away from the table and stepped over to a workbench where numerous tools were laid out. The first item he picked up looked like a simple tube about twenty inches long and three inches in diameter. "This is an air-launched grapple and rope. When you press the trigger button here near the bottom, compressed air shoots out a folding grappling hook that trails fifty feet of high-strength nylon line behind it. At the places I marked on that photo, that's enough for you to shoot it onto the building where it will catch on the architecture. You can then use the rope to climb up and onto the roof. The grappling hook is made of a very strong plastic and coated in rubber. It shouldn't make a very loud noise when it lands on the roof."

He set the tube back on the table and picked up the next item, a cordless drill with what looked like a sock hanging off the side, and fitted with a twenty-four-inch drill bit. "This started out as a standard cordless drill, the kind you can buy in any hardware store, but I've made a few modifications to it. The bit, on the other hand, is my own design. You can drill straight through up to twenty-four inches of wood, brick or concrete, but the length of the bit is based on spiral cutting technology. The long spiral you see that runs the whole length of it is essentially a cutting blade. Once you've drilled through, you can simply push the drill sideways and cut out a large section of whatever you drilled through. You'll be surprised at how quickly it works, and how silent it is, but the best feature is that I've added a small but extremely powerful vacuum attachment. All of the dust will be sucked up and blown into this sock, so it won't be falling into the room and giving away what you're doing."

Noah took the drill and looked at it closely. "So, as long as we pick a room with nobody in it, we should be able to cut through without being noticed?"

Jeremiah nodded his head. "Our intelligence indicates that their security doesn't use vibration detection. That being the case, it's a safe bet that if you can find an empty room and enter through the roof, no one will be the wiser. And, just to help keep it that way, I came up with a couple other little gizmos." He took the drill back from Noah and set it on the table, then picked up what looked like a six-inch-wide roll of duct tape. "This tape will stick to absolutely anything, and I've tested it on every type of material you're likely to find in that building. When you make your first straight cut, put a strip of this tape on it. Then, when you make a parallel cut, you can use another strip to secure a couple of these flat metal bars to keep that side from falling through, so that the first strip of tape will act as a hinge. That'll make a simple trapdoor that you can close behind you. Unless someone looks up and pays close attention, your point of entry should go completely undetected."

Noah looked at the tape and bars, then turned to Wally. "I think I like this guy," he said.

Buy The Wolf's Bite now:
davidarcherbooks.com/the-wolfs-bite

Be the first to receive Noah Wolf updates. Sign up here:
davidarcherbooks.com/noah-updates

ALSO BY DAVID ARCHER

Not all books have been made into paperbacks yet, but I'm working on getting them all formatted and available as soon as possible.
Up to date paperbacks can be found on my website:
davidarcherbooks.com/pb

ALEX MASON THRILLERS
Odin (Book 1)
Ice Cold Spy (Book 2)
Mason's Law (Book 3)
Assets and Liabilities (Book 4)

NOAH WOLF THRILLERS
Code Name Camelot (Book 1)
Lone Wolf (Book 2)
In Sheep's Clothing (Book 3)
Hit for Hire (Book 4)
The Wolf's Bite (Book 5)
Black Sheep (Book 6)
Balance of Power (Book 7)
Time to Hunt (Book 8)
Red Square (Book 9)
Highest Order (Book 10)
Edge of Anarchy (Book 11)
Unknown Evil (Book 12)
Black Harvest (Book 13)

World Order (Book 14)
Caged Animal (Book 15)
Deep Allegiance (Book 16)
Pack Leader (Book 17)
High Treason (Book 18)
A Wolf Among Men (Book 19)
Rogue Intelligence (Book 20)

SAM PRICHARD MYSTERIES
The Grave Man (Book 1)
Death Sung Softly (Book 2)
Love and War (Book 3)
Framed (Book 4)
The Kill List (Book 5)
Drifter: Part One (Book 6)
Drifter: Part Two (Book 7)
Drifter: Part Three (Book 8)
The Last Song (Book 9)
Ghost (Book 10)
Hidden Agenda (Book 11)

SAM AND INDIE MYSTERIES
Aces and Eights (Book 1)
Fact or Fiction (Book 2)
Close to Home (Book 3)
Brave New World (Book 4)
Innocent Conspiracy (Book 5)
Unfinished Business (Book 6)
Live Bait (Book 7)
Alter Ego (Book 8)
More Than It Seems (Book 9)
Moving On (Book 10)
Worst Nightmare (Book 11)
Chasing Ghosts (Book 12)

Made in United States
North Haven, CT
18 May 2022

19298328R00192